Taming

Him

Taming Him

KIMBERLY DEAN

SUMMER DEVON

MICHELLE M. PILLOW

POCKET BOOKS

New York London Toronto Sydney

POCKET BOOKS
a division of Simon & Schuster, Inc.
1230 Avenue of the Americas, New York, NY 10020

Published by arrangement with Ellora's Cave Publishing, Inc.

ISBN-13: 978-1-4165-3600-0
ISBN-10:   1-4165-3600-0

This Pocket Books trade paperback edition January 2007

10 9 8 7 6 5 4 3 2 1

POCKET and colophon are registered trademarks of Simon & Schuster, Inc.

Manufactured in the United States of America

For information regarding special discounts for bulk purchases, please contact Simon & Schuster Special Sales at 1-800-456-6798 or business@simonandschuster.com

Contents

Fever

KIMBERLY DEAN

Chapter One

"Man, Delia. Did you get the license plate of the Mack truck that ran over you?"

Delia Jenkins slowly lowered the cold glass of water she'd been rubbing against her burning forehead and glowered at her coworker. The grimace she found on his face killed any delusions she might have had about feeling worse than she looked. Her shoulders slumped. So much for the concealing powers of makeup.

"You silver-tongued devil, Rob," she said tiredly. "Now I know why you get all the girls."

"Oh, come on. You know what I meant." He threw her a lopsided smile that probably did bring all the girls running. The smile dimmed, though, as he stared into her face. Reaching out, he caught her chin. "You shouldn't be here, hon. You're sick. I can feel how overheated you are."

"I'm fine." Delia squirmed in her seat as the lie crossed her dry lips. His touch made her body temperature creep up another two degrees and although normally she would have enjoyed the reaction, she just couldn't take it now. She was already boiling over as it was. "It's just warm in here."

Trying to act casual, she pulled away and took a quick sip of water. Squinting, she tried to concentrate on the spreadsheet that took up most of her desk. She had to blink twice before the numbers came into focus.

"Nice try," Rob said as he leaned closer. "Now tell me the truth. What did the doctor say?"

She should have known. He wasn't going to let it drop. She set down her glass and looked at his handsome face again. Even it was starting to blur, which was a shame. A darn shame.

She let out a heavy sigh. She never should have told him about her appointment. It was just . . . Well, shoot, he'd invited her to lunch, and she hadn't wanted him to think that she was blowing him off. She'd waited a long time for that invitation; she wanted him to ask again. "Dr. Mosely said there's a bug going around. Nothing too serious. It's usually gone within a day or two."

"A day or two? You don't look like you'll last that long. Did he prescribe anything?"

She couldn't help but glance longingly at the drawer where she kept her purse.

"You haven't taken it?" For as much as Rob played up the carefree, GQ routine, there was an astute brain behind those dark eyes. "Delia."

She raked a hand through her hair and accidentally dislodged the pencil she'd tucked behind her ear. She bent over to pick it up off the floor, but a wave of heat moved with her. Dizzy, she sat still until her internal gyroscope righted itself.

Damn this fever!

She could feel it burning inside her, trying to escape through her very pores. With every degree her temperature rose, her anxiety level cranked up right along with it. She couldn't be sick now. She just couldn't!

"The doctor said the medication might make me groggy," she explained, "And I've got to finish doing the budget for this bid. Mr. Lloyd wants to look over it before we submit it tomorrow."

Rob slapped his hand down in the middle of her precious spreadsheet, fingers spread wide. "That's what's keeping you here? The bid? We've already got the job, Del. It's in the bag."

Sure it was. Delia rested her weary head in the palm of her hand and looked at the man who'd so casually perched on the edge of her desk. He practically oozed confidence. And why shouldn't he? He was good-looking, friendly, and outgoing—all the traits of a natural-born salesman. If he said that the Berkshire Hotel deal was in the bag, it probably was.

But contracts couldn't be signed without an official bid— and they certainly wouldn't be signed with a budget that didn't add up.

"Your part of the sales job may be done, Rob, but mine isn't," she said, trying to make him understand. "Please, just let me concentrate on this."

Determinedly, she stared down at the spreadsheet, but nerves made the muscles at the back of her neck pull tight. There was an error in here somewhere; she knew it. She just couldn't find it! She hadn't been able to see it on her wavering computer screen, and the printout wasn't any better. If she got all doped up on medication, she'd never track it down.

And there would go her job.

The thought made her feel even worse, and she hurriedly pushed it aside. She couldn't think like that. She had until her four o'clock meeting with Mr. Lloyd to fix things. She'd just have to do a low simmer for the next three, long, slow ticking hours.

Rob drummed his fingers on her desktop. "I'm not going to leave you when you're feeling like this."

"Rob, please. It's not that bad. Really."

Wearily, she wiped the back of her hand across her forehead. She was surprised when it came away dry. How was that possible when her brain felt like it was frying? Shouldn't she be sweating? She glanced again at her desk drawer. She hoped the antibiotics would work. The moment she got home, she was going to do battle with that childproof cap. Until then, though, she had numbers to crunch.

"Go home," Rob pressed.

"I can't."

She couldn't risk it. She'd only been with Lloyd Security Systems for two months. She needed this job. The market for bookkeepers wasn't exactly hopping; she knew that from personal experience. She'd been unemployed for six months before Jackson Lloyd had hired her. There was no way she was going back on that unemployment line. Not for a little hot flash.

Okay, a burning inferno. She could manage.

"That's it," Rob declared. Suddenly, he pushed himself to

his feet. The wheels of Delia's chair squeaked as she instinctively pushed herself back, but he rounded the desk and caught her by the arm before she could roll to safety.

She looked down at the unyielding grip. His hand was big, and his strength surprised her. His touch was cool compared to her hot flesh, and her belly squeezed. There were other, more needy places that would welcome that cool touch. "That's what?" she said distractedly.

"The end of my patience. You're going home if I have to strap you to that chair with duct tape and roll you there."

Her belly squeezed even tighter. Bondage? Ooh. She shook her head and laughed off his outrageous suggestion. "You wouldn't dare."

"No?" Still keeping his clutch on her, he rolled her to the supply cabinet a few feet away.

"Wait!" she sputtered when he found a roll of gray tape. She scrambled out of the chair and held up her hands to ward him off. "What do you think you're doing?"

"Taking care of you. Somebody needs to."

Delia rolled her eyes and summoned her patience. "Listen, Rob. I appreciate your concern, but you're not my boss. You can't send me home, and I don't want to go. I want to finish my job."

"You have finished your job—at least as much as you can. Stop worrying about big, bad Jackson Lloyd. I've got an in with him. If I say you need to go home, he won't have a problem with it."

Right. Maybe in Rob's dreamland. Not hers.

She let out a long, calming breath. It was time to compromise. A determined look had settled onto her coworker's face—one that told her he meant business. She'd seen that look before when he'd set his sights on the new computer services gal.

The pretty blonde had been in his bed before the weekend had rolled around.

Delia's lips flattened as the usual feeling of jealousy nipped at her. She'd been waiting for Rob's look to be focused on her, but not after he'd just told her she looked like roadkill. "I'm almost finished. Just let me double-check the numbers. Then I'll go."

He shook his head.

"I hate to show you this, but you're off your game today, Del." He walked her back to her desk and pointed at the spreadsheet. "Two plus two is four. Not twenty-two. You're going home."

Her jaw dropped in horror. "You're lying. I didn't do that."

She bumped him out of the way and leaned down to see better.

"I just sat there and watched you."

"Where?" She picked up her pencil and began searching for the unforgivable error. If only the numbers would stop dancing!

"Uh-uh. Come on." He plucked the pencil from her fingertips and dropped it on the desk. "Let's go."

"But—"

"No 'buts.'"

"But Mr. Lloyd—"

"Jack won't care. If he was here, he'd be telling you to get your shapely little butt home."

Delia gaped at her coworker. He couldn't be talking about the same Jackson Lloyd she knew. First off, her boss probably had no opinion whatsoever on her backside, but more to the point, since when had he not cared about something? She'd never met a man more focused, more intense. And when a job was up for bid? Forget about it. "He'll fire me."

"No, he won't. To tell you the truth, he'd be more pissed if you screwed up the numbers because your brain overheated." Taking charge, Rob pulled open her desk drawer and grabbed her purse. He slid the strap over her shoulder and nearly scooped her up into a fireman's carry before Delia yelped and backed away. Her shapely little butt promptly bumped up against the corner of her desk, and his eyebrows lifted in challenge. "Are you going to go willingly?"

She froze as her nerves flared once again. Was he right? Was she doing more harm than good if she stayed? She didn't know which was worse, leaving when she didn't have any sick leave time accrued or doing a poor job.

He never gave her time to decide. He grabbed their coats from the rack, swung an arm about her shoulders, and started to usher her out of the office.

Delia glanced fretfully over her shoulder at her desk. She never left it that messy—and she never left before ferreting out a misbalance. It would drive her crazy all night. "Shouldn't we call Jackson? Or at least leave a note?"

"I'll tell him."

The door swung open just before they got there, and

Delia came up short when her foot landed hard on the toe of a sharply polished shoe. Strong hands latched onto her waist before the top of her head could clip a man's chin. She came to an abrupt stop and found herself staring at a familiar tie and a well-shaped Adam's apple. Her heart lodged in her throat. Oh, God. "Mr. Lloyd!"

"Whoa," he said. "Where's the fire?"

Burning inside her chest. Delia felt a twinge of panic. Why couldn't she have fended off Rob for five seconds more? Just five teeny seconds would have saved her from this . . . this embarrassment. For heaven's sake, she'd nearly mowed her boss down. She did everything she could to make herself seem professional, efficient, and indispensable to the man, and here she was scuffing up his shiny loafer—caught as she tried to sneak out.

The shoe was the easiest problem to fix. "Your shoe."

She immediately started to bend down. To do what, she didn't know. Spit-shine it? His hands tightened, though, and her spine snapped straight.

"I'm so sorry," she said emphatically. "I didn't see you there."

"That's obvious," he said.

For a second, neither of them moved. They stayed together, only inches apart, in a near embrace. Delia had to remind herself to breathe. She inhaled shakily, and his tangy aftershave filled her senses. His big hands nearly spanned her waist, and the heat radiating through her thin, silk blouse branded her.

She'd thought she'd felt warm before.

His touch had her smoking.

The moment was swiftly gone. A glance from her to Rob had the expression on Jackson's face going hard. Delia sucked in her breath when he lifted her off his foot and set her firmly away from him. She teetered, though, and latched onto his forearms for balance. The strength hidden by his suit jacket stunned her, and she looked up quickly. She could have sworn she saw a muscle flinch in his firm jaw.

"You two going somewhere?" he asked.

Flames colored her cheekbones and, for the first time all day, the fever wasn't to blame. Meekly, she shuffled backwards. His disturbing touch dropped.

The way he was looking at her made her uneasy. His lips were flat in displeasure. His jaw was tight, and his eyes were . . . flinty. There was no other way to describe it.

Rob looked at Jackson for a long moment. Then his arm smoothly re-encircled her shoulders. Protectively. Almost possessively. "Ease up, Jack."

Her boss's demeanor went so icy, even Delia could feel it slicing through the shimmering haze of her fever. What in the world? She was too intimidated to look at him straight out, but she glanced at him through the curtain of her lashes. Understanding hit her like a lightning bolt.

Oh, dear Lord! Not only did he think two of his employees were cutting out on the day before a bid; he thought they were heading out for a quickie! She felt faint and reached out for the door handle. This couldn't be happening. She needed this job!

"Delia's feeling under the weather," Rob said smiling,

oblivious to the undercurrents. "I'm taking her home to bed."

Jackson's dark eyes narrowed, and Delia wished the ground would open up and take her. Why? Why had Rob felt inclined to mention her bed? Was he trying to make matters worse?

"Mr. Lloyd," she said anxiously. "I don't think you understand."

"I understand plenty." His piercing gaze swung over to her. "Are you finished with the budget?"

She flinched at the harsh tone.

"Almost," she said weakly. She knew she shouldn't have listened to Rob. The troublemaking hottie. She turned on her heel, even though the sudden move made the room spin. "I'll have it finished by our four o'clock meeting."

Rob latched onto her shoulder before she could get anywhere. "Uh-uh. Doctor's orders. She's going home."

Jackson's jaw hardened as he looked at the familiar touch, and he reached up halfway before stopping and letting his hand drop.

"Fine. Go home." He began loosening his tie. "I've done budgets on my own before. I'm sure I'll do them again."

Delia went dead still when he walked past her without another look. What did he mean he'd "do them again"? Without her? She turned to follow him, but Rob caught her by the arm and held her back.

She'd be damned if she'd go down without a fight. She'd worked those numbers until they were engraved on the back of her brain. "There's a problem somewhere in the materials and supplies," she said quickly. "I think it happened when we upgraded to the new motion detectors. Everything else balances."

Jackson didn't even look at her. "I'll find it. Go."

Delia dug in her heels when Rob tugged at her. "I'll be back tomorrow morning before the deadline."

Her boss ran a hand through his hair and sat down at her desk. The spreadsheet was already taking up more of his attention than her. "We'll talk about that later," he said gruffly.

Her eyes rounded. Had she just been let go? She nearly dove back to her desk, but Rob was already pulling her out the door.

Delia looked miserably over her shoulder. It wasn't as if she hadn't done anything! She'd had everything polished and ready to go three days ago until Jackson had found out that the motion detectors they'd been planning to use were in short supply. That meant not only new sensors, but new wiring, a new power system, and new mounting braces. Somewhere, somehow things had gotten entered wrong. If she could just look at the page for over five seconds without it blurring, she'd find the error. Her spine stiffened when she saw her boss plant his hands on her desk and start analyzing the calculations on her spreadsheet.

"Come on, Del," Rob said as the door swung shut, effectively blocking her view. He actually had the audacity to chuckle. "You'll feel better once you take your medicine and relax."

Relax? Was he nuts? How could she relax after what had just happened?

Suddenly, Delia felt deflated. Without a word, she let Rob lead her to the elevator. Why fight it? She wanted to go home so badly she could cry and, for all she knew, there wasn't a job left for her back in that office. Still, she couldn't let go of the picture of Jackson Lloyd brooding over her unfinished budget.

"Did I really put down twenty-two instead of four?" she moaned as the elevator doors closed. Talk about a book-keeper's personal version of hell. And hell was certainly where she felt like she was. With fires raging all around her. She lifted her hair off the nape of her neck. Why wasn't she sweating? Why couldn't she get rid of this insufferable heat inside her?

"Don't worry," Rob said as he forced her into her winter coat before putting on his own. "Jackson always gets grumpy when we get this close to a new job. His mind is on a million things right now. Your leaving will only be a blip on his radar screen."

It hadn't seemed like a blip. It had definitely been more like a big, fat, never-ending bleep. Delia closed her eyes in defeat. Her boss hadn't approved of her leaving. He'd made that perfectly clear.

"Would you go back and talk to him?" she asked.

"Let it go. You're making a mountain out of a molehill."

"Please?" The elevator finally arrived on the first floor, but Delia didn't budge. She turned her best puppy dog look on Rob, silently begging him.

"Oh, hell," he said, caving in. "Sure. If it will ease your mind, I'll go back and talk with Mr. Cranky. Just let me drive you home first."

"No, no." She stepped out of the elevator onto the main floor, but nudged him back inside for the ride up. "Go back now."

"And let you drive yourself?" He stepped out of the way of a harried deliveryman and grabbed her hand. "With the way your brain isn't working? I don't think so."

"Rob, *don't make me beg.*"

He threw her one of his patented smiles as he opened the front door of the building for her. "Jack really shakes you up, doesn't he?"

"Of course, he does. Can you blame me? You saw the look on his face."

"Yeah. I saw it." The winter wind whipped Rob's tie into the air as he walked by her side. Concern for her knotted his brow, though, as he looked down at her. Gently, he brushed her hair back and hooked it behind her ear. "How about a compromise? I'll go back and fix things if you take a cab."

"Deal!" she said, quickly agreeing. "Oh, thank you, Rob. I'll owe you one."

"Yes, you will," he said with a wink. Taking her arm, he led her away from the parking lot to the street.

Delia felt her face get warm all over again. He was looking at her differently—almost mischievously. A mixture of surprise and uneasiness settled in her chest. Had Jackson been right? Had Rob had more in mind than just driving her home?

Maybe she'd declined his offer too quickly.

And maybe she'd made her only good decision of the day. She couldn't imagine that she looked very sexy with glazed eyes, flushed skin, and chapped lips. Turning her back to the brisk wind, she signaled for a cab. "Go back to work, Rob. I don't want you to get fired, too."

He moved suddenly and caught her face with both hands. "Delia, you're not fired. I promise."

She went still. The unexpected touch chilled her inflamed cheeks. Stunned, she looked up into Rob's handsome face. He was watching her in fascination, almost as if he'd figured out a little secret. Her little secret. Delia's pulse jumped as, almost in slow motion, his head dropped. His lips brushed across hers, and her stomach gave a little leap. The kiss felt . . . nice. Soothing, even.

She gaped at him with wide eyes. When he saw her acceptance, he leaned in again. This time, his lips pressed more firmly and his arms wrapped around her waist to pull her close. Delia didn't know if it was the fever or arousal, but her body melted against his like butter.

His mouth ate at hers until her fingers clenched the back of his coat. When her knees started to buckle, he slowly backed away. "I'll drop by your apartment later to check on you. Okay?"

She smiled softly in wonder. "Okay."

Gently, he turned her around. Delia was surprised to find a taxi waiting curbside. She hadn't even heard it pull up.

He helped her into the car with a self-assured smile on his face. "Feel better."

"I will," she promised as she pulled on her seat belt.

In fact, she already did.

The cab pulled out into traffic, but she craned her neck to

watch Rob until he disappeared from view. Now, that was what she called a kiss! No wonder he had such a ladies' man reputation. The guy had moves.

And he'd used them on her!

Delia felt delightfully giddy until she walked into her apartment and reality poked its ugly head back up. She stared across the living room into her bedroom, and all she could think of was Jackson's reaction to Rob's outlandish declaration.

I'm taking her home to bed.

"You're not giddy; you're delirious," she berated herself.

She dropped her purse onto the kitchen table with a thud. How could she be excited about a few innocent kisses when she might have just found herself back on the unemployment line? She couldn't pay her bills with hormones.

Or hot flashes.

Good God, there was another one.

"Where's that stupid medicine?" she snapped. She yanked the tiny brown bottle out of her purse and began cranking on the white lid.

A sudden thought had her head snapping up. Had Jackson been looking out the window as she and his salesman had groped each other in the parking lot? Oh, hell. If he didn't give her a pink slip for leaving during the middle of a campaign, there was always inappropriate office behavior to fall back on.

Great. Just great.

He'd assumed that she and Rob were having a fling and she'd gone ahead and added fuel to the fire. "Good move, Delia. Superb."

There were no two ways about it. She'd just messed up a good thing.

"Ugh!" she grunted. The stubborn childproof cap refused to open. Turning, she yanked open her junk drawer and pulled out a pair of pliers.

Hope still niggled at her, though. Maybe she was worrying about nothing. Rob did have some pull with their boss. He and Jackson were more than just employer and employee. From what she'd been able to gather, the two men went way back. She wasn't certain, but she thought she'd heard Rob once say that they'd been college roommates.

That must have been quite the combination—outgoing party-guy Rob living with the quietly contained Jackson.

Her battle with the medicine bottle stopped as she tried to see the picture in her head. It never became clear. She just couldn't blend a young Jackson Lloyd with the man she knew. He was too brooding to have ever been a kid. Too intense. Dominant. Powerful.

A heat flare went off inside her, and she shook her head. Whatever tack Rob chose to take, she hoped he wouldn't make things worse.

She wiped her hand across her brow. For all the trouble he'd caused her, she just couldn't stay angry with him. He hadn't meant any harm, and he was such a fun, likeable sort. And sexy. She smiled self-consciously when she remembered his kiss. That had definitely been the most pleasant part of her very unpleasant day.

At least somebody thought of her as more than a calculating machine.

"But why did he have to pick the day I feel like a convection oven? Damn it."

The childproof cap suddenly popped open and pills spilled out. Delia gasped and pressed her stomach tight against the edge of the counter before half of them could roll off onto the floor. She sighed as she scooped up all but two and put them back into the bottle.

"And damn you, too, Jackson," she said as she held a glass under the water faucet. She threw the medicine to the back of her throat and washed the pills down.

With any other boss, she would have calmly explained the situation—with calm being the operative word. She just couldn't relax around the man. He put her on edge. It had started on the first day she'd interviewed, and it hadn't gotten any better. She couldn't point to anything in particular he'd ever said or done to disturb her. It was just his essence, the aura of the man.

He was so focused. So wickedly smart. So scarily quiet. She could never tell what he was thinking behind those dark, limpid eyes.

Except for today. He'd been angry with her.

Or Rob, she hadn't been able to tell which.

Delia felt fatigue sweep through her system. *Oh, just admit it. The man intimidates the hell out of you.* She turned toward the bathroom before she could run out of energy. Clothes hit the floor as she walked down the hallway.

Jackson was usually very adept at keeping his emotions to himself, but he hadn't been able to hide his displeasure today. She shivered as she stepped into the shower, but it wasn't due to the cold water slapping against her overheated body. The look in his eyes when he'd seen her and Rob together—it still made her insides quiver. He'd quickly made the assumption that his salesman was the one playing doctor, and she hadn't been able to get a word in edgewise to clear up the misunderstanding.

Get a word in? Who was she kidding? She'd hardly been able to talk at all.

He'd held her.

His hands had clapped onto her, and her muddled brain had ceased to function.

Hadn't he been able to feel the heat radiating off her? Swirling around them? Between them? She hadn't been lying to him. How could he have automatically jumped to the wrong conclusion like that?

She gritted her teeth at the unfairness of it all. "Well, that's his problem, not mine."

She turned off the shower so abruptly the pipes rattled. Whipping back the shower curtain, she stepped out of the tub—only to grab the towel rack when she nearly did a face-plant on her bathroom floor.

Whoa.

She took a deep breath, but the steam-filled air in the bathroom only made her feel more lightheaded. She went still. Either that medicine kicked in fast or she was getting worse. She closed her eyes and held on, concentrating on inhaling and exhaling. At last, her head cleared.

Carefully, she let go of the rack and caught a towel. That was it. She was through feeling guilty. She'd nearly fainted.

For heaven's sake, she wasn't a robot. She'd been a model employee ever since she'd started working for Lloyd Security Systems, but Rob was right. She was too sick to work today. Twenty-two! Her brain had overcooked. Jackson would just have to deal with it.

And Lord help her, so would she.

She felt like she was going to spontaneously combust.

Still feeling unsteady, she opened the bathroom door to let some cool air in. It swept in with a rush, but the relief was gone much too quickly. Delia nearly whimpered when she lifted the heavy towel to dry her shoulders. The friction of the terrycloth against her skin only fed the fire building inside her body.

The fever was rapidly consuming her.

Bed. She forced herself to focus on her destination. She had to get to bed.

Carefully putting one foot in front of the other, she headed to her bedroom. She opened the top drawer of her dresser and grabbed a pair of panties. She put them on slowly, making sure not to lose her balance. Opening the second drawer, she looked for a nightgown. She pulled a lightweight, summer chemise out from the bottom of the stack, but could barely stand the satin as it slithered down her body.

"This medicine better work," she said, wincing. The doctor had warned her that the antibiotics were strong, but right now, the fever seemed to be winning the battle. She raked her hands through her damp hair. Even the red strands felt warm.

Gingerly, she walked to the bed. It took her last bit of strength to pull back the covers and lie down. Sunlight streamed in the windows. It was still early afternoon, but her heavy eyelids drooped. She couldn't ever remember being so tired in her life.

Still, that wavering spreadsheet pulled at her.

"I hope you're up looking for that error all night, Jackson," she whispered as she snuggled into her pillow. It would only serve him right. She was the best bookkeeper that company was going to find. If he couldn't see what he'd be missing without her, it wasn't her fault.

She'd done everything she could.

Chapter Two

"Delia?"

A low voice seeped through the darkness. It nudged at Delia's senses, urging her to wake. To listen. She fought the intrusion. She was so tired. Oh, so very tired and uncomfortable.

"Delia, are you okay?"

The voice was insistent. Smoky and intimate. The timbre was familiar, yet out of place. She pushed through the thick layers of drowsiness and tried to think.

It was just so hot. She kicked at the sheets tangled around her legs. Her pillow lay on the floor, and the comforter sat in a lump on the mattress beside her. Even the brush of the heavy fabric against her skin was too much. She pushed it away, trying to find some relief.

"Hey. Come on. Look at me."

"Hot." So hot. The heat was consuming her.

The mattress shifted, and the back of a hand gently touched her forehead. "Ah hell. You're burning up."

Delia squirmed restlessly and looked up at the man who'd appeared so suddenly in her bedroom. He hovered over her, big and dark. Shadows hid his features, but moonlight lit the hand that still brushed against her face. In the recesses of her mind, she knew she should be frightened—or at least surprised—but his presence comforted her. She didn't want to be alone. Not while the fires of hell were ravaging her from the inside out.

But why was he here?

He shouldn't be here. Or should he? She vaguely remembered a promise to check on her.

It took too much energy to think. She pushed her hair away from her face and off her shoulder. Even it felt too oppressive. Her arm dropped to her side, and her hand bumped against a hard thigh.

The man. He was sitting close.

How had he gotten in again? Hadn't she locked the door?

She couldn't remember. Didn't care.

She closed her eyes and started to drift away.

Callused fingertips patted her cheek. "No, no. Stay with me. Open those pretty green eyes."

The firm tone made her obey. She rolled her head toward the voice and forced her eyelids open a slit. A light from the hallway shimmered around the silhouette of the man's body. He moved so the light no longer glared in her eyes, and she could see him better.

Dark hair. Dark eyes. Concern knotting his brow.

He'd come.

Relief made her sag against the mattress. He'd know how to fight this. He always knew how to take charge.

"Make it better," she begged.

His hand cupped her cheek, and a distinct curse passed

through his lips. Quickly, he reached out and clicked on her bedside lamp. The glare of the light made her close her eyes tightly. "No," she winced. "Too bright."

"Sorry." He turned the lamp down to its lowest setting. "Look at me, Delia. Please."

She didn't want to, but he asked so nicely.

"There you go." His thumb swept gently across her cheekbone. "Ah, damn. Your eyes are glazed. Your pupils are dilated, and you're way too warm. Why didn't you call someone?"

"Sleeping . . . the medicine."

"Medicine?" He nudged her when she began to nod off. "What did you take? Delia, this is important."

"Mm." She liked having him close, but the heat of their bodies was mingling. She wriggled away and covered her eyes with her hand. Too hot. Too bright.

He refused to let her be. "Where's your medicine, Delia?"

She tried to roll away.

He caught her shoulder and pressed her flat on her back. "Tell me, and I'll let you sleep."

Even through her daze, she heard the lie in his voice. She was too tempted to heed the warning. Sleep. She wanted to sleep. "Kitchen."

He was gone before she could say any more. The light was still too bright, but she didn't have the energy to lift her arm to turn it off. Instead she rolled away and curled into a ball.

That was a mistake. The heat only intensified as she folded into herself. With a whimper, she kicked the comforter onto the floor and stretched her legs out. She heard a rattling sound as he came back into her room.

"When was the last time you took a pill?"

She groaned. She'd known he was lying. He wasn't going to let her rest.

The mattress bowed as he sat down next to her again. He brushed her hair away from her temple. "How long ago since you took anything?" he asked.

Her forehead scrunched. Why was he asking so many hard questions? She couldn't focus. Couldn't concentrate. Oh, yes. The pills . . . She remembered them spilling onto the counter. "When I got home from work."

He turned his wrist to look at his watch. "Five—no six hours ago."

The bottle rattled again as he searched for the directions. "No wonder. It's worn off. You're supposed to take two every four hours. Stay here. I'll get you a glass of water."

Delia rolled onto her back when he left. Water. The idea was so appealing, she nearly crawled after him. Nearly. Just thinking about crawling was too much of an effort. Instead, she stayed still, trying to be patient, but the heat . . .

Oh, God. The heat. The mattress beneath her was absorbing her warmth and reflecting it back upon her, doubling her discomfort. She squirmed on the wrinkled sheets, but the fervor built until her back felt like it was on fire.

"Ahhh!" she hissed. She couldn't stand it anymore!

Lurching upright, she tugged off her chemise and threw it across the room. She lay back down, but even her panties felt too stifling. She grabbed the waistband and nearly rent the fabric in two as she shimmied her hips and pushed the material down. The silk clung to her legs until she managed to kick it off.

"You shouldn't have been here by yourself. You—" Footsteps from the bathroom came to an abrupt halt near the bed. "Hel-lo."

Water. He'd promised her water. She reached for it, swinging her arm wide.

She heard him inhale sharply, but then he was sitting down beside her and passing her the glass. "Here you go. Easy now."

Water sloshed over the side, wetting the bed as she swallowed almost convulsively. The moisture felt so good as it rolled down her dry throat.

"Wait. Don't forget to take the pills."

He shoved two into her hand and held the water away from her until she put them in her mouth. She groped for the glass and took a big gulp. The medicine stuck in her throat, but she forced it down. Anything to abate this damned heat. Anything! She settled back on the bed, and he picked her pillow off the floor. Carefully, he tucked it under her head.

She murmured, but kicked at the sheet when he tried to pull it over her nakedness. "No. I'm baking."

"All right. Relax and let the medicine go to work."

"It didn't help before," she said miserably.

He went quiet—almost dangerously so. She looked up at him, her vision blurring around the edges. Time seemed to slow, and the air in the room thickened. "You've been like this all day?" he finally asked.

"The fever," she said weakly. "It won't stop."

His jaw went tight. A muscle near his cheekbone ticked

once, then twice, before an all-too-familiar look of determination settled onto his face. "Yes, it will. You just leave it to me."

Suddenly, he was gone. Delia started to call after him, but hesitated when she saw him moving back to the bathroom. She sighed when she heard water splashing in the sink again. Water. Yes. More water was good. The faucet shut off, and she licked her lips. His shadow cast over when he came back to her bedside. She reached up for the glass, but he didn't give it to her.

"How does this feel?" he asked.

Instead of giving her something to drink, he lay something cool and wonderful against her forehead. It wasn't what she'd expected. It was *better.* Her tight muscles released, and for the first time in hours, her anxiety lessened. Oh, that felt heavenly.

"Good?"

"Mm." She reached up for the compress. She pressed it lightly and water ran into her hair, cooling the roots. She sighed with pleasure.

"Want more?"

Her eyes fluttered open. Their gazes connected, and that heavy feeling came into the air again.

He held another dripping washrag in his hand.

Her pulse skipped a beat. She stared at the cloth, lost in a dreamlike haze. She wanted its cooling effects.

She wanted his touch even more.

She always had.

"Lie back," he said softly.

Arousal suddenly swirled through her veins, riding along with the tide of heat. As delirious as she was, she knew what he intended to do—and she knew what line of intimacy it crossed. It was a line she'd shied away from. She'd been afraid to even approach it, but now, with him standing over her, it didn't even occur to her to say no.

He'd promised to make it better.

Wide-eyed, she settled back against the pillow, willfully putting herself in his hands. The never-ending heat looped around her. It spiraled out to him, and something fierce and hungry flashed in his eyes. The emotion was quickly sub-dued—

But not before she'd seen it.

Determinedly, he took a step forward.

Delia shuddered when he touched her. The cloth brushed against her jawline, impersonal and businesslike. It didn't matter. The flame inside her retreated—

Only to gather and regroup deep in her very core.

The intensity of it made her clench her thighs together. Oh, God. It had been playing with her before. Toying with her.

"Too cold?" he asked, hesitating.

She fought back a groan. "Too hot," she whispered.

In so many ways.

His breath whistled out between his lips, but that was the only reaction he allowed her to see. Like an automaton, he slid the soothing cloth down her neck. She tilted her head, already a slave to the pleasure. He was being so careful. So attentive. The cooling moisture swept over her shoulder and down her arm. He pressed the damp ball of material into her palm, and her fingers curled around it. Rivulets of water slid down her forearm.

"Ohhh," she gasped.

"Are you always this sensitive?" he asked, his voice rough.

"No . . . yes." She didn't know.

She was today. Despite his efforts to comfort her, the unexpected heat in her belly was blooming. Its power was concentrated—double that of anything she'd fought all day.

And it was growing.

"Does it hurt?" he asked.

Pleasure. Pain. It was getting harder to tell one from the other. "Good. It feels good."

"Then we'll try this for a while and see if we can knock that fever down."

For a while?

Heaven help her. She knew what he was like when he put his focus on something.

He set about his mission, and Delia was lost. Sensation buffeted her. Touch dominated, but all her senses were heightened. She could feel the damp terrycloth as it slid, rough and wet, against her skin. She could hear his deep breaths. Feel his undivided attention. Taste her own need.

Her vision narrowed until it was just the two of them.

But the fever fought back.

Deep inside her, a white-hot battle blazed. She began to squirm on the mattress, silently begging him as he stroked her. He was avoiding those parts of her that needed his ministrations the most. Time and again, he sponged down her

30

arms, her belly, and her legs. Always careful in his touch. Always avoiding where the heat was burning brightest.

"More," she whispered.

"I know, hot stuff, I know," he crooned. Her toes curled as he wiped the arch of her foot. "Go back to sleep. I'll be here when you wake up."

He didn't know. He couldn't know. If he knew, he wouldn't be tormenting her like this.

Any self-consciousness that Delia had left slipped away. Her nipples peaked, and her hips tilted. Her pussy was on fire. She let her thighs drop open. The air in the room felt cool as it puffed against her tender flesh.

He stopped momentarily and cleared his throat. Hard. "I know you're warm, but maybe we should cover you up."

She lashed out at the sheet. She couldn't bear it. Her fingers wrapped around his wrist and pulled his hand until it lay nestled between her aching breasts. His fist tightened and water rolled down her abdomen. It crept along the crease of her leg, down to the vee hidden by auburn curls. Ah, that was what she needed. "There," she whispered.

Silence. "You're killing me here, babe."

"Please." She opened her eyelids enough to see his dark eyes glittering down at her. He stared at her for a long moment before his gaze shifted to her breasts. The ache in them intensified as he studied her. She was ready to ask him again—to *beg* him—when she felt his first touch.

"Ahhh," she sighed.

"So perfect," he murmured.

His hand moved in small circles, carefully avoiding her

nipple. Her demanding flesh refused to be ignored. She could feel her nipple tightening, stiffening. It looked almost tawdry as it stood straight up in the air, itching for the terrycloth that lurked so nearby. As she watched, his thumb snaked out and rubbed the rough material firmly against the red areola. She arched on the bed and let out a cry.

He pulled back sharply.

She caught his wrist. "Don't stop," she said breathlessly.

"I'm not sure about this, Delia."

"Don't stop."

She pulled his hand back to her breast and whimpered when his fingers spread round her, capturing her.

God, she needed this.

He squeezed, and the heat inside her spiked. She'd been secretly waiting for this for so long. He was touching her. Intimately. Fondling and coaxing. The rush inside her head was dizzying. *This.* This was what she needed. It was the only thing that was going to ease her distress.

She let her legs spread apart. "Hot," she panted. "Burning up."

His hand stilled. "Oh, God. Don't push me."

"Help me."

He started to pull away. "We can't do this."

She clung to him. "Please."

"No. It wouldn't be right. I'm supposed to be taking care of you, not taking advantage of you."

She looked at him beseechingly. He couldn't stop now. He'd reduced her to a writhing, needy mess. If he left her, she'd be a pile of smoldering ashes by morning.

"I need it." She needed it more than her next breath.

Needed him. She'd trusted him to fight this battle with her, but if he couldn't. . . .

She caught the washcloth. "I'll do it myself."

His head snapped back, and he jerked the washcloth away. "The hell you will."

"Please!" she cried as his weight lifted abruptly from the bed. She reached for him, but he stood just out of her reach, looking down at her and breathing heavily. Suddenly, he turned. She propped herself up onto her elbows to watch him as he walked away into the haze.

He couldn't leave her like this!

She heard water running again, and her head dropped back. No. No more. She couldn't take any more teasing.

Silence bounced off the walls when he came back to the side of the bed. Water dripped from his hand onto the carpet as she waited in tense anticipation.

"For me," she whispered.

He stood still, almost as if fighting some internal struggle, but then moved fast. She collapsed back against the pillow when his hand dove between her legs and cupped her. Her hips thrust off the bed, half in an attempt to press harder against his touch and half in an effort to shove him away. The washcloth was colder than the others had been. It felt like ice against her tender skin.

"Is this what you need, hot stuff?"

She gyrated on the sheets. "Yessss."

"And this?"

His hand began to move. She bit her lip and closed her eyes so tightly, stars danced behind her eyelids.

33

"I'll take that as a *yes*," he said in a strained voice. He found his place at her side. "You better not regret this, Delia."

She forced her eyelids open enough to see his hand playing between her legs. The vision was blisteringly erotic. The fire in her body all radiated from her core. If he could ease her suffering there, she'd do anything.

Anything.

"Here?" he asked.

Her breath caught when the terrycloth pressed directly against her clit.

"Or here?"

A little cry left the back of her throat when his fingers burrowed between her swollen lips and found her opening.

"Or maybe there?"

Her hips left the bed entirely until her weight was balanced on her shoulder blades and her heels. He'd pushed the terrycloth up inside her using not one, but two fingers. His hands were big, but the added bulk of the washcloth made him feel huge. His fingers squirmed deeper and deeper until they were lodged inside her.

Then they began to twist.

"Oh, God!" Delia's body contorted, still balanced midair, as his devilish fingers curled inside her.

He wasn't teasing her anymore.

"Hurry," she begged.

Flames danced inside her belly, and tears pressed at her eyes. The need was so fervent, it was almost cruel.

She cried out loudly when his bare thumb found her clit. Just a few nudges had her spiraling out of control.

"Oh, oh!"

Reaching out, she caught his thigh, which was pressed hard against her hip. Her fingers dug into the taut muscles as the first wave hit her. His fingers pumped in and out until her pussy clenched down on him like a vise. Even then, his thumb played mercilessly with her clitoris.

Her head twisted back and forth on the pillow. He drew out her pleasure, holding her at the peak until he finally let her go over. At last, she fell back against the bed.

He gently brushed her hair away from her face, but she felt his hand shake. "Sleep," he ordered.

Delia could feel the tension in him, but darkness pulled at her. She didn't want to leave him. Not now. Not just when she'd realized how much time she'd wasted being timid. Unfortunately, fatigue wouldn't let her indulge any further. It overwhelmed her. For the first time in hours, the relentless heat had been banked. Her body needed sleep to fight the demon inside her.

"Let go," he whispered.

He'd promised he'd be here when she awoke. Feeling safe and cared for, she let herself slip away.

"She's burning up, Doc. I don't know if the medication is doing its job or not."

Delia snuggled into her pillow and wished for quiet. She didn't want to wake up. Not yet. Her sleep had been fitful. Too light and full of dreams. Dreams of fire. Dreams of demons. Dreams of sex.

She kicked at the covers that had once again found their

way on top of her. His doing, no doubt. She tried to blot out the soft conversation on the other side of the room, but she was too attuned to his voice. It invaded the recesses of her consciousness. Made her take notice.

"Last time she took it? About two hours ago."

She drifted in and out, catching only bits and pieces of the discussion that was surely about her. Two hours? She felt like she'd been asleep for two minutes.

"Hold on. Let me look." There was a short pause followed by a ruffling sound. "Yeah, here's one on the nightstand."

"You want me to do *what?*"

The raised tone of voice startled her, and she clumsily slapped a hand over her ear. Her senses were honed to too sharp of a point. He was too loud. The light from the bed-side lamp was too bright. Her skin was too raw.

The damnable heat was back.

Delia felt her distress return. She'd thought they'd beaten it, but there it was smoldering deep down inside her.

Why wouldn't it leave her alone?

The muffled voice didn't go away. "All right, Doc, if you say so. Give me a minute."

She heard the phone settle onto the nightstand, but was surprised when strong hands caught her by the waist. She looked at her caretaker blearily. He shouldn't touch her. Not now. Things happened when he touched her. Wonderful, scary, exhausting things. She groaned when he rolled her onto her stomach.

"Shh," he crooned. "I didn't mean to wake you."

She sagged onto the pillow. Whatever the doctor had

given her was powerful. Her brain was filled with haze, but the heat that prickled her body was still winning the fight. Her skin felt tender. Everywhere he touched her burned.

Her waist. Her back.

Her butt.

Her head snapped off the pillow when his touch slid down to the curves of her backside. *Did he really think it was shapely?* She wasn't given time to ask, because her thoughts scattered when he parted her cheeks.

"What?" She jerked when a wet finger rubbed intimately against the tight bud of her anus. "No!"

"Easy," he murmured. He licked his finger and moistened her carefully. "Doctor Mosely wants me to check your temperature. You haven't cooled down at all."

Her brain couldn't sort out his words. He shouldn't. She shouldn't let him. She reached back to clutch at his wrist, but his touch was firm.

"Relax."

She couldn't relax. Alarm bells screamed inside her clouded head when something cool and hard pressed against her. Instinct told her it was wrong. She fought the intimate intrusion, but he was insistent. The hard, cool thermometer determinedly sought entrance—and finally gained it.

"Ahhh!" Her fingers bit into the pillowcase as the device slid up inside her rectum. It was small. It provided only the slightest physical discomfort, but with it, the driving heat returned.

And the need.

Only this time, it was raging.

"Not again," she whispered tightly.

The power of the desire scared her. There was no buildup this time. It hit her straight on at full force.

Delia squeezed her eyes tight, trying to fight the wildness inside her.

What was wrong with her? She never lost control like this. It required too much trust. In *him,* a man she barely knew, yet whose respect she wanted deeply. How could he respect her if she behaved so outrageously?

"That's a good girl," he said behind her. He settled his hot palm against her bottom and left the thermometer buried deep.

She groaned. She needed him again. Needed him more than her inhibitions could hide. She tried to remain still, but her hips had a mind of their own. They rolled to the side, trying to get his touch where she wanted it the most. He pressed her back down against the mattress.

"It will only take a moment," he said. "Hold still."

Hold still? It was like asking her not to breathe. She ground her forehead into the pillow. She didn't need a temperature measurement to know her body was on fire.

"Delia," he said warningly. "Stop it. The doctor is still on the phone."

The caress of his hand was in direct contrast to the firm tone of his voice. If the touch was meant to soothe, it had precisely the opposite effect. Her fervor cranked up a notch. He felt her muscles tense, and his fingers spread wide to try to hold her down. This time, she didn't let him. Drawing her knees to her chest, she lifted her hips high into the air. She heard his sharp intake of breath, and she pressed her face more tightly into the pillow.

"Fuck," he said in a low, tight voice.

Yes, fuck. She wanted to fuck.

She wanted it enough to relinquish control to him. Enough to put herself into his hands and trust him to take care of her. She rocked her hips, making him stroke her. Respect her or not, he had to help her. If he didn't, the fire would rage unrestrained and only cinders would be left.

"Uh, Doc?" His voice cracked. "Are there any side effects of this medication I should know about?"

"What kind? Um . . . *sexual*?"

Delia reached up and grabbed the headboard. The heat was building. "Hurry," she moaned.

"It's the fever?" He cleared his throat. "What would you recommend I do?"

There was a long, heavy pause.

"Yeah, I heard you," he said gruffly. "Are you sure?"

His fingers brushed against her clenched butt cheek, and Delia cried out. Her pussy throbbed, and she felt dampness drip against her thighs.

He muffled the phone against his shoulder. "Wait 'til I get off the phone, hot stuff. And hold still!"

Her back arched when she felt his touch drift toward her most private place. His fingers brushed against her pursed opening, and she shuddered uncontrollably when the thermometer moved.

"Oooh," she groaned.

"Christ, Delia."

She couldn't help it. It felt too sinfully good. She had to bite her lip as he slowly pulled the thermometer out of her.

"Damn it, you're at 104. She's at 104, Doc."

Numbers meant nothing. Need did. Her hips swung determinedly toward him.

His hand clapped onto her backside, and his fingers bit into her overheated flesh. "You're sick, baby," he hissed. "I'm not going to do this."

His touch didn't move, though. If anything, his fingers dipped deeper into the crevice between her butt cheeks. Delia's hips craned higher to meet him. She turned her face on the pillow, and their gazes collided.

A muscle pulsed along his jaw, but he kept his concentration on the phone call. "Right. Keep up with the medication, cold packs, and . . . ease her distress." He nodded. "Sorry about the late call, Dr. Mosely. I'll keep you updated."

He dropped the phone noisily into its cradle, and Delia couldn't wait anymore.

"I *need*," she whispered. It was such a mild word for the fire licking through her veins.

"No," he said firmly. "Not like this. After you feel better."

"Don't leave me like this," she begged. "The doctor said—"

"I know what the doctor said," he replied sharply.

He rolled his shoulders uncomfortably. It was a habit she'd noticed about him at the office. He only did it when he got stressed—and that wasn't very often.

"You don't know what you're doing," he said.

She knew what felt good and what didn't. "Please. It's the only thing that helps."

He shook his head. "You'd hate me when you snap out of this."

She rubbed her butt against his hand like a cat begging to be petted. She couldn't think that far ahead. All that mattered was now. "I'll hate you if you make me suffer."

He made a soft sound and looked away.

"I'm suffering," she whispered.

"Damn it, Delia. That's not fair."

His voice was so gruff; it momentarily drew her away from her obsession. Oh God, had she read him that wrong? The possibility made her heart ache. Hesitantly, she glanced over her shoulder. "Don't you . . . Don't you *want* to?"

His gaze flashed to hers. "You know I do," he said hoarsely.

"Then why?"

"I'm trying to do the right thing here. I'm trying to put you first." He rolled his shoulders again. "Ah, fuck it!"

"I'll go to hell for this," he muttered as he reared back and began to tear at his clothes. They fell onto the floor next to hers, and his belt lashed against the wall before dropping with a thud. Delia inhaled deeply when he pushed down his jeans and shorts in one smooth motion.

He wanted her.

For a moment, she hadn't been sure and it had scared her more than the fever. Now, she knew for certain.

And it excited her even more.

The room wavered about him, but his body was starkly defined by the light still shining from the bed stand. She couldn't tear her gaze from him. His muscles were sleek and taut. She hadn't had a clue what lay under those dark suits he wore. Power radiated from his body, yet he'd been so tender with her.

She glanced down and licked her dry lips.

His cock was thick and hard. It strained upward toward his six-pack abs, and his balls were already drawn up tight. He was big and, from the purplish-red color, she knew he was hot.

Not as hot as she was.

She was at 104 and climbing.

She wiggled her hips shamelessly as he climbed onto the bed behind her. The mattress dipped as his knees bumped against the inside of hers, spreading her wider. A thrill ran through her at the surreality of it all. Earlier today, a simple kiss had pleased her. Now, she was lifting her pussy, begging for penetration.

Things between them were going so far so fast.

She pressed her forehead against the pillow and wrapped her arms around it. Still, her hips jumped when his thumbs touched her. She'd never felt so acutely aware of her body in her life.

He spread her distended lips wide, and the tip of his erection found its place. "Are you sure?" he grunted.

Of him? Or herself?

"Do it," she moaned.

Her air left her lungs in a sudden *whoosh* when he thrust into her. He pushed in hard and long, entering her to the hilt with one roll of his hips. Delia's lungs immediately forgot how to function. She went without air for interminable seconds until they began to fill and expand rapidly.

"Ahhhhh," she cried.

The one, little sound was like a starting pistol. His hips began to swing back and forth, and her fingernails raked along the cotton sheets. Oh God, she hadn't known it would be like this. He felt huge inside her. His thrusts were hard and jagged, increasing the friction until she thought she'd go up in flames.

"You're like a furnace in there," he groaned.

His arms wrapped around her, and his hands caught her breasts. Twin points of fire burned in Delia's nipples when he pinched them. Her air rasped hard in her throat. He wanted more than the fever to submit.

He wanted her.

"Oh, God!" she choked out when he used his hold to pull her to an upright position.

He was pounding straight up into her as she straddled his lap, and his hands were everywhere. One stayed at her breast, but the other slid down her stomach to delve between her legs. She felt surrounded by strength. She could feel the muscles in his thighs and arms clenching as he held her. Inside her, his cock felt invincible. He touched the place where it was plowing away, and white-hot heat suffused her.

Her warrior. Her protector. She'd known he'd fight this for her.

Reaching back, she threaded her fingers through his soft hair. She craned her neck around and pulled him down for a kiss. His tongue batted around inside her mouth with as much gusto as his thickness pumped in and out of her below. She broke the kiss and pressed her head back against his shoulder as her body began to strain toward completion.

"I've wanted to do this for the past two months," he growled into her ear.

She rubbed the forearm against her belly and reached back to catch his hip. They were moving together now in a rough, sexual dance. She could feel every brush of the crisp hair on his chest against her back, every bump of his balls against her bottom. "Why didn't you?" she managed to ask.

"It's called sexual harassment."

"Harass me harder."

He groaned and the remainder of his gentleness fled. His hands bit into her flesh as his hips surged. Delia closed her eyes tightly. He was working deeply now, not even bothering to pull down more than few centimeters before hammering right back up into her furthest reaches.

She bounced on his lap. His breaths hit her ear and dampened her neck. Her senses narrowed to two points— the breast caught in his hand and the very heart of her being so thoroughly ravaged. Her teeth ground together as they went higher, hotter, harder.

Suddenly, she crested.

Her mouth opened in a silent scream. Heat lashed through her body until her muscles went limp. He kept her upright on his lap until she felt him shoot inside her. After a long, poignant moment, he collapsed onto the bed with her still caught in his arms.

"Hell's waiting, but what a way to go," he said behind her. He fought to catch his breath. "You nearly burned my cock off, hot stuff."

Hot stuff. She stirred against the pillow. She'd been called a lot of things because of her red hair, but never "hot stuff." She liked it. It made her feel sexy.

He made her feel sexy.

And sated. The fever had finally retreated.

"I . . . I didn't know it would be like that," she said in awe. No matter how many fantasies she'd had, she'd never dreamed she'd actually make love with him—or that her fantasies would pale in comparison. "I didn't know it could."

"Good," he said, satisfaction clear in his tone.

He pulled her closer and settled them into a more comfortable position, but made no effort to pull his softened erection out of her. Delia gently squeezed her inner muscles to hold him in place and was rewarded with a soft grumble in her ear.

"And don't even begin to think that's because of your damned fever," he said, his lips brushing against the shell of her ear. He nipped her earlobe softly. "Because it's not. Not by a long shot."

Chapter Three

Delia's eyes fluttered open sometime later. She didn't know what had awoken her; the night was still deep and quiet. So was her room. The light on the bed stand that had bothered her for so long was finally extinguished. Settling against her pillow, she looked at the sky outside her bedroom window. The curtains framed a constellation of stars, but she couldn't judge the time.

All she knew was that it was late. Late and apparently cold outside the apartment building. Moonlight reflected off newly fallen snow, making the night take on a serene luminescence.

Lying still, she mentally took stock. The heat inside her—it wasn't gone, but it was bearable. Her body slumped in relief. It had been so bad before, she'd thought she'd implode.

And she had.

Her comfortable stillness took on an edge. Before . . . Snippets of erotic memories floated through her head. The heat. The wanting.

The man.

She listened hard and heard breaths joining hers, echoing

softly throughout the room. Slowly, she rolled onto her back and looked to the other side of the bed—the side that was normally empty.

Tonight, it was definitely filled. With six feet of pure masculinity.

She sucked in a quick breath. He was still here.

Just like he'd promised.

She could see him sleeping in the hazy moonlight. He looked like a worn-out child, lying flat on his belly with his legs spread wide. Self-conscious, she felt her face flush. He had good reason to be tired. Her demands had wrung them both dry.

For the first time, she could see why.

Oh, my.

Her body hummed in appreciation. She'd been so consumed before, she hadn't taken time to appreciate the details. And the beauty of his form was definitely in the details. He was luscious—all muscle, sinew, and smooth, male skin. Her gaze drifted hungrily down his body. He surpassed all the secret fantasies she'd held about him.

Every last one.

Slowly, she propped herself up on her elbow to get a better view. She'd never expected this to happen, but now that it had, she wanted to imprint the memory on her brain. Even relaxed in sleep, the muscles of his body were clearly defined. He was well-built, but not brawny. How did a man get a body like that? Weights? Running? Boxing? Her body melted. He had the body of a fighter.

Her fighter. Her defender.

Her fingers itched to run through his dark, rumpled hair. There hadn't been time to touch him before. It had all been him touching her . . . everywhere. Even now, one of his hands was stretched out toward her as if ready to protect her. Goose bumps sprang up on her skin. She wanted to return the favor. Desperately.

She wanted to kiss him again. She wanted to nibble and suck. She wanted to brush her tongue against his and lap up his dark taste.

She wanted to take him inside her again.

Only this time, she wanted to take it slow and easy.

Arousal pulled at her, and her hand sneaked out of its own volition. She watched curiously as it slid down his back. How had she managed to keep herself from pouncing on him for so long?

"Keep looking at me like that, and I'll be on you whether your fever needs it or not."

Startled, she snatched her hand back. "You're awake."

"And so are you." He stretched like a jungle cat and wrapped his arms around the pillow under his head. His dark eyes focused on her, lazy, yet alert even in the dim light of the room. "You were supposed to stay asleep this time. Aren't you feeling well?"

His drowsy gaze trailed along her figure, and awareness shimmered down Delia's spine. She was naked. Stark, buck naked. She hadn't cared before. She'd hardly realized it, even with all the lights blazing. Here in the intimacy of the darkness, though, she suddenly felt vulnerable. A chill ran through her, and she shivered. She reached for the sheet, but it had been ripped off the bed and was now securely wrapped around his hips.

She tried ineffectually to cover herself with her hands. "Would you—"

"Now she gets shy," he muttered underneath his breath.

Apparently, he wasn't acquainted with the feeling. He rolled to loosen the covers, and her eyes widened when she saw the shadow of dark hair and the swelling between his legs. She knew that swelling intimately. She'd felt it spreading her, filling her.

Her pussy clenched with remembered pleasure, and she couldn't help but stare.

He fluffed the sheet before pulling it up over the both of them. She gratefully tucked the fabric up to her chin, but was surprised when he caught her and pulled her across the bed. Her nipples stiffened when they bumped against his rock-hard chest.

"Oh," she gasped. The chill was chased away. Suddenly, she found herself wrapped up, face-to-face with him in a crowded cocoon.

His dark gaze was steady on hers. "How do you feel?" he asked.

The intimate question made her cunt throb. She could only think of one answer with his body caressing hers and him looking at her like that.

But that wasn't what he meant.

She shifted nervously. This sudden familiarity between them was unsettling, especially considering how distant they behaved at the office. Their relationship was quickly becoming more personal than she was ready to deal with. More emotional. Somehow, the raw, physical closeness they'd experienced earlier had been easier.

"Delia?"

Shadows pressed all around them, and she didn't know what to say. Her head still hadn't cleared. She felt confused, wary, uninhibited, and needy. Definitely needy. His legs brushed against hers, and it was all she could do not to wrap her thigh around his hips.

His hand swept down her back. "You feel a little cooler."

She didn't know about that. Shivers followed his touch down her spine, and she could feel warmth starting to unfurl in her veins. She bit her lip anxiously. It was like that with him. Every time he got close, her body roused. Yet if he stayed away, she hurt.

He gave her a soft shake. "Hot stuff, tell me you're okay."

"I'm fine," she said. She fought the reverie that was trying to pull her under. "Better."

He watched her closely as his hand slid down further, and Delia snapped to attention when his fingers nudged between her legs to cup her from behind. The position forced her bottom to spread to accommodate him. His thick wrist snuggled into the tight crevice and pressed firmly against the puckered bud of her anus. The touch was like a match to her flame. Her body jolted as fire suffused her nerve endings.

"Sore?" he asked softly.

She glanced away and tried to contain the craze surging inside her. How could he expect her to talk when he was touching her like that? "A little."

He bent his head so he could look into her face. His mouth flattened. "Regrets?"

"No," she whispered. Her body lay rigid against his as she fought her basic urges. Her hands were flat on his chest, but she kept them stiff so they wouldn't wander. She didn't regret what she'd done; she couldn't. The need had been ferocious. She'd had no control over it. She remembered, because she was starting to lose her grip all over again.

"Frightened," she admitted.

His brow furrowed. "Of me?"

Yes. Of him. Of the situation. Of the demon swirling inside her. She saw the glimmer of hurt in his eyes and opened her hand over his heart. She let her fingertips caress him as they were dying to do. "Of myself," she said shakily. "I don't usually act this way. I don't beg men to . . . do . . . you know."

She rocked her hips, and they both became acutely aware of where his hand was.

The lines on his forehead smoothed, and he cupped her possessively. "I know."

Did he? Even after the way she'd behaved today?

"The heat," she tried to explain. "It's inside me, and it wants to get out. I have no power over it."

"Don't try. It's exhausting you, baby. I can see it." He stroked her face, and her lashes fluttered when his fingers caressed the pulse throbbing in her temple. "Just let go. I'll take care of things."

She took an unsteady breath even as her hips rocked against the cradle of his more intimately placed hand. She'd never admit it, but she *was* frightened of him. Not physically.

51

No, she knew instinctively that he'd never hurt her. It was this sudden turn in their relationship that unnerved her. She was out of her comfort zone. Maybe even out of her league.

"I'll take care of you, Delia." His lips brushed across her forehead. "Any way you need."

He emphasized his point by strumming his thumb along the sensitive folds between her legs. She flinched, and her breath heaved in her lungs.

"You can't be surprised," he said, reading her reaction. His voice growled close to her ear. "We've been circling each other like two hungry tigers ever since you started working at Lloyd."

She shuddered. They had. The glances. The absent brushes of hands over paperwork. The deep inhales of each other's scent. Her belly clenched.

Unbidden, her hands circled around to his back. Her fingers scraped down the hard planes of his shoulder blades. The muscles contracted, and her nails bit into him. "But you never said anything. Never did anything . . . Until today."

"Yeah, today," he rumbled. His hand fisted in her hair. "Today pushed me past my limits."

She knew all about being pushed past her limits. The fever inside her was starting to rage all over again, and with it, her reticence was fading fast. It was so easy to lean on him, to let him be the strong one. She snuggled closer and brushed her lips down his collarbone. "Why today?"

His grip on her tightened. "It doesn't matter," he said gruffly. "Just know I'm ready to stake my claim."

So was she.

She pushed her mental and emotional concerns aside. It was easier that way. Tonight was about the physical, and she needed it so badly.

She wanted to touch all of him at once. Her body rubbed against his as her hands and mouth wandered. She dipped her head down and boldly licked his nipple. "I've been waiting for you."

He groaned aloud when her hand slid between their tightly pressed bodies and wrapped around his stiff cock. "Delia," he groaned.

She stroked him eagerly, pumping her hand up and down as he became thicker and hotter. Two months was a long time to wait. She couldn't wait any more. She swung her thigh over his hip, and their hands batted against each other in their impatience to position him.

Slow and easy be damned. It wasn't going to happen this time.

"It's starting again," she said anxiously. The heat was right there at its pinnacle. She let out a whimper when his broad tip found her notch.

"I know, hot stuff." His voice was rough, but his hand was gentle as it slid around to cup her bottom. "I can feel it, too."

"I need you!"

The hand on her backside anchored her as he thrust into her. Her neck arched as stars exploded behind her eyelids. The heat began to seep out of her core into her extremities. Her fingertips blazed across his skin as she touched him everywhere she could reach. "Oh, God. Yes!"

"Damn," he groaned. "You're on fire again."

He lifted her leg higher around his waist and began to pound into her, fast and hard. Passion was already over-whelming Delia's senses. Fire had even entered her lungs; she felt it with every breath she drew. She slid her hand away from his neck and down to his hip. Her fingers clenched.

"The flames . . ."

"Hold on to me, baby." His breaths were hot against her ear. "I'll put them out or we'll go down in them together."

And so the night went. Delia couldn't count the number of times she woke in feverish need that only he could douse. From the front, from behind, with his hands, with his mouth—his stamina kept pace with her the entire night. The fire reduced her inhibitions to ashes. Anything that would bank the blaze was acceptable.

Beyond acceptable. *Craved.*

After four hours had passed, he fed her more antibiotics. Her temperature refused to abate. Time and again, he rolled her onto her stomach and slid the thermometer deep into her ass. Each time, he swore when he read the result. Cold compresses were constantly swept down her overheated body. Twice, he stood her under a cool shower, and when that didn't work, he resorted to calling the doctor again.

"Come on, hot stuff," he said as he hung up the phone. "It's time we got serious about this."

Delia looked at him weakly. The past few hours had drained her strength. The fever was winning. She squirmed on the bedsheets, trying to find relief, but there was none. Even the curtain of her hair falling over her shoulder was too much. She spread the long strands across the pillow away from her skin and covered her eyes with the cold compress he'd given her.

"Doctor Mosely said we need to bring your temperature down *now*." He took the compress from her eyes and tossed it toward the bathroom. It landed on the floor with a *splotch*. "You need to be comfortable enough to sleep—and not for these little fifteen minute patches you've been taking. Your body's restorative powers need time to work."

"Can't sleep," she said tiredly. "The sheets are blistering my skin."

"I know, baby." He rubbed her shoulder gently before standing. It took some searching, but he found his jeans and pulled them on. He looked at her determinedly as he stepped into his shoes. "We're going to fix that."

His voice had taken on an edge. It was one she'd heard before, but not tonight. Her eyebrows drew together when he swept a blanket off the floor and came toward her. She tried to back away, but he caught her and pulled her across the sheets. She struggled when he wrapped the blanket around her and plucked her up into his arms. "No," she said. "It's suffocating me."

"You'll want it soon enough."

"What do you mean? What are you doing?" She clutched at his shoulders when he carried her out of the bedroom. She looked around in confusion when he took her down the hallway and headed straight for the front door of her apartment. What was he thinking? "We can't leave! I'm not dressed. Neither are you!"

55

"It's four o'clock in the morning, babe. Everyone else is asleep." He juggled her into a more secure position and grabbed her keys as he walked by the kitchen table.

Was he out of his mind? It was winter. She might be baking, but she'd seen the crystal stillness outside her window. She knew what it meant. It was freezing out there. He didn't have a shirt on and all she had was a blanket. This was crazy. "Let me put some clothes on first! I don't want to go to the hospital *naked*," she hissed.

His jaw remained firm.

"We're not going to the hospital. At least not yet."

Security-conscious even in the middle of the night, he locked her apartment door and started down the hallway. Delia looked around nervously. It was late, but she had neighbors. Mrs. Sneed, in particular, liked to keep close tabs on her. They were being quiet, but knowing the old lady, she'd wake up and want to know what was going on.

Delia would like to know that herself. She pushed the blanket away from her face and neck. Between it and his body heat, she was about ready to pass out. She shook her head to stay alert. "Tell me where we're going."

He jabbed the down button for the elevator. "The doctor had one more idea."

She kicked the blanket until at least her feet were bare. Another idea? Finally! "Anything," she said. "The heat's driving me mad."

His arms tightened protectively. "Be careful what you wish for."

She glanced at him sharply, and his profile wavered. She

waited, but he steadfastly refused to return her look. It made her nervous. Nervous enough to flinch when the elevator dinged, and the door slid open. "Tell me," she said.

He carried her onto the elevator and used his elbow to hit the button for the ground floor. A muscle worked in his jaw as he leaned back against the elevator wall. She almost thought he wasn't going to answer until he started talking.

"If I took you to the hospital now, they'd put you in an ice bath," he said quietly. "Your temperature had come down three degrees, but now it's back up. It's been too high for too long."

An ice bath? Uneasiness settled in the pit of her stomach.

His dark gaze finally locked onto hers. "The hospital staff could take care of you, but they wouldn't let me help you. Not the way that you need."

Her eyes widened when his meaning became clear. The fever had reduced her to her most primal needs. Together, they'd only found one way to slake them. If he wasn't there . . . Even if they did let him in the room with her . . . She couldn't have the whole world seeing her like that!

The bell rang, and the elevator door opened ominously. His hands tightened on her, but he didn't move. "It's your choice," he said gruffly. "The hospital or me?"

She knew what he intended to do, and it wasn't a choice at all.

Still, he'd said he'd take care of her, and that's exactly what he'd done all night. He'd nursed her, showing a gentle side she hadn't known he had. He'd coerced her into taking her pills, betraying the assertive side she knew all too well.

He'd held her, he'd bathed her, and he'd made love to her. She had to trust him in this. "You," she whispered.

A soft sound escaped from the back of his throat, but his eyes darkened. His face hardened in determination, and he strode out into the main lobby like a man on a mission.

Delia braced herself as they neared the plate glass windows. It looked like a postcard outside. Puffy white snow clung to tree limbs. Moonlight reflected off the layer of powder that blanketed the earth. Everything looked so pretty and inviting.

She knew better.

She knew how the wind could whistle, the snow could bite, and the air could pinch. She cringed even though her body was scorching. It just might be too much. "What's the temperature out there?" she whispered.

His lips brushed against her temple. "You don't want to know."

He wouldn't tell her; that could only mean one thing. It was going to hurt. Second thoughts assailed her. "I don't know about this."

He stood poised in front of the door that led to the apartment complex courtyard. "We have to do it, Delia. You've been running a high-grade temperature for hours. Your body's going to start turning on itself."

His voice became strained, and he cuddled her closer. "We can't mess with this piece of wonder."

Her heart pounded against her chest, and she felt his thudding against her side. She'd never heard him so serious. It scared her, but not as much as going to the hospital and having to do this without him. She needed his steadfastness. She needed his support. She needed him.

She summoned what little strength she had. "What do I have to do?"

"Just hold on to me."

Done. She was already holding him so tightly her finger-nails had left half-moon indentations on his shoulders. She heard the door open. Scared, she pressed her face against his neck. The cold night air swept through her hair. It felt good yet dreadful at the same time.

She wrapped her arms around his neck, sharing her heat with him. Why hadn't he gotten dressed? He didn't need to come out here like this. He wasn't proving anything to her. "You stupid he-man. You're going to get sick, too."

"Then you can return the favor."

Snow scrunched under his feet. Fear swamped her when he stopped walking. He'd carried her to a shadowed area be-neath a tree in the courtyard. Watching her intently, he let her feet drop into the mound of snow.

Delia gasped from the pain. It felt like she'd just stepped on a bunch of little daggers. "Aiiieee!"

"I'm sorry, baby," he said gruffly. His callused hands shook as he cupped her face. "I hate doing this to you."

"Then don't," she said through clenched teeth. The pain was sharper than she'd prepared herself for. Her entire body began to quake. He was right about the blanket. She clung to it, wrapping it around her as tightly as it would go. What had they been thinking? "I don't want to do this. It isn't going to work."

"Try to remember it's for your own good."

"Don't say that." Her feet danced awkwardly in and out of the icy snow. Puddles were forming around her toes, but the prickle was just as sharp. "Things that are good for you taste bad, make you uncomfortable . . . or *hurt*. This hurts!"

"I know, but it will only be for a little while. I swear. Just focus on me."

She shook her head. "I can't. Take me back inside."

"Try to hold on."

"It's too cold. Give me the keys."

"No."

She held out her hand. He could be a taskmaster, but he wasn't cruel.

"No!" A shuttered look came over his face. "Goddamnit, if you want me to be the bad guy, I will."

She gasped when he suddenly fisted his hand in the blanket between her breasts and yanked it off her. Without ceremony, he dropped it behind him, leaving her naked to the elements and anybody who might be looking out a window into the courtyard.

"Hey!" she yelped. "Give that back to me!"

"Later." He stepped in front of her to block her way when she tried to reach for it. "We do this first."

She looked at him in shock. He stared right back.

Delia didn't know what to do. The night air brushed her body intimately. It scraped against her nipples and prodded between her legs. Heat and shivers alternately racked her. The contrast was too much. *She needed that blanket!*

She tried to go around him, but he was quick. Every way

she turned, he was there. As a last-ditch effort, she lunged at him. Breathing hard, she climbed him and wrapped her legs around his waist to get her throbbing feet out of the snow. "Enough," she said firmly. "I've changed my mind."

"I haven't."

She felt tears press at her eyes. He'd given her everything she'd wanted tonight. Why couldn't he give her this?

His cool hands swept down her back and encircled her hips. He was going to push her away. She prepared to fight him—but then his head dipped. The kiss he planted on her lips was hard and tumultuous.

Passion tore through Delia, diverting all other thoughts.

"Don't let go," he growled when he came up for air.

Her eyes widened in panic, but then he was kissing her again. The skyline tilted behind his shoulders, and her arms and legs constricted around him. He didn't drop her, and he didn't let her go. Holding her as if she were the most precious thing in the world, he went down into the snowbank with her.

And pinned her there.

Delia shrieked when the cold hit her back, her neck, and the curves of her bottom. The snow felt like needles piercing her sensitive skin. She lurched upright, but his heavy weight bore down on her, trapping her. His lips came down hard again, swallowing her gasps and pleas.

She tore her mouth away and writhed in distress. She tried to dislodge him, but his strength more than doubled hers. Those muscled arms that had held her so tenderly all night were now holding her down. "It hurts," she sobbed.

Tears streamed down her cheeks, but his face remained set in stone.

"Just a few more minutes, hot stuff," he said in a ragged voice. "Come on, now. Do this for me."

She could finally see what lurked in his dark eyes. Concern. Anguish. And resolve.

His head dipped, but this time his mouth caught her breast. He sucked her nipple deep. The heat of his mouth was at such odds with the cold underneath her, Delia was stunned motionless. His mouth tugged insistently, suckling and nipping. She closed her eyes and moaned. The sensations were too intense. Her body wasn't built to withstand this dual assault.

"Oh, I can't do this. Not now."

"You can and you will. Stay with me, baby," he crooned.

His kiss drifted lower and skimmed across her belly. His tongue dipped into her belly button, and her lungs heaved. He'd made love to her all night, but not like this. He was dominating her, making her respond, forcing her to pay more attention to him than the cold. His teeth raked across her skin, low on her abdomen, and her body jolted.

She couldn't fight him and the fever at the same time. She had to submit to one.

"Look at me," he ordered.

Her eyelids felt heavy as she strained to open them. He'd leveraged himself up onto his knees to straddle her. She looked up at him, bleary-eyed. He looked like a dark devil as he loomed over her. She didn't understand the edge to his voice until he scooped up two handfuls of snow from beside her.

"We've got to get you cooled down one way or the other," he said, his voice almost fierce.

Before she could comprehend what he meant, he turned his palms and ground the crisp white crystals onto her breasts. The chill flayed her.

"Ah!" Her back arched, and her cry rent the air. She tore at his hands, but he cupped her tenaciously as the snow melted into icy water. Streams ran over her body, seeking crevices and finding them. She lurched, but he kept fondling her aggressively, working the cold into the very tips of her nipples.

"Stop!" she gasped.

His mouth came down hot on her belly, and his tongue was wicked. He licked up the excess water, causing heat bolts to shoot through her system, but the ice stream had started to run through her veins. "It's too much," she whined.

He'd gone too far.

Her fingers threaded through his hair and bit into his scalp. He was trying to help. Her frantic brain comprehended that much, but it didn't stop her from fighting him. She squirmed in the melting snow, trying to buck him off, roll him over, or just *escape*.

One hand left her breast, and she thought she'd been given a reprieve. All conscious thought left her, though, when he scooped up another handful of snow. He braced his other hand against her breastbone to keep her from moving. Her heart thudded against his palm. Their gazes locked, hers showing trepidation, his lit with a combination of regret and desire.

"Open your legs," he demanded. One denim-covered knee pressed insistently between her thighs.

"No!" she gasped. She couldn't take that. Not that!

She clawed at him, trying to find a way to make him stop. He wouldn't. She could see it in his eyes. She whimpered when the pressure increased and her thighs gave way. Before she could recover, both his knees were inside hers, spreading her wide.

Suddenly, he moved up over her. Delia flinched, but then he was kissing her with white-hot intensity. It clashed with the glacial shock that tore through her system when he shoved the handful of snow against her cunt.

Her body went rigid.

He was cupping the cold powder against the part of her that burned the hottest.

And the brightest. Her sensitive nerve endings screamed.

Her mouth opened in a silent cry, and his tongue dove deep. Shudders of pleasure and distress rocked her body as his cold, wet fingers began to probe.

"I'll make it better," he promised. His voice sounded tight. "I swear. We'll get through this together."

His fingers were persistent. Delia bucked and swayed, but she couldn't shake him. He lodged his fingers deep and began to draw out her own, hot moisture.

She cried out when she felt the demon rise inside her again.

"Turn it loose, hot stuff. Let me at it." He moved until he hovered over her way down low and dipped his head. Her fingernails bit into his shoulders when she felt warm puffs of air caress her inflamed pussy.

"Stop this," she cried. "Get off me!"

"Shh." Still curling his fingers inside her, he let his mouth touch her. Her thigh muscles clenched. Opening his mouth, he used his tongue. He laved it over her, licking at her swollen tissues and delving into the sensitive dips.

"Ooh! What are you . . . ? Oh, God."

"Tell me what feels good, Delia. Tell me what you need."

"I don't need this."

"Yes, you do. We both know you do."

He replaced his fingers with his tongue, and her discomfort swiftly morphed into pleasure. "Oh, damn you. Yes! Right there."

"Like this?"

"Yessss."

Suddenly, it didn't matter that icy water was pooling between her breasts and under her body. The fever was back at fighting strength, but he was there to take it on. He spread her legs wider to give himself more room, and snow worked its way into the crease of her bottom. Her body roiled, but he just snuffled at her with more intent.

"Ahhh!" Her fingers clawed at him, leaving scratch marks on his shoulders and the back of his neck.

Curtains fluttered when she cried out, but Delia didn't care. Her lover did.

His head swung towards Mrs. Sneed's window, and he let out a curse. Quickly, he grabbed the blanket. He swung it around his bare shoulders and up over his head, hiding the private interlude from the old woman's prying eyes.

Delia felt waves of heat and cold alternately roll through

her body. It was too powerful to last long. He ate at her, drawing out her wet juices and driving her upward. He settled down deeper into the vee of her legs. With the blanket over him, she couldn't see him. Couldn't prepare herself.

She jerked when his mouth latched onto her clit. The suction was tight and hot. She felt herself climbing. Her head rocked back and forth, grinding into the snow until her hair was sopping. The wet tendrils lashed against her shoulders, but he still didn't stop.

He grabbed more handfuls of snow. They hit her torso in soft splashes, making her squirm. Her hips pumped steadily against his mouth.

"I can't," she whimpered. "No more. Make it end."

He urged her legs back toward her chest, and soft smacking sounds echoed from between her legs. She reached under the blanket and cupped the back of his head.

"Please, I can't take it."

"Just this," he said. "Take this."

Suddenly, she felt a handful of snow rub against her lifted bottom. Unhurriedly, he scraped his thumbnail against the top of the crack of her ass. Burrowing between her cheeks, he trailed the cold snow all the way down to her anus.

The icy pad of his thumb pressed against her there hard.

He nipped at her clit at the same time, and Delia came.

She came with a rush. Opening her eyes, she felt herself catapulting toward the stars. She clung to him as the swells hit her, one after the other. It went on for a long, long time. When the quakes turned to tremors, she fell back into the snow, not caring about the cold, the wet, or the muck.

She was replete.

"God, hot stuff," he said, breathing heavily. "You just went off like a fucking volcano."

He braced his hands against his thighs as he fought to get himself under control. Finally, he wiped his mouth with the back of his hand. "Now we can go back inside. Let's get you cleaned up."

With unsteady hands, he wrapped the blanket around her and swept her into his arms. He pushed himself to his feet and adjusted her until his grip was sure. The look on his face was so severe it should have frightened her, but Delia just curled her body toward his.

He didn't intimidate her anymore. She was a strong, independent woman, and his protective instincts turned her to mush.

"What about you?" she said softly into his ear as he walked swiftly toward the building. His stiff erection was bumping hard against her hip, but she was suddenly more concerned when she felt the shudders running through him. He'd been half-naked out there, too.

"This wasn't about sex," he grunted as he let them in with her key. The lobby door swooshed shut behind them. He pushed the up button for the elevator and tucked the blanket around her more closely as they waited. "I don't think your fever broke, but you're not so flushed. How do you feel? Tell me you're better."

She looked at him, stunned.

It hadn't been about sex—and he actually meant that.

Her heart squeezed. Feeling incredibly humbled, she

opened the blanket and wrapped him inside with her. She pressed her breasts against his rippled chest. She had body heat to spare, and he needed it. "I'm better."

His stern countenance disintegrated, and he pressed his face hard into her neck. "I'm so sorry I had to put you through that."

"You made it a lot more pleasant than it could have been." She wove her fingers through his soft hair and kissed the sensitive spot behind his ear. "Thank you for not taking me to the hospital."

He took a deep breath, but didn't lift his head. "If this doesn't work, that's where we're going."

She caressed the tense muscles at the nape of his neck. "It worked," she whispered.

She threw one last look out the window over his shoulder and saw the lewd snow angel they'd left under the tree. His treatment had been unorthodox, but it was something she'd never forget—both for the sexual revelations and for the depth of the caring it had exposed. She'd never dreamed she'd find that in him.

She nuzzled his ear as the elevator door opened. "It worked," she whispered. "Now, take me back to bed. It's time I took care of you."

Chapter Four

Delia slept. She slept for hours in a deep sleep, never once budging from the spot on the bed on which he laid her. It was only the morning sunlight pouring through the window that finally roused her. She woke with a groan. She didn't feel rested. Her head was still foggy, and her body felt as if it weighed a thousand pounds. Why had she woken?

She squinted as the sun nearly blinded her. It was bright. It filled the corners of the room, reflected off the white sheets—

And stoked the ever-present fire inside her.

Her hand instinctively went to her belly. That was why. Anxiousness threatened to overwhelm her. The low burn was still there, simmering deep in her core. She could feel it. It was controlled for now, but she knew the signs. She knew where they would lead.

She rolled onto her back and restlessly kicked off the sheets. Had that dip in the snow been for nothing?

She'd told him it had worked.

And it had—but only for a while.

She couldn't ignore her fear any longer. This fever had

taken her by surprise, and she didn't have the strength to fight it on her own anymore. Not even with his help. She was ready to go to the doctor.

But not like this.

She squirmed on the bed and tried to ease the throbbing that had started between her legs. It wasn't simmering any longer. It was as if she'd kicked the embers and fed it the oxygen it needed. The hunger was roaring back to life.

Feebly, she looked across the rumpled bed to her lover. He'd been up with her all night, but sleep had taken him down for the count. His strength needed replenishing, too. He looked as if he wouldn't wake for hours.

And she needed him.

Her gaze drifted over him longingly. His hair was still tousled, but this time it was of her doing . . . as were the scratches on his shoulders and the faint hickey on his neck. She watched as his chest rose and fell. A dark shadow of whiskers had appeared along his jawline, and she pressed her legs together tightly. She could imagine how that prickly hair would feel along the tender skin of her inner thighs.

The quickening set upon her again. Hard.

Her gaze slid down the canvas of muscles until she saw the part of him that could ease her ache. Even after such a never-ending night, a morning erection still rose. Desire made her shiver, and she glanced up at his face again. She hated to wake him.

Yet she had to do something.

Her body tingled when realization set in. There was only one option. She was going to have to handle it herself.

Nerves assailed her.

Could she do it? With him lying so nearby?

The fire inside her told her she had to. She couldn't wait any longer.

Lying back, she took a deep breath. It didn't have the calming effect she wished for. Excitement and trepidation sizzled through her veins.

She stared blindly at the ceiling, unable to watch what she was doing. Slowly, she slid the hand on her stomach lower. Her fingers came across the tangle of red hair that he'd found so fascinating. Her muscles quivered, but she didn't stop. Spreading her legs, she let her fingers explore. Hesitantly, they slid through the tender, wet folds of her pussy.

She winced softly. Their sexual marathon had left her sore, but the tenderness didn't matter. Her need outweighed it a thousand times over.

Anticipation made hurry. She reached deeper and bit her lower lip as two fingers slid into her damp channel. Her heels dug into the mattress, and her body bowed.

It was good, but it wasn't the same. Her hands weren't as big as his—or as sure. She wiggled her fingers and timidly began to pump. She closed her eyes tightly as her thumb nudged her clit.

"Need some help with that?"

The rumble of the low voice made her eyelids fly open. Her head jerked to the side, and she found him watching her. Caught! She felt her face flush with embarrassment. The mattress shifted as he rolled onto his side and propped his head into his hand. His actions were lazy, but his eyes were alert.

So was his cock. He'd lengthened and thickened in the short time since she'd last stolen a peek at him.

She jerked her hand away from her crotch, but he caught her wrist and pressed it tight against her curls. "Don't let me stop you."

"I can't," she whispered. "Not in front of you."

"Why not? We've done just about everything else there is to do." Weaving his fingers through hers, he gently wedged their joined hands back between her legs. He'd barely begun to teach her the movement when his dark gaze flew up to her face. "Damn it, Delia. You're on fire again. Why didn't you wake me?"

She groaned as her hips rolled up to meet their combined touch. "You needed your sleep."

"I've dealt with less sleep before and lived. For God's sake, you're the one I'm worried about." He let her fingers go and penetrated her deeply, examining her for himself. The lines of his face drew tight. "Come here."

She gasped when he rolled onto his back and took her with him. His strength still surprised her. He lifted her as if she were light as a feather and settled her over his hips. She straddled him uncertainly as he let her weight come down onto her knees.

"There," he said. "Use me."

She spread her fingers wide on the muscled chest beneath her. Why argue with him? He was what she really wanted. Really needed.

Reaching down, she wrapped her fist around his thick erection. He grunted at her soft touch. A ghost of a smile lit her lips as she looked into his eyes. She'd been shy with herself; with him, it felt natural. Gradually, she impaled herself. It wasn't as easy as it had been last night. He'd ridden her hard, and she was swollen.

His neck arched as she took him to the hilt. "God, you're like a blowtorch."

"Help me put the fire out."

His fingers bit into her waist. "One time," he said, breathing hard. "One time and then I'm taking you to the emergency room."

Delia's head fell back, and her hair brushed against the small of her back. She savored the connection between them. She couldn't get enough of the feel of his cock stretching her. She loved how his fingers clutched at her. Her ears craved his grunts of satisfaction. She began to move and a moan of delight left the back of her throat.

"Christ," he hissed. His rough hands came up to cup her breasts possessively. "You are so beautiful."

After hours of moonlight loving, the sun was glaring. It left nowhere to hide. Everything was out in the open and brilliantly displayed. Emotion mixed with the heat burning inside Delia's chest, and she went a little crazy. Her hair swung wildly about her shoulders as she shagged him in quick, rough movements. Her breasts bounced in his hands, and her bottom slapped against his hips. The fever inside her roared, and the tingle at the back of her neck told her she was close.

She was going to come, and she'd hardly gotten started. One, two . . . On the third pump, her muscles clenched.

Her thighs gripped his hips as she ground herself onto him. Shimmering waves of heat and satisfaction swept through her. She went lightheaded and felt herself break out in a sweat. Suddenly, her body was coated with moisture. Droplets ran down her temples, and she shivered at the river running down her back.

"Yes!" he barked beneath her. His hips slammed up so hard, her knees left the bed. "That damned fever has finally broken."

Delia's eyes flew open. The constant haze that had filled her head finally cleared. Her mind focused on his voice. His familiar, authoritative voice. Her gaze snapped to his face.

"Mr. Lloyd!"

Shock hit her, and she nearly fell off him.

His eyebrows lifted in surprise, but understanding made his features turn hard.

"Oh, no, you don't," he growled. He caught her in his arms and rolled until she was flat on her back beneath him.

Delia's breaths went short in her chest. Jackson Lloyd was in her bed. In her bed? He was in her, buried about as deep as he could go. They were connected as a man and woman, and it mortified her. She was taking her boss—a man she could barely talk to on the best of days. When she thought of the things they'd done . . .

"Damn it. Don't back away. You're not going to do this to me. To us."

She couldn't respond. Oh, God. What must he think of her?

His face took on a ferocious cast.

"Spread wider," he demanded. His hands caught the insides of her thighs and pushed her legs outwards until she had no defenses left. She lay open and vulnerable to his intimate thrusts, and he drew them out to make sure she knew exactly what they were doing together.

"Don't look at me that way," he said. "You knew it was me. Goddamnit. You knew it was me!"

Words couldn't escape her tight throat. Conflicting emotions rocked her. Had she known it was him? She'd known she was safe. She'd known she was wanted. That was as far as her clouded brain had gotten.

"You thought I was Rob."

The skin at his cheekbones pulled tight. His teeth ground together as his head dropped in defeat. His hips, though, weren't giving up.

Delia didn't know what to say. The look in his eyes had captured her. He was angry, but there was also hurt in those dark depths. Deep, cutting hurt. She lay still, accepting his thrusts, but remained uncertain as to what she should do.

"No," she said, finally finding her voice. "I didn't think you were Rob."

He lodged deep inside her and stared at her face. The tension in the room skyrocketed. "Then what did you think?"

She couldn't get enough air into her lungs.

Last night, she'd been confused. The fever had affected her thinking processes.

But never once had she thought she was making love with Rob.

"I wasn't thinking at all," she admitted in a tiny voice. She squirmed beneath him uncomfortably. "My head . . . I think I was delirious."

His hips rolled. "So I was convenient? It didn't matter who I was as long as I kept the fire in your pussy banked?"

She shrank back from his harsh words, but he had her pinned against the mattress. Nailed was a better description. He was hard, thick, and determined. If anything, he'd sunk into her even deeper.

"No," she said on a soft cry. Oh, God. He was nudging against her very cervix. Her head rolled on the pillow. "It wasn't like that."

Any old stud wouldn't have done. She hadn't needed *servicing*. She'd needed him. Even now, knowing who he was, her body was still heating, straining to meet his.

He caught her face in both hands and made her look at him. "Then why are you so surprised? Why are you so upset? Christ, Delia. Is it really that hard for you to be with me?"

"Yes!"

Her dream lover was Jackson Lloyd! Before, her instincts had always told her to run whenever he'd gotten close . . . And she suddenly realized why. He'd been right. They'd been quietly circling each other for months. She'd flirted with Rob, but that had been because he was safe. Safe and harmless.

Jackson was anything but.

"You scare me," she whispered.

He snapped back as if she'd just hit him. The look on his face was stunned. Crestfallen. "I'd never hurt you," he said hoarsely. "You've got to know that."

"I do." Oh, why had she said anything? She didn't want to get into this. "It's not that."

"Then what is it?"

The tone of his voice made her shiver. He wasn't going to let it go. She'd thought he'd been intense at the office; in bed, he was overpowering.

"You . . . You make me feel things that I shouldn't. I don't know how to act when I'm around you." Reaching up, she covered her face with her hands. "You make me lose control enough as it is, but after last night . . . Now you know."

She felt his tense body relax and then he was coaxing her hands to the side. "Is that all? Hell, hot stuff, you're not the only one who went wild last night. You should have warning signs posted on you. Don't you know you scare the shit out of me, too?"

Hesitantly, she peeked at him. "I do?"

"Fuck, yeah, but I'm not going to let that stop me." He looked her dead in the eye. "Are you?"

Slowly, he wedged his hand between their bodies. Watching her closely, he flicked her clit. The sensation brought her need back with a rush. It percolated out of her core and bubbled through her veins. Her thighs tightened around his hips, but he refused to move. His lungs worked like a bellows as he braced himself over her, watching her face. Assessing her.

"Look at me," he said. He fingered her again, and she groaned. "We're good together. You can't deny it."

She couldn't. Not with the way her body was betraying her. She ran her hands down his back, trying to encourage him to move. To thrust.

He shuddered, but stayed stock-still. "You've got to make the choice, Delia. Do you want some unknown dream lover or me?"

She wrapped her legs around his hips.

"What do you want, baby?" he growled.

She couldn't fight it anymore.

"I want you." She caught his shoulders as her back bowed. "*Jackson!*"

His control snapped, and he began to pound into her.

Delia clung to him like a life raft in a storm. Her need had been strong all night, but now it threatened to incinerate her. The heat was blinding. Her teeth scraped along his shoulder, and she held on for dear life. "What's wrong with me? Why won't it stop?"

"You're in heat, baby," he growled. He thrust so hard and so fast, the headboard rattled against the wall. "I don't care about the doctor's diagnosis. You needed to mate."

Mate. The word was enough to make her come. The orgasm slammed into her hard, and he wasn't far behind. He thrust one more time, nearly sending the headboard through the wall into Mrs. Sneed's apartment, and his body stiffened. He spurted into her for what seemed like forever before he sagged onto her.

They lay there together, his weight pressing her into the mattress as the urgency dissipated.

Delia went quiet.

Jackson Lloyd was her lover. The whole man. Every side of him.

Timidly, she ran her fingers down his spine. It was going to take some adjusting to, but he was still the same man he'd been in the darkness. Sexy. Bold. Caring. He'd be good to her. He'd be good for her. There was no reason to be nervous.

Other than the fact that he held her livelihood in his hands.

Her eyes widened. The day was already half over. "The bid!"

"Rob's taking care of it," he murmured tiredly. He nuzzled the side of her neck, and she felt her cheeks flame as he slowly disconnected their bodies.

The budget. That was probably the reason he'd come here in the first place. He'd needed clarification on something—the sensor quotes, her spreadsheet . . .

Her thoughts came to a screeching halt. Oh, God. Her spreadsheet.

He'd found the error and had come here to fire her.

"Rob's terrible with numbers!" She pushed at Jackson's shoulders. "Let me up. I'll go in and make sure everything's ready. We've still got some time."

He moved to her side so she could breathe more easily, but kept one leg thrown securely over her hips. His dark eyes were alert, but he seemed more curious than angry. "It's ready. I cleaned up your spreadsheet last night and gave him the final numbers before I came here. Don't worry about it."

"But . . . I don't understand. If you didn't come here about the budget . . ."

"Are you asking me why I showed up at your apartment in the middle of the night?"

She hesitantly nodded.

He tucked a strand of her hair behind her ear. "Twenty-two."

Her eyebrows drew together. It wasn't what she'd expected to hear. "What?"

"Twenty-two. I knew you were sick when I found that error. You never make mistakes like that." His fingers brushed across her cheekbone, and the look on his face sobered. "That's when I knew it was serious. I got over my jealousy real fast."

"You were jealous?" she choked out. "About what?"

He actually looked embarrassed. "You caught me by surprise when you left work so suddenly, and when I saw Rob with his arm around you . . ."

"I knew you got the wrong impression!"

"What was I supposed to think when you two started sucking face on a public sidewalk? You want to talk about envy? That old green monster took a huge bite out of my ass."

The kiss. Delia was horrified. She hadn't known he was watching. She never would have let Rob kiss her if she'd known.

The realization made her come up short. She never would have let Rob touch her. A flirty little kiss or two was okay, but if he'd asked for anything more?

She would have been tempted, but Jackson was the one. They'd been gearing up for this for two months. It was he that made her feet stumble, her words clumsy, and her heart slam against her rib cage.

She looked at him in wonder. "I thought Rob was your best friend."

"He is—the little prick. He staged that whole thing and thought it was funny, too."

"He did what?"

For once, Jackson was the one who acted uncomfortable. He let out a long breath and ran his hand through his hair. "He knew how I felt about you," he said quietly. "Hell, he's known since the first day I interviewed you, and he's been goading me to do something about it ever since. Yesterday, though, he kicked his plan into high gear."

"But . . . I don't understand."

"Let's just say we had a man-to-man talk when he got back to the office."

"Oh, no." Delia didn't like the sound of that. "You two didn't. I never meant to come between the two of you."

"Relax. That pretty boy face of his is just fine." Jackson reached out and began to toy with her hair. He seemed entranced with the way the red strands wrapped around his fingers. "You'll find a receipt for a new trash can, though, when you get back to the office."

Delia couldn't help it. The thought of Jackson Lloyd losing his legendary control—and over her—made her feel all warm inside. It wasn't the feverish heat she'd felt over the course of the night, but a warmth that went deep into her being and wouldn't go away. She finally understood what that mischievous smile on Rob's face had been about. "He told you to come check on me last night."

"It's the only thing that saved his puny butt. That, plus the fact that he kept his hands to himself." Jackson glanced at her uncertainly. "Are you disappointed?"

She lifted her head and shyly kissed the mark her teeth had left on his shoulder. "No."

He cupped the back of her head and held her look. "Somebody needed to take care of you—and it was going to be me."

"I'm glad it was," she murmured. Finding him in her bed had been a surprise, but it was turning out to be a good one. It was just going to take her a while to merge her night lover with her day boss. Still, knowing what she did about him . . . his power, his compassion, his mouthwatering body, his un-blinking focus . . . ooh, the possibilities were endless.

A thought occurred to her, one that had bothered her even in her delirium. "But how did you get in?"

He pulled back and looked at her with one eyebrow lifted.

"Oh, that's right," she said with embarrassment. He was a security expert.

"That's it." He pushed himself off her and hovered above her on all fours. "It's time to take you in for that checkup."

Delia protested when he gathered her up in his arms and carried her to the bathroom. "You're not still taking me to the doctor."

He set her on her feet and reached out to turn on the shower. "The hell I'm not."

For some reason, standing upright beside him totally naked brought back her shyness. She knew she was being silly, but she grabbed a towel from the rack and wrapped it around herself. "But . . . I'm better. I swear."

He looked at the towel with a scowl on his face. "You had a rough night, hot stuff. I want to make sure you're okay."

She reached out and caught his arm, surprising herself when it felt natural to do so. "But Jackson . . . Dr. Mosely knows."

"Knows what?" The hard look on his face softened. "That you've been horny as a mink?"

Her cheeks flamed, and she looked away. There was no ignoring him, though, when he caught her towel and tossed it aside. He wrapped his arm around her and pulled her close. Her breasts flattened against his chest, and Delia felt her heart thud when she looked up into his face.

Jackson Lloyd.

Her lover.

He looked at her languidly, and she recognized the gleam in his eyes.

"So let old Doc be jealous," he said. "I'm the one who got to play firefighter."

Her breath caught when he lifted her and entered her in one smooth motion.

He groaned at the tight clasp of her body. "And, baby, I'm not giving up the job."

He stepped under the spray of water and pushed her up hard against the shower wall. He looked deep into her eyes as water sluiced down their hot, sticky skin. "I want to fuck you again, Delia," he whispered. "I want your eyes open and your mind clear, so you know exactly who's doing you."

Her fingers dug into his shoulders, and she brazenly swiveled her hips. She had a lot to learn about the man, but this was one side of him she knew well. "I thought you said 'one time.'"

He laughed—yet another uncharacteristic reaction that she was going to have to get used to. She didn't think it would be too hard.

"Your fever hadn't broken then," he said with a grin. He thrust slowly, and the grin slipped into a groan. "We'll make it two."

She locked her ankles around his back and arched into him. She could hardly believe it, but it was even better now that the heated fog had left her brain.

"Or maybe twenty-two," she said breathlessly. "It depends on how you do the math."

Epilogue

Heads up! Check out Camera 1 in the lobby."

"Whoa. Look at those legs."

"And that hair." The man behind the monitor sighed dramatically. "I've always had a thing for redheads. Wonder what room she's in."

"*Mine*," Jackson said firmly. He pushed himself away from the wall against which he'd been leaning, and the Berkshire security team suddenly became all-business. To make sure they stayed that way, he planted himself behind them and crossed his arms over his chest. "That camera's slightly off center. Try adjusting it five degrees to the right. I should be able to see both the front door and the main desk when it's in stationary mode."

Keyboard keys began clicking furiously, and the sound made him ease up a bit. The hotel team was doing one last training run on their new camera system. He had confidence it would live up to their expectations; he just felt it best to make sure none of these computer geeks eyed his woman too closely.

He stole another look for himself. Rob and Delia were

now in center frame. Really, he couldn't blame the security guys. Although they had an important job watching out for the safety of the hotel's guests and employees, the routine could get monotonous. When a looker like Delia came on-screen, she was bound to draw attention.

He knew. He'd spotted her the moment she'd stepped inside the front door.

"Adjust the focus," he instructed.

He'd been going crazy waiting for her. He'd spent the last three days working at the hotel to smooth out the inevitable kinks that always seemed to pop up whenever a project was supposed to finish. He didn't mind the long days. It was the long nights that had nearly killed him.

He'd made the mistake of taking a room without her.

The two nights alone had been two nights too many. They hadn't slept apart since her bout with that damned fever, and they wouldn't ever again if he had anything to say about it.

He watched as Rob and Delia showed their identification to the front desk and obtained their temporary security passes. Delia said something to Rob, but he just waved her on. The cute Asian concierge had captured his attention. Jack snorted. One of these days that boy was going to go down for the count, and when he did, he was going to fall hard.

Jackson knew how that felt.

"Keep running through the checklist," he instructed the team. "I'll be back."

Trying not to act too anxious, he headed out of the secured room and down the empty hallway. This was the part of the hotel that guests never saw. The walls were stark white, the floors were concrete, and pipes ran exposed along the ceiling. It was in this secluded world that the heart of hotel operations beat. For clearance reasons, this would be Delia's first visit.

He couldn't wait to show her what they'd accomplished.

He waited impatiently for the elevator to arrive. When it did, it was well worth the wait. Delia stood inside looking fresh and gorgeous. God, she was a sight for sore eyes. "Hey, hot stuff," he said gruffly.

She smiled at him softly. "Hi, boss."

Suddenly, Jackson found it hard to breathe. He'd never grow immune to that intimate grin. It had taken him a long time to ease her into feeling comfortable around him. Coaxing her out of her shyness had had its upsides, but things were definitely better now.

She was his.

And he was hers, through and through.

"Get over here," he said, catching her about the waist.

She flinched when he pounced so suddenly, but quickly softened against him. Jackson knew he was being rough, but he couldn't help it. He'd had no idea how hard it would be to be away from her. The kiss he gave her was hot, deep, and raunchy, but she didn't shy away. She felt the urgency, too.

"I missed you," he growled against her lips.

The torment in Jackson's voice made Delia want to melt.

"I missed you more," she said. She truly had. She'd been aching for his touch for days. It had gotten so bad, she'd taken to wearing one of his shirts to bed. Two nights alone had seemed like forever. She didn't ever want to go through that again. Feeling bold despite the cameras she knew were in this hallway, she swiveled her hips against him. "Can't you tell?"

He groaned. "Damn, you should have stayed here with me."

She nuzzled against his neck. "You were busy. We both were. Besides, I didn't want to get in your way. You had a job to do."

His hands bit into her waist. "You're never in the way."

She smiled at him tolerantly. "Right. Just like you're never in my way when you bring me receipts two weeks late."

He looked pained, and she kissed his cheek. It was hard to remember back to when he'd intimidated her so. She patted her hands on his shoulders placatingly. There were people watching, she knew. "Now, what about that tour you promised me?"

With curiosity, she looked down the hallway. She'd wanted to see where he'd spent so much of his time. It was different than she'd expected. The glossy façade of hotels was all she'd ever seen. "Is that really Command Central down there?"

Jackson looked over his shoulder down the barren hallway, and she could see the wheels turning in his head. She knew he'd gotten special permission for her to come up here. He'd liked it when she'd indicated interest in more than just than the number side of the business.

"We'll do that later," he said abruptly. Reaching behind

her, he jabbed the up button for the elevator. "Right now, we need to go to my room."

"Jack!" Delia gasped. The doors opened, and he started nudging her inside. She tripped over her heels and caught his shoulders as he backed her up against the wall. "What are you doing?"

"The security boys can wait." His eyes took on a gleam that she recognized. "*I can't.*"

She couldn't either, but this was so unlike him. Where was his focus? His sense of responsibility? They had a job to finish. As much as she wanted to be with him, they needed to fulfill their obligations first.

Jackson seemed more interested in nibbling on her ear. She pushed at his shoulders. "We can't run off like this," she said, trying to convince herself as much as him. "You have to be there for the final walk-through."

He punched the button for the 7th floor with relish. "Berkshire hotel management signed off on the project an hour ago."

Her jaw dropped in surprise. They'd signed off early? That was unheard of. "Are you saying we're done? We've completed all our contractual work?"

"Done, completed, finished, crossed-off, and double-checked." He pulled back and looked at her with that penetrating gaze of his. "I wasn't going to spend another night without you."

"Oh, Jackson." Her fingers bit into his broad shoulders. The project had been a major undertaking for the whole company. It had taken months, and they'd had more than a few setbacks. To hear that they were really and truly done stunned her.

It also made her a little uneasy.

His look didn't waver. "This is a big milestone for us, Delia."

"I know," she said, her throat going tight. In a way, she'd tried not to think about it. They'd gotten together on the night before the bid—but now the project was over. "What happens next?" she asked hesitantly.

"We celebrate," he said, firmly squashing any doubts about their future.

The elevator doors opened, and he grabbed her hand. Delia followed happily as he led her through the maze of stark, utilitarian hallways. Just when she was completely turned around, he opened a door and they walked into another world. The lush surroundings of the guest portion of the hotel were disconcerting, but Jackson knew exactly where he was going.

"I figure two more days in this hotel room should take the edge off." He stopped in front of Room 715—the room she'd called repeatedly just to hear the sound of his voice. He pulled her into his arms for another quick kiss. "Then I thought we'd go on vacation."

"Vacation?" She blinked. She hadn't been on vacation for years. Unemployment tended to do that to a gal.

"Anywhere you want to go. Hawaii, Florida, the Caribbean—somewhere I can get you into a bikini. Preferably with a thong."

Delia couldn't help it. She blushed. She'd asked him once if he thought her backside was shapely.

He did.

Jackson's eyebrows drew together. "What's the matter? Don't you want to go away with me?"

"I do," she said. She moved closer and brazenly rubbed her hand against his crotch. "I was just thinking that somewhere with snow might be fun."

He made a strangled sound and jabbed his key card at the door lock. It took him three tries before he got it open. "Stupid security," he grumbled.

She nipped at his earlobe. "That security will be paying for my thong."

"Good point." He tugged her inside and slammed the door behind them. "Get out of those clothes."

Delia laughed and reached for the tie at the side of her dress. She'd come prepared. She pulled on the belt, and the wraparound dress gaped open to reveal the sexy lingerie she'd bought just for him.

He nearly went down on his knees before her. "Oh, baby."

He grabbed her, and they tumbled onto the bed together. Delia moved underneath Jackson as his hands roamed eagerly. She'd missed the feel of his weight pressing her into the mattress. She'd missed the sound of his breaths as he slept beside her. She'd missed the breakfasts he made her.

She'd missed him.

"You feel warm," he said as he undid the front closure of her bra. He cupped her breast, and she bit her lip in pleasure. Her nipple was already prodding the center of his palm.

"Are you feeling okay?" he asked abruptly. The look he shot her was concerned and suspicious at once.

Delia sighed. He looked over her like a mother hen. She couldn't sneeze without him wanting to call Dr. Mosely. "I'm fine," she said. "It's ninety-two degrees outside. Of course, I'm hot."

His lips slowly curled up in a sly smile. "You can say that again."

She felt her heart flip. God, she loved this side of him. More and more, he was loosening up that rigid personality of his. Every day, he let her see inside him just a little bit more.

She cocked her head as she looked up at him. "Don't you ever get sick?"

"Nah." He watched as her nipple perked up under the coaxing of his thumb. "I'm too mean to get sick."

She caught his face with both hands and made him look at her. "Don't you want to? *Get sick,* I mean?"

He finally got the message. She knew, because his entire body went rigid atop her.

He cleared his throat. "Well, now that you say something, it is getting awfully hot in here."

She stroked her hands down his chest. His muscles were taut as steel. "Need me to take care of you?"

With a shuddering breath, he leaned his forehead against hers. "Hot stuff, I need all the TLC you've got."

Perfection

SUMMER DEVON

To the inspirational gang, Sooz,
Logan, and especially Sorrell. Woof.

Chapter One

Allie grabbed her pad and resisted the urge to rub at her face again. Two hours since she'd accidentally sprayed herself with Grease Off and her nose still stung—and she suspected she looked like a demented rabbit.

She made her way to the back booth. "Hi, what can I—" she began, and sneezed again.

"God bless you."

She didn't usually notice voices. These three words rose above the buzz of the regulars and spilled through her like warm cream.

He was rolling up his sleeves. She glanced at his hands, long fingers. The thick wrists, the muscular forearm. Whoa. Here was a problem more serious than a sneezing fit.

Something that had lain happily dormant inside Allie stretched and yawned at the sight of that male arm. Oh no. No, no. She'd crossed men off her menu long ago, and this was one spicy dish she'd be a fool to sample. He'd give her heartburn—or heartbreak, and she'd had her fill of that.

She ought to turn around and get back to work. She

stood, staring at deft fingers turning the cloth of his plaid shirtsleeve. Just a hand, right? Not a poem.

A long red mark marred the perfection of his arm. A cut. He glanced up at her.

Even the diner's fluorescent lighting couldn't diminish the nice line of his jaw and golden skin. But the eyes meeting hers provided the final nudge that woke parts of her body that had been just fine asleep, thank you.

Blue-green eyes flecked with gold held her in a gaze that reached right in and stirred her. It brought on that heavy, ticklish ache deep inside. The nearly painful warming of frostbitten hands doused by warm water.

Damn. Even the tips of her breasts woke up and saluted the man who'd played reveille to her body. She crossed her arms over her breasts. As if she didn't look foolish enough already for gawking, her pencil had to clatter to the floor.

She hardly cared about how she looked now because she was too busy inwardly cursing.

Her snoozing libido had awakened. Just friggin' wonderful.

Bryan caught the waitress staring at him. He shouldn't have come into the place, but it had looked crowded enough with men—he'd hoped the curse would have been hidden in the fog of testosterone. But no, she'd found him, poor him. Poor girl. He shifted sideways away from her. "Coffee, please," he said, putting a note of impatience in his voice.

"Uh, yeah. Right." She turned to leave and he released the breath he'd been holding.

As she strode to the counter, he took an automatic inventory of her from the back. Sensible dull shoes, pretty good legs, curling brown hair pulled into a careless ponytail. Work-reddened hands, nice lines to her rear ... He breathed in the diner's air of fried food and coffee, and detected another, more intriguing aroma. The waitress. She wasn't half-bad. Or maybe he was finally noticing that he hadn't had sex in months.

Not interested. He was only looking for the one woman. Most men wanted Ms. Perfect, but Bryan needed her.

Ms. Perfect was the only thing could turn off his weird-ass creation of the pheromones that Metcher Corporation loved and that he called "the curse."

Dr. Nathan had let loose with that little secret just a week ago—bedding the perfect woman would cut off Bryan's "come and take me" chemical. The next day, Bryan had slipped out of town and hit the road.

"Where'd you get that cut?" The waitress was back, sliding a thick mug of coffee onto the table.

Funny, she almost sounded like she was making conversation.

"Accident," he grunted. An accident named Jill. Or maybe Lill. He hadn't stuck around long enough to find out. He'd thought someone over seventy might be safe and had struck up a friendly chat as he stretched in the parking lot at a rest stop. Who knew an old lady would have such a grip? Or that fake fingernails could be so strong?

Allie reached out to his arm, and the back of his neck prickled. When her fingertips brushed his skin, she gasped and her pupils dilated.

Here we go again. He needed this coffee and he really didn't want to get another cup to go but . . . He grabbed his leather jacket.

She snatched back her hand and turned as red as the cut-rate ketchup on the table. "I know how that goes. I had a dumb accident this morning." She broke off with a laugh, clearly embarrassed, and shoved at her hair, tucking a few loose wisps of hair behind her ear. "Sorry. You don't to hear about it. I'll get your, ah, I forgot your cream."

He dropped his jacket onto the bench, but kept his eyes on the waitress as she walked back to the counter. He'd learned to be vigilant; trouble had a habit of ambushing him whenever he let down his guard.

Then he watched her for entertainment purposes and found himself wondering what she'd been about to say. He missed talking to women. Too bad she wasn't "the One." Yeah, she was cute but not perfection. Bryan had supposed that must be the stereotype pinup with shining blond hair, huge breasts, and endless legs. Nothing like this waitress, who couldn't have been more than five foot three and had a rounder-than-photo-perfect figure. But all those soft curves had his hands itching. In the old days, he'd liked the sensual roundness of a full-figured woman. Back when he liked sex and women.

He'd get a life again soon. It would probably take only that one time in the sack with *the* woman, Dr. Nathan had said.

Of course Nathan had said a lot of things. He left out a lot, too—like how the stupid experiment would make Bryan hyperaware of women's signals, or that he'd become a flame and they'd turned into so many horny moths.

Bryan rubbed his eyes and settled his shoulders against the booth's plastic back. Four-thirty a.m. He'd get some sleep, maybe stay at the shabby hotel that stood behind the diner.

When he opened his eyes, the waitress stood in front of him, clutching her pad to her as if he might try to bite it. "Anything else?" she quavered.

This one had a weird attitude. He risked a smile. Instead of taming her and bringing on a little mew of pleasure the way his smiles usually did, it seemed to make her angry. She cocked an eyebrow and served him with a scowl as if he were taking up her valuable time. That amused him. He knew the symptoms of lust—no one knew them better.

The woman swallowed, and her body gave off the deepening aura of awareness. The front pleats of her drab brown uniform peaked over alert nipples. Even if he weren't tuned to those symptoms, he had the curse, so she had no say about her lust. She'd want him no matter what, even if she hated his guts.

The waitress apparently didn't think much of him, the way she avoided coming close to his booth as if he had some kind of weird disorder.

He did, of course, though she didn't know that.

"Excuse me. Would you like anything else? Sir?" She sounded annoyed, but he knew better. Their eyes met and at once she immediately shifted her gaze to the scuffed linoleum floor. How far would he have to push her before she melted and gave him the feral, hungry look?

She hugged herself. Her dilated eyes and deep breaths told him it would take nothing more than a rub or two at the right parts of her body to make her open her legs and beg him.

The scene playing out in his mind roused an interest he thought had been killed off. Maybe he'd say yes to her. After all, Ms. Perfection, if such a person existed, would probably be asleep. No chance to get at her at the moment.

He glanced at the waitress's blue plastic name tag. Allie— a perfect name for a waitress. She gave off the scent that told him she wanted him as much as most women did, but again he was amazed to realize he really didn't mind.

Sex was all she'd want from him, of course, but he'd pretend it was something warmer.

"I was wondering what time you got off of work," he asked.

She plunked the silver creamer down on the table, hard. "I don't."

"What?" He raised his eyebrows, surprised.

"I work twenty-four hours a day, seven days a week. Got it?"

Maybe she was married? Probably not. She wore no ring, and the intensity of her response made him think that she hadn't had any kind of encounter in a long time. Or maybe she was so abused she couldn't suffer her own desire?

"Yeah, got it, Allie," he said, and grinned at her again, this time with real sympathy. For once his pity wasn't for himself, but for this woman who seemed to dislike her own body's response. He could identify with that.

She twitched and drew in an audible breath at his smile, like he'd brushed his fingers over some sensitive part of her body. Hurt or turned on? Might be the same thing to her.

"You okay?" he asked.

"Why wouldn't I be?"

"Hey, come on. I'm just being polite," he protested.

She gave a sniff and pushed her hands into her apron pockets. "Oh. Right. I'm fine. Thanks. For asking." She shot him a glance, half-smiled, and muttered something like "Then again sanity isn't in the job description."

She took a step closer and he braced himself, one hand on the table, one on the bench ready to shove away from the booth when she rushed him, but she didn't cause the usual scene. Nor did she leave. She shifted from foot to foot and fiddled with something in her pocket, as her body screamed "take me" at him.

He wasn't sure what to do—damn, he'd forgotten how to make small talk with females. "So. Allie. Why do you work the night shift? You a student or something?"

"I'm a waitress." She waggled the grimy order pad at him. "See? There's a big hint."

Before the delighted Bryan could ask another question, Allie turned and retreated to the safety of her station behind the counter, where most of the diner's few other customers sat.

He leaned back in the booth and studied her as she worked. How come she'd managed to walk away? Perhaps she was a worker in the sex trade? He doubted it. Yeah, prostitutes tended to be immune to him, but despite her attitude, Allie was most definitely was aware of him.

He could feel her awareness of him even as Allie swapped smart remarks and hoots of laughter with the cook. Not a fainthearted woman. The crowd in the diner was all men, but she held her own in the flirty and caustic exchanges that were something like a floor show for the customers.

A burly truck driver got to his feet and tossed down money. Allie came by to collect the bill. "Hope you left a tip this time, Jer. Am I gonna have to stop giving you extra coffee to teach you waitresses deserve our tips?"

The driver leered and waggled his hips. "Hey babe, how about I give you more than just my tip?"

She snorted. "How 'bout I saw the whole thing off with a rusty butter knife?"

The easy grin that lingered on her lush mouth flattened into a hard line only when she looked back at him. And she did that often, turning away quickly when he met her eyes.

Bryan enjoyed the show and idly wondered what she'd say if he told her the truth. Not that the women had given a crap about what came out of his mouth, if it wasn't his tongue, ready to please them, to taste their pussies.

Would Allie believe him? One of the first females who'd hurtled into his bed screamed at him when he said that she felt nothing but a chemical response. "No, I love you," she'd howled.

"But you only met me an hour ago."

She had kissed him, almost clawed at him. "It's love, it's love. I need more," she moaned. When she'd taken his hardening cock into her mouth, he had been obliged to abandon discussion.

Allie wanted him, of course, but for some reason or another, she didn't want to want him.

She ventured over, carrying a full pot of coffee.

He risked being obnoxious. That part could be fun. "I know you want me," he said in a low voice, just to see what she'd say. He guessed she'd go for denial or maybe just ignore him.

She started. Her large dark eyes narrowed as she looked him up and down. "Yeah, so?"

"Shit, you know it's fake." He burst into relieved laughter.

"What do you mean? What's fake?" She went pale and rocked back on her sensible black shoes. Oh, damn, she must have thought he mocked her. Too bad she didn't answer with a sharp retort the way she did with her other customers.

He pushed the mug towards her so she could refill it. "Listen, no, sorry. I'm not laughing at you."

"What's so funny then?"

"Hmm. Me, I suppose."

"Uh-huh." Her voice was flat, but the corner of her mouth twitched up a little. She had a gorgeous mouth. Now that she bent close enough for a visual inspection he saw she had freckles under a creamy, smooth complexion. "You're funny enough, but I guess I come in a close second."

When she reached across the table to pour the coffee, the sweet musk of her arousal rose over the scent of bitter coffee. As she drew nearer, her pulse quickened under the delicate skin of her throat. Bryan didn't have the overwhelming need to run. In fact, his own pulse took a jump, and not with fear.

He eyed the coffee and his stomach rumbled with real hunger for food for the first time in a long while. "I've changed my mind about food. What do you have here that won't hurt me?"

She put down the pot and pulled out the order pad and a pencil. "Just stay away from the sausage. We do decent eggs."

"I'll take three eggs," he said. "Scrambled, please." He was suddenly salivating for a midnight breakfast—or maybe for a midnight snack, clad in a mud-brown waitress uniform. He shifted on the seat, tipping his head to follow her stroll across the faded tan tiles. Nicely shaped legs, no doubt about it. They'd be smooth under his hands, and delicious wrapped around him.

The bell over the door jangled, and a man and woman bustled in. The new woman made a beeline for Bryan even before she caught sight of him. She must have had a hell of a lot of animal instincts.

Shit. Bryan knew he couldn't hide, but he slid into the corner of the booth anyway. The middle-aged woman had spotted the source of her attraction and was making her way to the back of the diner.

No fights, Bryan prayed. He felt for his money and pulled out some bills in case he had to get out quickly.

"Do I know you?" The dark-haired woman breathed wine into his face as she eased into his booth and shoved the length of her body against him. Alcohol increased the response.

"Dawn, shag it over here." Her companion sauntered over and gave Bryan a scowl.

"Nice meeting you, ma'am." Bryan gave a slight nod. "Sir."

Dawn's red-nailed fingers were on his knee and then slipping to his crotch. Whoa, she didn't mind moving quickly. He could move faster, though, and caught her wrist. "No ma'am. Sorry, but I'm really not interested."

Her vermilion mouth twisted into a smile. The large, balding companion inched closer, casual, but wired. Bryan couldn't read most men as well as he could women, but it didn't take supernatural powers to see the guy was pissed off.

"What's going on?" The big guy's nostrils flared as if he'd caught scent of fresh skunk.

"I'm just meeting a new friend." Dawn laid a hand on Bryan's thigh again, and her bracelets clinked.

The man's fists clenched. Bryan, who'd grown skilled at brawling lately, looked the guy over and decided that if he had to, he could take him down. He'd be easier than the last jerk who'd gone after him. This one looked more baboon than gorilla.

Bryan eased himself away from the woman's clutches and half-rose to his feet, reluctantly ready to give her a push to get her out of the way. His stomach grumbled in protest—real hunger pulled at him—but it didn't look like a meal was in the cards tonight and he didn't want to take the diner apart. He felt like he owed the sour, honest Allie.

"Dawn and Joey!" The waitress strode over to the table and leaned her hip against the table and set the plate of eggs down. Her hesitant, confused manner had evaporated. "I see you're getting to know my boyfriend . . . um, Bob."

Dawn and the baboon gaped at her. Bryan choked.

Allie ignored him. "Dawn, you scoot out of there. You look too darned good in that new blouse—you're way too tempting."

Dawn giggled but didn't stop staring at Bryan.

Allie pointed to a booth at the front of the restaurant. "G'wan, you two. I got your coffee waiting for you in your usual spot." She turned to Bryan and, without meeting his amused gaze, added in a chatty manner, "Glad you got to meet these two, hon. They are a couple of my favorite regulars."

"Boyfriend?" Bryan muttered after the two wandered off to the front of the diner. She moved even faster than the woman who had trapped him in her apartment by tying him to her bed as he slept.

Allie smiled after the grumbling Dawn, not at him. And her answer had nothing to do with him, either. "I had to say something. She's single-minded when it comes to her, er, pursuits. Bob."

Bryan exhaled and sat down. "I suppose I owe you thanks."

Her gaze met his briefly, and for once her full mouth remained quirked in an easy smile. "Hey, don't strain yourself."

"Okay. I won't. Thanks won't kill me, I think." Almost flirtation. He poured cream into the coffee. She seemed more relaxed. Maybe she wouldn't walk away if he didn't push too hard, so he waited. A normal conversation. And with a woman.

Allie continued, "Dawn's gone after men before, but usually she's a little less obvious about it." She put her fists on

108

her hips and turned her full attention to him. "What *is* it with you?"

He grinned. What a lovely, dispassionate, almost irritated tone she used.

Allie saw the grin spread over the man's face, saw his white teeth, and she stopped breathing as her whole body screamed at her to take Dawn's place next to the stranger. The picture filled her mind again. She was kissing him, touching him, pulling him down on top of her as she ripped open that shirt of his, begging him to yank up her skirt . . .

No. She didn't trust bodies, hers or his. Especially not her own.

"You want to know what's wrong with me?" He spoke in a low, intimate tone. "I'll tell you when you have time."

She leaned toward him. She did not seriously flirt with customers. But her next words contradicted that rule. "I get off in two hours. You can tell me then." She wondered at the odd breathless quality in her voice.

The playful gleam in his eyes disappeared to be replaced by a weary look; she'd apparently disappointed him.

"Huh. Don't look so delighted." She straightened up. "You said you wanted to meet me after work and—"

The corner of his mouth hitched as he tugged the plate of eggs closer. "Fine. Good."

Allie wished the place would get busy. The pounding awareness of need touched every step she took, every plate she hefted. She wanted to avoid thinking about the man lurking in the corner. Nightmare or a winning lottery ticket—she didn't know which yet. But nothing else would sway her attention until she found out. She focused on him like lightning to a rod. A thick, driving rod, bet he had one. Her insides clenched just imagining it.

Dawn ignored her pie and craned her neck to watch the stranger as he ate. Allie grew breathless near him. Was he a movie star?

She wiped down the counter, surreptitiously studying him. Long legs, athletic, a muscular but lanky sort of man. A nice body. Wide shoulders, thick dark hair in need of a cut. She supposed his face was handsome enough, thin and angular. Oh, and the eyes, oh God . . . He glanced up at her and when their gazed locked, her fingers curled with the need to stroke the man's skin, discover the texture of his hair, the rough stubble darkening his cheeks . . . *Stop it right there.* He made it clear he knew all about his appeal, and she didn't need a vain twit in her life. She'd already been down that road more than once.

Dawn stood and stretched, pushing out her large chest provocatively in the man's direction. He tensed, his fork paused halfway to his mouth. Allie managed to ignore her own body's clamor as she watched wariness transform his eyes and tighten his body. Dawn swayed toward his booth, but he'd already gotten to his feet, too, and threw down money fast. He turned to leave as if he knew something was in the air.

Sure enough, dopey Joey followed Dawn. Joey grabbed at the man's shoulder and his voice rang out through the nearly empty diner. "All she's talking about is you, mister. I'm sick of it, and you."

The stranger didn't look confused—or surprised.

Joey tried to give him a shove, but the man just bent a shoulder so Joey's push lost its power. He easily slipped past Joey, and continued toward the door. When Joey's swing came, Allie shrieked, but "Bob" twisted again and kept walking, barely speeding up. He'd apparently known that was coming, too.

"Hey, watch it," she shouted, but even as she called out, she saw that the stranger knew what he was doing. He'd lived through this before—other women, other places. The man had said she wanted him. She thought he was just being an asshole, but . . . Who was he?

Tagge burst from the kitchen.

"What the hell you doing now, Joey?" he bellowed.

"Why you always blaming me," Joey shouted back.

Allie dropped her rag onto the counter. "A dustup with another customer," she told Tagge. "It's okay now."

Tagge ignored her reassurance. "Joey, what is it with you?"

"Never mind." Allie patted him as she pushed past, but she didn't pause or worry. The two men didn't feel like a night was complete without a good bellow at each other.

She ran to the front door. "Bob" was striding away, heading toward a dusty blue car that had the anonymous look of a rental.

"Wait," she called and then crunched across the gravel toward him.

He froze, but when he turned to her, the weariness was

etched in the fine lines around his mouth and eyes. He was more than just tired—the look of wary sorrow pierced her, as potent as the lust he inspired. She had been about to say goodbye, but she changed her mind.

He spoke gently. "I'm sorry. I gotta go."

"No, no, don't go," she begged. She put out a hand to touch him, but at his frown, she moved her hand up to hug her own arms. She hoped he'd think that she was warming herself up against the cool predawn air rather than struggling against the instinct to touch him. She didn't think the guy was fooled.

He was taller than she'd guessed. She squeezed her eyes shut so she wouldn't see all that gorgeous guy in front of her. Still she wasn't entirely surprised to feel she'd instinctively stepped closer. She waited for him to gather her close and kiss her face and mouth and . . .

The car door squeaked as he yanked it open. "Bye, Allie."

"Hey. You-you were going to tell me something," she babbled to stop him. "Don't leave until you explain. If you go now, you might leave something worthwhile."

The door slammed and she opened her eyes. His brows were drawn into an impatient vee. To her disgust, even the lines of his crooked frown made her hot for the man.

"What do you mean? Damn, are you talking about just sex?" He put his hands on his hips, legs apart, a posture of indignation.

"Since when does a guy get angry about being offered 'just sex'?" She laughed—and his frown relaxed, maybe because of her amusement.

She shrugged and admitted, "I don't know what I meant. I was just talking to keep you from leaving."

"Why do you want me to stay?" he pressed.

A good question, but she gave the only answer she could. "Why not?" She crossed her arms over her chest. "I'm the one who's taking the risk, right? Everyone around here knows me. I'm Allie Hamden. You're the stranger. Heck, I'm the one who should be suspicious and asking a million questions."

"Go ahead. Ask them."

Their breath formed light clouds in the chilled silent air. The early light gilded the lines of his face, the heavy eyebrows over those eyes. When he rubbed his chin she heard the rasp of unshaven male skin. As if in response, her own skin prickled.

She shrugged. "Well, um, it's okay. I can ask later. If you want to come back in. We can talk after I get off work soon."

"Do you have a place I might sleep?" he asked at last, and she was surprised to hear an apologetic note. "I'm really beat. I was thinking of checking in here but—"

"Yeah. Sure. There's a suite we waitresses can use." She waved at the hotel. "I'm off soon. Just, just wait a bit. Please?"

Don't beg. She put her hands behind her back and twisted her fingers together. *For God's sake show a little dignity.*

He gave a single nod. "Sure. Thanks."

"Hey, you're getting better at that gratitude thing."

His smile made him look younger and even more of a heart-stopper. She could feel her own teeth grow dry as she grinned back like a fool.

Allie forced herself inside to finish off her work. She

hauled the garbage to the rear, grateful for the quiet time. In the cool air of a brand-new morning, she pulled in a deep breath. At least she couldn't smell the garbage, thanks to the thorough cleaning her nose had gotten earlier.

The man. Suddenly she understood he had done her a favor.

Hang time was over. Somehow this succulent stranger had awakened more than her libido. He'd jolted her to the dull reality of her life. *Time to wake up, Allie.* Feeling and sensation opened to her like a menu of potential delights. Sex was a dish best served hot, boiling hot, and Allie felt a throbbing hunger rise with every moment she fantasized about the man. If tonight was a one-night stand, she'd live with it.

Once she got back in the diner, she'd make an effort to be as friendly to him as she was to any customer. No more bad mood because the sight of a stranger in blue jeans and flannel shirt had jerked her from a comfortable sleep.

What if he'd walked away while she was cleaning up? Dang, in the songs they usually did, right? She emptied the garbage cans and beamed at nothing in particular. Even then, she'd have had the few minutes to savor the return of her body's hunger. Not resent it.

But when she swung through the door to the dining area, her heart thudding with fear or anticipation, he still sat wedged into the corner of the bench as if he was hiding. He stared out the window, studying the passing cars.

Was he some sort of fugitive? Based on her past record with men she'd trusted, he might well be a mass murderer.

Tagge came out from the kitchen and locked the front

door. He apparently didn't notice the last customer, the stranger.

Allie followed Tagge to the kitchen. "Why'd you lock up?"

"Mary called to say she's gonna be an hour late. She'll open at seven for breakfast, but I'm outta here. You go on out the back way when you're done with cleanup."

He pulled off his apron and tucked his shirt in before yanking on a jacket.

"See ya, hon. But listen, don't be too bad." He winked at her and she knew he'd seen the dark-haired man after all— probably watched her drag him back into the diner.

She rolled her eyes—Tagge whistled "Strangers in the Night" as he went out the back door to his pickup.

An hour. She'd sit with the man, talk to him, before she let him into the apartment. She wasn't the fool she'd been once upon a time. She hoped.

She set up the coffeemakers for Mary, poured out the last of the old coffee into two cups, carried them over to his table.

After drawing the venetian blinds to show the diner was closed—only for that reason, she told herself—she dropped down into the booth across from him. "So. What's your real name, Bob?"

"Bryan." His fingertips tapped a steady beat on the scarred tabletop, and he occasionally leaned back to lift a blade of the blinds and peer out. Uh-oh.

"What are you running from?"

"You wouldn't believe me."

She managed to hide the gasp. It wasn't her imagination—he was some kind of fugitive. Damn, damn, damn.

But she didn't jump up, unlock the door, and heave him out. Not stupid old Allie.

Instead she said, "Try me."

The tapping stopped. He picked up the coffee, and she felt the seat next to her dip slightly. He'd stretched his long legs under the table, and now his beat-up sneakers rested next to her thigh. She fought the urge to move closer and rub her hands over his calves, to see if they were as muscular as they looked under the jeans.

"Ever heard of Metcher Products?" he asked.

"Sure. They make deodorant, right?"

He nodded. "I worked for them. In their Maryland lab."

"You some sort of scientist?"

He laughed. "Not hardly. I was in construction and got laid off. A friend got me a temporary job as a lab rat. A guinea pig."

He tipped back his mug, and she had time to admire the strong golden column of his throat. And wonder what kind of trouble a lab rat could get into—gnawing on the supplies? "Go on," she prompted.

He cupped the coffee mug in both hands as if drawing comfort from it. Long tapering fingers she imagined stroking her, clutching her in passion. A hard jab of longing surprised a tiny moan from her. The quick raise of a dark eyebrow showed that he'd heard and maybe even understood it. Embarrassed, she forced her attention back to his words.

"They're messing around with cologne. Stuff that's more than just scent. But," he hesitated, "the point is they screwed up with me."

"Why are you in trouble because they screwed up?"

He took a long drink before answering. "You know the answer."

"No, I don't."

"I meant you feel the answer." His unearthly, gorgeous eyes studied her. "Why are you bothering with me? Huh? Because of Metcher. Aw hell, I'd explain but I bet Metcher Corporation would sue, get me thrown in jail." He snorted. "Hell, they'd love to have that much access to me."

Allie's insides dipped. Great, a conspiracy nut. Was he telling her she trusted him because he wore some kind of perfume he'd stolen? Maybe the man was nuts after all. "What is it that I'm supposed to be feeling? Go ahead and tell me."

"Lust," he grunted.

Her skin grew hot with her blush. That was true enough, but he could probably see it in the way she gawked at him. She'd never been good at hiding her feelings.

That didn't mean she wouldn't make the attempt. "You don't know what you're talking about."

"Hell," he snapped. "I can almost taste your . . . desire."

She drew away, annoyed at herself for her surge of fear, tinged with even more nonsensical lust. But she was more annoyed at his lunatic annoyance. "What are you getting all bent about, Bryan? I don't understand."

He rubbed his unshaved chin with a large palm, and his mouth quirked into the trace of a grin. "Yeah, and I don't suppose I can explain."

She should have marched him to the door and ordered

him out, but the return of humorous despair in his voice and face made her say, "Might as well try. I've got nothing planned today 'til noon."

Allie pressed her shoulders against the back of the booth and rested her clasped hands on the table, clearly clamping down on the surges of desire Bryan could taste in the air. "Go on. Tell me why Metcher deodorant is why I'm lusting after you."

Bryan stared into her cocoa-brown eyes. Maybe she was interested, and not just putting on a show to get him into the sack.

Not that the thought of sex seemed so appalling just now. Five months. That was how long he'd gone without a woman. A month after the curse took over his life.

Faced with almost the first woman who didn't crawl all over him, moaning—and he took out his anger at Metcher on her?

"Allie." He sighed. "I'm sorry. I'm acting like a jerk."

She smiled and widened her eyes. "You mean you're not always a conceited jackass?" She tilted her head. "What's wrong with you?"

He opened his mouth to tell her details, but stopped. Could she get in trouble with the corporate sharks if she knew too much about the damned project? He wanted to stay here, for at least a day or two. He sure didn't want to risk losing his temporary safe harbor or hurt the person offering him shelter.

"I contracted some kind of, um, condition. No, nothing contagious. They've paid me plenty to recompense me. It-it's why women come on to me."

118

In the silence, she rested her chin on her hand and her solemn dark eyes stared into his.

"Okay, Mr. I'm-Too-Sexy-for-My-Pants, I admit I'm attracted to you. I feel something," she said at last. "But I think you feel something, as well."

He drew in a sharp breath. Jesus, it was true. For the first time in weeks he felt like a regular human again, and she could see it, too. Hell, weirder still was that she had noticed he was something more than an object to relieve the fierce ache between her legs.

Her dark eyes sparkled with amusement. "Ha. You look like you opened one of those fake cans of peanuts and a bunch of springy snakes jumped out at you."

"Damn, I feel like that." He gave a sudden laugh that surprised him almost as much as his increasing desire. "I loved those stupid things."

She nodded. "Yeah, no one was ever fooled by 'em. Or by the plastic spiders you could freeze in the ice cubes."

"Or—" he laughed so hard he could barely get out the words "—or dribble glasses." For some reason this dumb conversation struck him as the funniest damn thing he'd ever heard. When he managed to get his inane laughter under control, he noticed her staring at him, the hunger for him obvious in her heavy-lidded eyes, the heat practically shimmering from her skin. Good, smooth skin, he noticed. Would it taste like rich butter and cream? Or sweet maple syrup? Either way, he could lick her all up from her button nose to her sensibly shod toes and everywhere in between. Especially everywhere in between.

Time to pay the piper. She'd come after him now. But instead of revulsion, he felt his pulse quicken and his belly swoop with interest as her lips parted and her tongue flicked over her teeth.

He waited to hear the inevitable commands. *Kiss me. Take me. Screw me.*

"You have the greatest laugh," she said instead. "A belly laugh."

He got up, walked around the table, and slid in next to her, the vinyl still warm from her body heat. Her back went straight, pushing out those appealing rounded breasts. Ah, she was so tightly strung. He'd help her relax.

His cock stirred, just a little, at the thought of touching her, and he wanted to sing with relief. She'd helped him already, giving him back the thrum of desire. He'd give her a gift in return.

"Now what are you doing?" Her voice hitched with desire—or maybe frustration. Escaped strands of curling hair framed her heart-shaped face. "You get all bent out of shape when . . . well, about, um, sex. And now you're . . . I don't understand what you want."

He propped an elbow on the table and rested his cheek on his hand so he could watch her gulp deep breaths and her eyes darken with lust. Very nice. "Okay, that makes two of us who don't know. I'm clueless. Maybe we should worry about what you want."

"Me?" Her surprise, bordering on indignation, made him smile.

"Sure. You, Allie, my fine waitress. What do you want?"

Chapter Two

Bryan wasn't sure why he had such a strong urge to give Allie the gift of whatever she wanted from him.

Serving the server for a change.

Maybe because she'd made him laugh. She was no ravishing beauty, but her round features looked damned cute when she grinned or glowered at him and her dark eyes brimmed with an in-your-face determination.

She reminded him that females were more than panting, grabbing animals. Still, he automatically flinched when her hand tentatively brushed his shoulder.

She hadn't been captured by the chemical pull of him yet, for she drew back at once. "What's the matter?"

"Bad memories," he said.

Her back straightened, and she scooted a couple of inches away. He didn't feel the heat rising from the side of her body. Surprising—he had a twinge of regret that she didn't try to touch him again. When the spicy moss scent of her interest reached him, for once he didn't suffocate. Under that scent was another more elusive fragrance he didn't recognize.

He wished she'd put her hand on his shoulder again. His

body tightened and he grew harder. He wanted to explore the source of that scent. Hell, he wanted her.

Astonishing to realize that more than sleep, he craved burying himself in this woman's body.

Well, well. Bryan had the urge to touch a woman again. He'd experiment, see if he could take her to the edge without feeling like he had to cut and run. He couldn't allow himself to go too far or it would turn her lust into craziness. That had happened to another woman on a couple of memorable occasions.

He'd manage their hunger, allow them both to taste pleasure. The challenge intrigued him. "So, go on, Allie the waitress. Tell me what you want."

She shrugged and flushed. He liked the way her pale skin showed all of her emotions. "Um. Why don't you tell me about Metcher? Or about bad memories?"

The delectable aroma of carnal longing abated slightly, and he could taste more of the underlying scent. Fear? That was new for him. He'd never been able to sense anything but sex from women.

He wondered if the symptoms of awareness were going to keep getting worse. Maybe he'd start reading minds next. Tapping into women's thoughts and not just emotions? Frightening. But . . .

Might as well use the signals. "Nah. Let's skip them. Tell me, are you afraid of me, or afraid of wanting me?"

She glowered at him. Annoyance evidently evaporated her fear, as he'd hoped it would. "You really are something, you know?" she said, "I don't think I've ever met a man so full of himself."

"It's a fact, ma'am. Nothing but."

"Huh." She wrinkled her nose in a smirk of disgusted amusement and picked up her coffee.

He was almost glad she didn't believe him—and he was thoroughly glad she seemed able to control herself around him. "Never mind, Allie. Tell me why you're scared. It's because of sex?"

"No, not scared," she murmured and shoved at her hair. "More like . . . About the time I get my act together, when I manage to get on my feet, my life falls apart. The reason is always a man. Stupid, huh."

"Tell me," he coaxed.

Allie didn't want to talk about herself. She examined his face with its strong angles. Even if he wasn't too thin, he'd be a striking man rather than a pretty boy. "You know, you don't eat enough."

Her hand had tingled so alarmingly when she'd touched his shoulder; she risked tracing a small, fresh scar on his cheek. Sure enough, the sensation ripped through her body. Her stomach clenched tight with lust.

"I eat plenty. Tell me about the men who've hurt you." His tone informed her that he wasn't going to drop the subject.

The losers weren't important right at the moment, after all. When she opened her mouth, she discovered it was easy to talk about the first one. "There was this teacher in high school. I told my best friend about him and she told someone. You know how it goes. It turned ugly. He was real popular and the kids hated me when he got in trouble. He claimed I'd been pursuing him and that I was sick, pretending that we were lovers. I remember he said he only felt sorry for me. I didn't want any more crap from him or anyone else. I just . . . left."

She could barely remember what Mr. P. looked like, though she vividly recalled the sounds he'd made on top of her in the backseat of his red compact.

"Shit. You mean he got away with hurting you?"

She shrugged. "No big deal. I didn't miss school."

"Poor Allie," he murmured.

She shrugged again, more dismissive. She didn't want pity. What she wanted to do was jump this man, a total stranger, and force him to help her completely forget the rotten apples. A tall order. She wondered how she'd phrase the request. "I got my GED. Anyway, the teacher wasn't the worst."

"You're kidding. Who was?"

She'd had enough of the conversation. "He's long gone. But listen, you said whatever I wanted? I don't want to make a laundry list of losers."

"Okay. Fair enough." He drew in a deep breath, as if testing the air. "Mmm. You're less frightened. Can I help get rid of more fear?"

She was lifting her mug to swallow the last of the coffee, but at those words, she put it down, almost dropped it. The man might be a mind reader. "Why do you think I'm still frightened?"

Astoundingly gentle, he put his hands on her shoulders to twist her to him. "I can read you, Allie."

She snorted. "Yeah, some book."

"A page-turner."

He leaned toward her, and his ragged breath fanned her cheek. She grew so dizzy with his presence, the signs of his own interest that she had to close her eyes. "Oh, yes," she murmured, "please, yes."

His lips brushed hers, teasing, too soft and gentle for her sanity. She groaned and tilted sideways to gain access to the intoxicating taste of him.

"Easy." He spoke against her mouth. "We have all day."

She didn't mean to ask, but the words slipped out. "Is that as long as you can stay?"

He pulled back, but his square strong hands gripped her shoulders harder. "Yes. I'm sorry. I have to leave because—"

She reached up and pressed her finger against his warm mouth. "I'll take it."

She'd take what he could give without more questions. Once again she was trusting a man—giving herself to him— and this time she didn't even know the guy.

He leaned in, slow and cautious, almost as if he understood how bewildered she felt. Or maybe he was holding back for a reason of his own. As the tip of his tongue lightly traced her lips and teased her, she closed her eyes and moaned.

The first intimate touch drew heat from her mouth to her belly, all the way to her fingers. Her toes curled with a sharp jolt of longing. Just from a kiss. His firm mouth on hers was skillful and practiced, nothing tentative—yet entirely new.

She broke away and nuzzled at his neck, trying to breathe him in, but her nose was still stunned from the face full of cleaner she'd gotten. Perhaps she caught the hint of night air and musk on his skin.

She slid her hands up the wall of his chest and savored the light groan she drew from him. He pulled her closer and her heart sped up.

The kisses grew deeper and more urgent; his hand pushed through her hair and cupped her head. She heard the sound of her own moan. *More, more, more.* The hungry slide of his mouth on hers drove her crazy.

His other hand reached for her breast and caressed her through the thin nylon uniform. The big hand almost covered her full breasts, once her bane in high school, now her glory as the pad of his thumb made teasing circles over her nipples. Even through the layers of cloth the sensation of his touch was raw and vivid.

"It's gonna be fine," he spoke gruffly, sounding almost surprised. "This will work. Yeah. It'll be very good."

He pressed her down gently on the seat and kneeled above her.

"Take off your shoes," he ordered.

She toed them off, and even as they thumped to the floor he slipped his hands up her legs, under her skirt. Befuddled by a heavy fog of desire, she would let him do whatever he wanted—as long as he touched her. Only a few moments ago, she'd been frightened that he'd push too far too fast, but now he moved deliberately, far too slow. She twisted on the seat, needing more. *Touch me everywhere,* she wanted to moan. Where had this frantic craving come from?

She reached out her arms to him. "Please."

"Wait," he said. "Hush." With a twitch and a yank, he expertly pulled down her pantyhose and her plain white cotton bikini briefs. As if she were a child unable to do the job herself, he bent her legs and gently disentangled them. He looked at the haphazard bundle in his hands and then grinned into her face. "I'd guessed silk."

From her lust-soaked daze she blinked at him. "What?"

"I had decided you wore silk under that uniform."

"I'm not a silk kind of person," she said, and squeaked with pleasure as his warm palms glided up her thighs.

"Oh, yes you are," he whispered. "All silk. I know these things."

His smile was as cocky as his attitude. Cocky. *Whoa.* She looked down at the bulge in his jeans. He was ready and so, astoundingly, was she. Usually she heated slowly. Now she could set damp wood on fire. The air touching her seemed to stoke rather than cool her skin.

He yanked at her dress. "Let's get this brown thing off."

She nearly lifted her arms so he could pull it off, but a flash of good sense penetrated the fog. "No, not here." Her sane self had awakened again.

Not anywhere, she reminded herself. She wasn't the sort to go too far with a stranger. But maybe some more kisses. Yes. They could be necessary. If he didn't put his mouth on hers, she might expire.

"No sex. Just kiss me," she panted.

"Sounds good to me. Wonderful plan, in fact." How could he speak so easily? She could barely form coherent thoughts, much less words.

He leaned over her and angled his mouth against hers. He didn't shove his full weight on her, but through his jeans she could feel his erection, hard and long, wedged between her legs. She pressed up and wiggled, impatient for more. Had she really settled for kisses? Was she nuts? This man offered a feast of new feelings, rich, delicious desire. Goodbye again, sane self.

He gasped and rocked rhythmically against her. He wasn't so calm after all.

He reared back, pushed her uniform up around her hips and stared down at her naked lower body. She closed her eyes; the sight of his heavy-lidded admiration embarrassed and aroused her. "Lovely," he muttered. "You're gorgeous."

His gaze was too intense, yet she felt gorgeous—ripe and ready. Reaching for his strong shoulders, she pulled him to her and wrapped her legs around his hips, hiding from him and feeling his potency at the same time. The rough cloth, his arousal rubbing against her bare, tenderly swollen crotch brought her to the edge of frenzy. But he was drawing away from where she needed him.

"No," she gasped and her hands scrabbled at his sides as she attempted to pull him to her.

The cool air brushing over her thighs and between her legs didn't calm her. She arched her back in frustration. The fake leather seat squeaked as he slid down. His hands grasped her hips firmly. He kissed her belly, her thighs.

Her eyes snapped open when his warm tongue swirled over her clit.

"God." She hauled herself up on her elbows to stare down

at him. "Bryan," she panted. "I don't even know your last name."

The blue-green eyes looked back, amused and heavy-lidded with arousal. What a sight—that glorious man be-tween *her* legs.

"Hartigan," he muttered, and his tongue glided over the tender skin at the crook at her thigh.

"Hey," she protested, even more breathless.

He looked at her, his eyebrows raised in mock surprise. "You said only kissing. It's kissing. Don't you like it?" He dipped his head and planted a noisy smack on her curls.

She shivered with eagerness and a tinge of embarrass-ment. "Oh, yeah, I-I do. But I mean, um, for you. I haven't had a shower since yes—"

"Hush," he commanded, his voice husky, and he slid back down so she looked at the crooked part in the top of his silky dark hair.

The sudden, gentle onslaught of his lips and tongue took her by surprise. Almost at once her body flew back into alarming and complete arousal. A five-alarm fire. No one had ever lavished such attention on her before. Heck, even *she* hadn't. Brand-new sensations rushed through, overpow-ering her and washing away any embarrassment. She could not escape the waves of her response even if she'd wanted to.

"Oh, no," she whimpered over and over, "that feels so good. That's so good."

She was dimly aware that she sounded like an idiot, but he only hummed his approval. The sound vibrated through her, added to her frenzy.

She touched his soft hair, wove her fingers through it. She twisted under his touch, needing more. He didn't unzip his jeans, the way she'd feared, hoped, and expected. Instead he slipped his fingers high up into her, and she felt rather than heard herself cry out. Only a few hard thrusts of his hand and pleasure threatened to flood her body beyond endurance. She arched up to meet him. A sudden explosion—waves of an enormous orgasm shook her body.

Perhaps she blacked out, for she didn't remember him moving up to return to her mouth. He kissed her, heat in his plunging tongue. His own desire reached through her languid post-orgasmic stupor. Another spasm of eagerness gripped her belly, and she woke entirely.

"God, I'm turning into a crazy woman," she gasped against his neck as she ran her fingers over the broad muscles of his back over his belt to his hard butt. "I can't get enough of you."

He froze. A second later, he pulled away. The seat squeaked as he sat back on his heels, breathing hard.

"Oh, no, shit. I'm sorry," he said softly. She was surprised to see that he looked unhappy, even appalled. *Great way to kill a mood, Allie.*

"No, what I meant was thank you. I haven't felt this good in . . ." Her voice trailed off.

When was the last time she'd felt so alive, filled with tingles of excitement and drowsy relief at the same time? Never.

"Bryan," she whispered. She reached up and touched a lock of the black hair curling over his forehead. "Please, come back here. If I'm a sex-crazed lunatic, at least I'm a happy one."

He grinned at her—not his self-satisfied smirk. This was a shy, goofy grin. He asked, "So you're not going to scream if I get up and walk away?"

"Scream? No, of course not. But, um, do you want to go?" She glanced at the erection pressing against his jeans—still very pronounced and tempting. She ran her tongue across her kiss-swollen lower lip. Maybe she shouldn't have been so hasty when she'd turned down his initial offer. Suddenly sex felt . . . necessary.

He carefully lay back down, next to her now. For the first time, she noticed how narrow the booth was. Amazing neither of them had slipped onto the floor. Dang, if both of them had dropped to the ground without drawing apart, Allie doubted she would have noticed.

He wrapped his arms around her and pressed his mouth to her forehead and then her lips. "No. I don't want to go," he murmured. "Thank God."

"After all it's your turn, isn't it?"

He frowned but didn't pull away as her hand found the snap to his trousers. She unzipped him and slipped her hands into the jeans. Her fingers explored the silken skin of his cock, and she squeezed the heavy, hard thickness. A perfect combination.

He groaned. "Allie. Thank you, but I-I can't lose control. When I'm with a woman . . . oh-h-h. That feels so. Good."

"You can. I'll help. Ummm," she hummed appreciatively as he thrust against her fingers.

His breath hissed through clenched teeth. "No. I'm afraid it'll make it worse for you when—"

Someone thumped at the door, banging angrily at the glass. Bryan jerked away and sat up quickly. He looked fatigued rather than alarmed. Almost as if he'd been expecting it.

Allie slipped out of the booth and picked up the bundle of underwear and hose on the floor. She should have felt tawdry, being caught necking in the diner. Instead she felt a frisson of fear because of the way Brian pushed himself up against the wall to peer through the cracks in the blinds. He was experienced at life on the run. Icy trepidation chilled her. This man might be dangerous, an escaped prisoner perhaps, and she'd eagerly offered him her body.

"Damn." He winced as he zipped up his jeans. "They've got Elsie."

Bewilderment replaced her fear. "Who is Elsie?"

"A dog." He ran his hands over his face. Even in the darkened dining room, the circles under his eyes showed his tiredness. "I'm gonna go to the kitchen. If you want the reward, you can lead them there. Otherwise, well . . . I'll see you later either way."

"Reward?" she said, but he'd already disappeared through the swinging door. She pulled on her underwear, grimacing as it touched her sensitive, extremely damp crotch. She pushed the pantyhose into her apron pocket, slipped on her shoes and went to the door. Parting the blinds, she looked out at three men in dark, nondescript suits. FBI? Something official. After Bryan. God, what had he done?

At the back of the group stood a pale, thin man with a golden retriever. The dog. Didn't police usually use nasty, snarling breeds?

"We're closed," she shouted through the door.

"We only need a minute of your time." The gray-haired buzz-cut one in the front held up an identification of some sort. Not FBI, she was relieved to see. She studied the badge. Some kind of private security agency perhaps—they couldn't really arrest Bryan could they?

They stood watching her, waiting. Clearly they wouldn't take no for an answer.

She sighed, leaned against the door, and unlocked it. The men surged forward, but they weren't nearly as excited as the golden retriever that wore an excited happy dog smile and panted as it pulled against its collar.

It yanked past the men in suits and went straight for Allie and pawed at her feet.

"Hey, no dogs allowed in here."

"This is a drug-sniffing dog, ma'am." The thin dog handler narrowed his eyes at her.

"Drug-sniffing?"

The dog stood in front of her and gave a few frenzied sharp barks.

All the humans turned to face her.

"Excuse me, ma'am." The dog handler cleared his throat. "But do you know a man named Bryan Hartigan?"

She made a show of glancing at her watch. "Look, we have to open in a half an hour and—"

The gray buzz cut interrupted. Despite the suit he had a military bearing and looked like the type who had major tattoos somewhere on his body. "There's a ten thousand dollar reward for him."

She managed not to gawk. "Who is this guy? Is he a murderer?"

She must have looked alarmed because the buzz-cut one hastened to reassure her. "No ma'am. He is not a danger to the public. But he has stolen valuable research material."

The cologne? Her belly turned over with dismay. He must have taken a flask of the stuff or something. The dog was lunging at her. It planted its paws on her chest and licked her chin.

At least the dog was nice. "Hi sweetie." Allie automatically scratched its ears and let the dog pant into her face before the thin man pulled it down.

She'd always been a fool for rambunctious golden retrievers. Not nearly as dangerous as good-looking, rotten thieves. For an instant she was tempted to toss these guys Bryan, apparently her latest turkey. She almost opened her mouth to say, "He's waiting in the kitchen." But no matter who he was, he'd done nothing to her—other than give her a few of the most memorable moments of her life.

Instead she rubbed the dog's head and stalled for time. "What's this guy look like?"

"She knows," the dog handler said, and Allie thought he was talking about the dog until he added, "No way Elsie would have this kind of response unless there's been some physical contact. He's got to—"

"Excuse me, mister," Allie interrupted, narrowing her eyes. Her heart thumped hard, as if she were afraid, but she wasn't aware of any emotion other than annoyance. "If you're accusing me of consorting with a thief or drug dealer or whatever, you and your dog can go back outside. And, hey, do you have a search warrant? Don't you need one of those?"

Buzz-cut guy shifted uncomfortably and folded his arms. "Well, you see ma'am, we're from a corporation. It's a private matter that hasn't been handed over to the law as yet."

Something in the way he avoided her puzzled stare made her ask, "So this guy hasn't broken any laws?"

"We didn't say that," Buzz cut said. "You gonna cooperate with us, ma'am, or will we have to talk to the manager?"

She twitched her shoulder into a shrug. Bryan would be able to hear this conversation if he stood near the door, and she hoped he'd take off. She hadn't liked that look on his face—defeated. Maybe she didn't want to hand over her heart to the man, but she wanted him to get away from these weird semi-law types.

"What do you want from me?" she said.

Buzz cut whipped out a photo. A happier Bryan leaned against a porch and squinted at the camera. He was dressed in jeans, maybe even the same faded close-fitting pair he had on, but there were no circles under his eyes, no shadow of a beard. His arms were folded and he wore a tool belt. He looked tanned. And delicious. Her mouth suddenly flooded with longing for the taste of him again, her body yearned for the erotic rasp of his unshaven cheek against her breast—

One of the three spoke. "Ma'am?" and she realized she'd been staring at the photo hungrily.

"So you recognize him?"

"Yeah, maybe he came through here, but if he did, it was hours ago."

There, she wasn't entirely lying.

She handed back the photo, wondering if she'd ever see that face again. No more losers, she reminded herself. *Please, save me from my stupid need for losers.*

The man with the dog circled the room. Elsie jumped up on the seat of Bryan's booth and started barking happily.

"Did he sit there?"

"Maybe. Probably." She crossed her arms over her chest as her breasts prickled at the memory of what else he'd done in that booth. The dog looked over at them, puffing and delighted, her tail waving. The coffee cups. But Allie had automatically moved them to the counter where they didn't look out of place.

The dog jumped from the booth. It trotted to the kitchen door and scrabbled at it, whining. The handler opened the door, and the dog went to work at once, sniffing around the doorway.

Allie hoped Bryan had come to his senses and left, but she didn't want to look. She sat down at the counter and rested her chin on her unsteady hand.

The dog and handler disappeared into the kitchen.

The two other men stood in a semicircle. One of them, the young blond one, tried unsuccessfully to hide a yawn. His tie hung crookedly, there were circles under his eyes, and he needed a shave. Bryan had led them on a good chase.

She swallowed. What they would do to him? "So what is this guy guilty of, exactly?" Her voice trembled. She feigned a yawn so they'd chalk it up to tiredness.

Buzz cut sniffed. "He took off with some top-secret formula or something."

The washed-out blond laughed and spoke up for the first time. "He *is* the top-secret formula."

"Watkins," Buzz cut said in a warning growl.

Allie ignored him and looked at the pale guy. "What the heck does that mean—he's the formula?"

"You got any coffee?" the blond guy said, nervous now.

Allie drew on her two years of rousting drunks from the diner. "We're not open. If you're gonna bug me and keep me here after my shift is over, tell me about the man you're looking for."

"He's got some kind of thing going on. His perspiration. It's valua—"

Buzz cut interrupted. "That's enough."

Allie ignored him. "His sweat?" She tried to remember what Bryan had said about being a lab rat. Something about the tests they'd done on him had made a change.

"Yeah. That's all I know." The blond shot a nervous glance at the tough buzz cut, and Allie could see he knew plenty more but wasn't going to say another word.

The dog and handler came back out of the kitchen. "Elsie lost the scent." The dog gave a large sneeze. She still wagged her tail, but with less enthusiasm.

Elsie clicked across the linoleum floor. She whined and nosed at Allie's side until Allie absently scratched the dog's ears. The dog handler leaned over and spoke to Buzz cut. They stared in her direction. No wonder Bryan ran. She hated the sensation of being studied like a bug under a microscope. Why didn't they leave? Had he done something to her? No good orgasm goes unpunished, she glumly thought.

Allie drifted to a stool. She sat down and brushed a hand over the counter, swiping at imaginary crumbs.

"Miss . . . um." Buzz cut squinted at her name tag. "What's your last name, Allie?"

She considered lying, but figured she had nothing to lose. "Hamden."

The three men had moved close. The cold threat of their impersonal smiles drove her to her feet.

"Miss Hamden," Buzz cut said. "We just want to ask a few questions."

Allie managed to force an answering smile onto her face. She inched away. Sure enough, the two larger of them shuffled closer. "Sure, ask them. But I gotta go home soon and—"

He rested a beefy mitt on her shoulder. "We'd like you to accompany us to a facility."

She twitched away. "What kind of 'facility'?"

"A laboratory. It's not far away, and we'd be happy to give you a ride there." He spoke in a friendly casual manner, but Allie's heart shot straight into her throat.

"Why?"

"We'd like to ask a few questions, maybe perform a non-invasive test." He pointed a stubby finger at her arm. "On your skin. And of course we'd compensate you for your time."

The same skin that Bryan had kissed. "And if I say no?"

She shouldn't have used such a belligerent tone. His hand clamped onto her shoulder again, and Mr. Personality swiftly gave way to Mr. Tough Guy. "Miss Hamden. We have evidence that you are in possession of stolen research material. I assure you that if you don't cooperate, we could make life . . . difficult."

Stolen research material? What the hell had Bryan done to her? She pulled away from Buzz cut and smoothed the front of her dress. Had Bryan slipped something inside her while she was in the throes of an orgasm? Yes, he'd shoved in those amazing fingers.

She almost laughed. Big bad guys giving her a hard time and she could still wander into a haze of lust thinking about Bryan's hands. No wonder he was such hot property.

Buzz cut spoke up. "There is no need to worry, Miss Hamden, I can assure you that it will well be worth your while to come with us."

Oh, no. "Um . . ." She ignored the panic rising in her. She needed a plan. "Sure. I have to go get my purse. Okay? It's out back." She waved at the kitchen.

What had that overly attractive bastard done to her when he touched her? She was going to find out, and not from this scary group.

"Be right back," she called and pushed into the kitchen before they had a chance to protest. Silence met her. Someone had turned out the lights. She ran through the kitchen and shoved open the door.

Behind her she heard the squeak of the other door. Panicked, she took off and sprinted away, aiming for the back of the hotel.

Footsteps thudded up behind her and hard fingers grabbed her arm. She opened her mouth to scream. Fingers clamped over her lips and she tasted . . . him.

Chapter Three

B ryan pulled Allie to a halt. His whisper was fierce. "What's going on? Why do you look like you're under attack? Did those bastards frighten you?"

Two large plastic containers of spices, cayenne and garlic powder, dangled from his other hand. Only a half inch or less of spice remained in them.

Out of breath, she gasped, "The men. With Elsie. They want me. To go with them. They say they want to do tests on me and—"

His grip on her arm tightened. "Allie, damn. Come on."

"Hey, but wh—"

He yanked her hard, and she broke into a run again to keep up with him. At the shadowy edge of the parking lot that curved behind the hotel, Bryan stopped abruptly and slid his hand around her belly to stop her. His touch started a swirl of heat in the pit of her stomach, which only grew with his warm whisper in her ear. "Wait a sec."

Leaning against the wall, he eased around the corner for a look. He cursed. "Elsie found my rental car. They're all over it. I'm just gonna leave it. Do you have a car?"

"At the service station. I'm-I was going to stay here, sleep until about noon when they said it would be ready."

"Damn. A couple of them are heading back inside." He turned, and resting his hands firmly on her hips, pushed her in front of him. "Run. To the woods."

She wanted to stop and argue, but the grim straight line of his mouth convinced her to run now, ask questions later. When she looked over her shoulder, she saw him jogging close behind, sprinkling the grass with the spices.

A small muddy stream ran through the woods.

"Into the water," he ordered.

"What?"

"Just run for a few yards. To the other side."

She would have demanded answers, but she was almost out of breath. He ran along easily behind her, splashing through the murky water.

"Only a little farther," he urged.

Thorny underbrush scratched at her bare shins and grabbed at the hem of her uniform. Allie muttered a curse. No one-night stand was worth this. Well . . . She glanced at him and grimaced. Okay, so she'd still swap scratched shins for that tongue on her clit, but much more of this and he wouldn't get her phone number for a second date. He pushed her to scrabble through the trees until they couldn't see any evidence of the road or hotel. He called a halt in a small clearing lit by the pale sunlight. An old beer can and the sound of distant traffic was the only signs of nearby human habitation.

Allie folded her arms over her stomach and leaned over,

panting. Her legs were covered with scratches. "Right, why did we just do that cross-country run?"

He didn't even look winded, damn him. "I wanted to keep you away from the Metcher types."

"Why? You already knew I wasn't going to turn you in." She leaned against a tree trunk, fearing his answer.

"I was worried about you."

"Why?" She tossed her hands in the air, the panic ringing through her. "Why did they want me? What have you done to me? What did you put in me?"

His mouth tightened. "I don't have a clue why they want you. They told me that I wouldn't have any effect on the people I . . . er . . . touched. And I didn't put anything in you." The grim look passed and his eyes narrowed thoughtfully. "Not entirely true. I put my fingers inside you." He examined her, up and down. "Very nice indeed, too. Tight and lovely."

She made a strangled sound as her insides dipped in agreement. It had been lovely.

He must have interpreted her gasp as impatience because he said, "Okay, okay, I dragged you away because—well, it was just instinct. When you said that phrase, 'run some tests'—I went into some kind of overdrive."

Protective overdrive, she reflected. She believed him. "You scared me to death."

Damn, she wasn't certain the fear was gone. Letting him pull her into the woods couldn't be a good idea. He was so large and he made her lose her control so entirely. She'd already forgotten his last name. And there was a matter of the guys in suits wanting to haul her into a lab because of him.

He gave her a sheepish look. "Sorry, I just reacted." He shoved his hands into his pockets and backed away from her. Mind reading again, she supposed.

"I guess I don't blame you. I didn't like them." She rested her hip against the tree. "How long should I wait?"

"If you want to avoid them, you'll have to stay away for hours. They'll keep an eye on the hotel." He sat down on a large flat rock. "They came in two cars. I know Watkins, he's the younger guy, from the lab. They'll take my precious dirty laundry from my car and send it off. The enforcer and Elsie's guy—I never met them—will slip the desk clerk an enormous bribe so they can wait for me to appear."

"Precious dirty laundry?"

He snorted. "You heard Watkins. My sweat is more valuable than diamonds."

"You're kidding." But it was an automatic response. "Wow. Damn. Bryan. Have you been running a long time?"

"Only a week." He rolled his broad shoulders. The weariness in his voice told her it felt much longer. "But it didn't take long to figure out these guys. Or I should say I know their modus operandi. That's the expression I want, right? Their MO?"

She frowned. "The day manager won't put up with them hanging around."

"They have deep pockets and really want me back."

She remembered Buzz cut's menacing face. "God, I'm glad they didn't get you."

"Or you. Shit, I'm sorry. If you somehow got some of this stuff, believe me, they won't make your life easy."

His words echoed the threat made by Buzz cut. The one Bryan had called the enforcer. She was suddenly very glad they had left the diner behind. Even if her feet were soaking wet.

He shook the nearly empty container of cayenne. "I'd never tried covering my tracks before, but it seems to have worked." He turned his head and squinted at her speculatively. "Thanks for not sending them into the kitchen after me."

"Well, after all . . ." She blushed and didn't continue. Her body tightened and swooped when she remembered his touch.

He gave a wolf's grin. "Hey. I promised whatever you wanted, remember?"

Golly, she half-hoped he'd forgotten. No, more like quarter-hoped he had. The other three-quarters of her cheered at his words, but she said, "I can't believe you'd think about that when you've got those lunatics chasing you into the woods. Heck, they're chasing me and sex is the last thing I'm thinking about. You have a one-track mind."

The grin softened but didn't vanish. "Yeah, you're not kidding. I haven't for a long time."

Something in his gaze made her push away from the tree and walk over to stand next to him. Touching him had moved up on her agenda.

He held out a hand to her. She grabbed it, thinking he wanted her to help haul him to his feet.

Instead, the large callused fingers gave a yank downward, and she lost her balance, landing across his thighs.

For a moment his delicious warmth enveloped her; then he easily turned her around and placed her between his legs and pulled her back against him. Cozy. No, not quite that. The breeze and the tickling underbrush grazed her bare legs, and she felt almost naked. She couldn't relax. She was too aware of his strength and the temptation of his overwhelming male presence.

Boy howdy, she didn't want to lose it with him again, not with a man on the run, a stranger who could make her drop into a swoon just with a smile. And who'd apparently pulled her into his peculiar adventures. She cleared her throat. "If you didn't steal anything, do they really have the right to chase after you?"

She felt his shrug against her back, and then his voice rumbled against the length of her. "I signed a contract that gave them rights to my, er . . . bodily products, until such time that there was no more evidence I'm producing the magic elixir."

She twisted around so she could watch his face, though it was hard to read his expression in the dappled early light of the clearing. "Why'd you sign that contract?"

"I knew they hadn't succeeded in getting anyone to produce the pheromones. I figured I'd pick up some easy cash. It was a lot of money. A hell of a lot more, once I started showing signs of what they wanted. That was six months ago." He reached up and brushed a curl from her face. "Mmm soft. About two seconds after I spotted you, I wanted to bury my face in your hair. The urge is getting stronger."

Her heart sped up, but she managed to twist her head

away from him. "Bryan, come on. What are you going to do now?" she gasped.

He tucked back her hair, and she tried to ignore the stroke of his finger gently outlining her ear. "I have a plan."

"What is it?"

He didn't answer the question. Instead, he said, "Good thing they've paid well, since they've nearly caught up with me twice in the last week and keep stealing my dirty laundry. I'll have to get more clothes and get another car."

Valuable sweat. She thought about Dawn's response and her own aching fever for the man.

He had to be right about the chemicals rousing females. His presence was too potent. She had trouble drawing a steady breath. Leaning back against his chest, she slid her palms along his thighs. Being aroused didn't seem like such a bad deal. Chemical or no, the sweet languor sweeping through her veins overwhelmed any lingering caution.

He gave a shuddering jerk and hugged her, enfolding her in heat, his swollen interest pressing against her back. She rubbed herself against it, just a bit, struggling to pretend she wasn't interested. Ha, as if she could fool him. Her nipples tightened beneath her dress. "What are you gonna do? Wait until they give up on you? Doesn't sound like that's going to happen anytime soon."

"I found out there might be a way to stop my body from making the stupid pheromones."

"Pheromones? That's what they want?"

"Yep."

"What's your plan?"

He nuzzled the nape of her neck. The brush of his face tickled her skin and made shivers run down her spine. His hands traveled up her arms, rubbing heat into every pore. "You had a long night at work, and then I drag you into the woods." His voice deep and low rumbled in her ear. "I at least owe you a back rub."

His fingers worked at her shoulders, pressing, kneading the tight muscles. She stifled a groan, but not of relaxation. The large warm hands worked their deft way down her arms, chafing her skin into tingling awareness.

Back rub, front rub, bottom, top, she wanted his hands everywhere they could reach. She wiggled against him trying to turn around so she could touch him.

"Shh," he whispered, and he wrapped one arm around her to hold her still while his other hand covered a breast, capturing her aching nipple through the dress and bra. The hand left her breast. He slid his fingers languorously over her belly, hitched up her dress, and moved between her legs.

Yes, there! Maybe those pheromones made him a mind reader, too, because he seemed to know exactly what she craved. She yelped and redoubled her efforts to turn and reach his mouth with hers. But he had her pulled hard against him. No mercy.

His strength overwhelmed her even as desire shot through her. For a moment her fear was real—he could do anything he wanted to her. He trapped her so thoroughly, she couldn't even move her arms, which were pinned to her sides.

At once his large hand stopped pushing under the elastic band of her panties. "Say the word. I'll let go."

The rasp of his voice sent yet another uncontrollable tremor of desire through her. She didn't speak, only pressed her head back on his shoulder. He chuckled and tightened his hold. With one hand he stopped her, and with the other he made her frantic.

"You're already slick," he breathed. He circled her still sensitive clit, and then suddenly he plunged two blunt fingers into her.

She groaned and rocked against his hand, shocked at her own eagerness. More, more. She wanted more, she wanted him . . . She pressed her mouth to the rock-hard arm that held her in place. She kissed it, tasted the surprisingly silken skin, strained her body against the enticing restraint, in frantic need to get at him.

"It's okay. Go on." His heated breath in her ear was enough to send her over.

"Now!" she shouted, meaning she needed him now. Or that she was coming . . . now. The arm across her tensed, the fingers caressed her. And she shouted again. For a moment she could not breathe, his touch brought the spasms crashing through her and banished everything else.

When the world reasserted itself, she slumped back against Bryan's solid body, annoyed and grateful. Bossy man, thinking he could control her like that. Mmmm, yes, indeed he could.

She sat for a moment, listening to the distant drone of cars, the occasional birdcall, something pattering on the leaves.

Allie gave a shaky laugh. "Thank you for the . . . back rub."

A drop of water landed on Bryan's neck.

Uh-oh.

He shifted, trying to find a comfortable spot on the rock. He allowed the arm holding Allie still to relax.

When Allie had writhed against him, eagerly whimpering, the small animal cry sounded too close to noises he'd heard another woman make. Panic had hit him, but he couldn't stop stroking the lush wetness, bringing more of that response. And he remained aroused, painfully so.

He'd held on to more than her body as she'd climaxed—he'd had to restrain himself from pushing her down and thrusting into her slick, tight heat. At that instant he'd almost turned into an animal—as crazed with lust as any of the women who'd jumped him. He couldn't help himself with Allie—amazing, since self-preservation should have sent him running at the first signal of her overwhelming excitement, or at least banished his erection.

He gathered her onto his aching lap and eyed a nearby tree. Would she mind being shoved up against the rough bark while he pushed into her over and over until he exploded? Yeah, probably.

Or maybe he could lie on his back, with her on top?

Another drop of water landed on him. She didn't appear to notice. Her sweet mocha eyes were half-closed in drowsy repletion, and her breath came evenly now. In a soft bed on a rainy afternoon, he'd like to loop her into a lazy embrace and watch her sleep after he'd loved her long and hard. But the rough rock digging into his legs and the distant woof that might have been that damned Elsie brought him back to reality. Looked like he'd have his rainy afternoon, at any rate. He certainly hadn't seen the clouds coming.

The other woman, the perfect one, might make him normal to the rest of the world again, but Allie was the one who gave him the gift of savoring life again. Damn, he did enjoy savoring her, especially.

He'd keep her warm in a chilly shower. Steam would rise from him, enough to heat them both.

" 'S raining," she murmured, not sounding as if she much cared.

"Yup." He shifted her delicious weight. "Sorry."

"It's okay." She opened her eyes and stroked his jaw with gentle fingers. "Don't care just now."

He'd succeeded in avoiding talking about his plan for the moment, but had driven himself into an almost intolerable state of arousal. He dipped his head and inhaled her sweet perfume. The scent of the diner food, soap, and, under that, Allie. He held his fingers near his face; they were coated with the scent of her excitement and pleasure. A dizzying sweetness that made him hungry to taste her again.

The drops were falling more purposefully. They'd soon be soaked. Bryan stretched out his legs and flexed the arm which ached slightly from holding the bucking, frantic Allie. He was aroused, but some other elusive sensation warmed him as well.

Happiness. Despite a long list of reasons, it was a stupid reaction—still running away from Metcher idiots, without his clothes or a car again—Bryan felt happy.

The only part of the equation that seriously bothered

him at the moment was his search for that perfect woman and how to explain that little hitch to Allie. Because he had to if he wanted more than a day with this waitress.

If he had his way, he'd keep her safe from the Metcher gang, at least until he knew she wouldn't get hassled.

At his side. Or even closer. He stroked the silk skin of her arm. Was his appetite for her really why they sat in this grubby little clearing?

Damn. She wasn't really in danger from Metcher. He had to face the fact that if she kept hanging around with him, she was going to get more unwelcome attention. His appetite for her had to be the reason he'd dragged her away.

She hadn't signed a contract. They couldn't force her into anything.

He was fooling himself about the danger to her, and probably had been since he'd grabbed her arm outside the diner and forced her to run away.

He heaved a sigh, less happy now. "Allie. Metcher doesn't have a hold on you. Christ, they can't arrest you. Go on back to the hotel, and maybe they can help you somehow."

"Nope." She tilted her head back and stuck out her curling tongue to catch faster-falling raindrops. "I don't trust them. You said you have some sort of plan. Maybe I can help you."

She wiggled excitedly in the shelter of his lap bringing up a groan from him. "Oh, I can help! I just remembered. My friend Kim lives less than a mile from the restaurant. She's away. I know she wouldn't mind if we . . . um . . . borrowed her place."

"I don't know if it's such a good idea," he began.

"It's a fine idea." Without looking behind her to make sure he followed, Allie jumped up and set off toward the small bungalow. "Let's go."

Kim would be delighted to know Allie used the Love Shack.

Allie, on the other hand, grew less sure about the idea once she started tramping through the damp woods. Alone in a house with Bryan. Sinking deeper and deeper into his bizarre problems, or deeper into his arms, and that soft mattress in Kim's Love Shack. Oh, heck, life was short. Tomorrow she'd go back to being plain Allie the waitress. Allie's back tightened with the awareness of his presence just behind her.

Chapter Four

Allie found the key behind the propane tank and shoved her shoulder at the door. As Bryan brushed past her in the doorway, she saw he held the empty spice canisters. He underhanded them into the trash can in the corner.

She tossed the keys on the coffee table and flopped onto the junky green couch, hoping he didn't notice her nervousness. "Your elixir. Essence of Bryan. What is it again? Pheromones?"

"Yeah, a kind of signal to the world that announces I'm here for you females. I have no way to control it."

"Oh really?" She rubbed at the goose bumps forming on her arms. Her skin prickled simply in response to his nearness. The man was like a magnet, and she wanted nothing more than to cling to him. He must have noticed because he smirked at her. "Hey. I told you. I exude sex."

She folded her arms over her chest. "You don't just exude it. From what I've experienced you're pretty good at the follow-through. You enjoy your gift."

"I do right now. With you. C'mere."

Allie shook her head. "It's weird, Bryan. What I feel

around you, I mean. It's a little scary. It's good, but I feel . . . It's like I'm caught in an undertow." She didn't add that the sensation he created was addictive, and she couldn't afford to become an addict to a man who was just passing through. Her body protested with a stab of desire that made her even more aware of the heavy throb between her legs.

He held open his arms. "Just a hug, okay? I've missed hugs."

"I don't know, Bryan. I guess I ought to show you the bed, okay? You said you needed rest."

Bryan almost laughed. For months women had literally thrown themselves at him. Here was the first woman he wanted, and she was trying to get him to go to sleep. Alone.

"I'm no longer so tired. How about you?" Instead of pointing to a bedroom and telling him to get away, she cursed softly. Staring into his face, she stood and walked straight into his arms. Allie laughed, a throaty, sensual chuckle. "I guess we could rest together," she said, in a tone that made it clear she knew they'd be doing more than resting. At least at first. She let him draw her in, snuggled against his chest.

He wished more than chemicals pulled her to him, but he loved the feel of her. And at least she knew the score with Metcher.

Bryan pulled her tight against him, and her soft curvy body fit as if she'd been made to tuck into the crook under his arm. He took in a deep breath and willed away the world—everything outside the small dark room where they stood, slightly damp and out of breath, clinging to each other. He palmed her bottom and gave it a soft squeeze. The sensation of Allie pressing against him was just too perfect to complicate with any other nonsense.

Perfect?

He pulled away to examine her face for flaws. Even a cursory inspection revealed quite a few—a slightly crooked tooth on one side that gave her smile personality. A generous sprinkling of freckles that made her nose adorable. That lush, rounded body would exclude her from the standard pattern of beauty—not that he had any complaints. Her hair was not gilded gold or raven, just soft and brown. She was a far cry from perfection, but he wanted her with a desperation he hadn't felt in years. Perhaps ever.

Ms. Perfection sounded like chilled marble compared to this armful of warm and wriggling Allie.

Oh, hell, it didn't matter for now. The months of despising his body and the touch of others didn't exist when Allie pressed her lips to his throat.

You can't fall in love an hour after meeting someone, he'd told more than one woman since the curse had hit him.

What about three hours?

Until he got his life back, he wasn't going to worry about it.

In fact he wasn't going to think about anything but the welcome sensation of Allie standing on tiptoe now, and filling his mouth with her kisses and pressing her curves against him. Purely sex for her, perhaps, but he'd give her pleasure she'd never forget.

She groaned and burrowed against him. Her hands clawed his back as she restlessly rubbed her body against him. He tensed. Another echo from the past. Guilt and need did battle inside him. If only he could forget about the chemicals and believe her response was real. He cradled her face in his hands and tilted her up. "Allie," he whispered.

She came out of the trance. A slow smile spread across her face. "You're worried." She reached up and grazed his forehead with two fingers, maybe smoothing away the alarm she saw.

Tenderness. How long since he'd had a gentle touch on his skin. He brought his mouth down on hers for a light kiss that blossomed into lush moist urgency. Allie fever.

"Mmm." Now her breathy moan only increased his appetite, so he blinked at her when she pulled away to search his face.

"It's the whole funky pheromone thing, isn't it," she murmured. "The scratches on your arm and face. And you flinch sometimes. What happened?"

He didn't want to talk. He wanted to kiss and stroke her. His own mounting excitement meant he could press her to the floor, the bed, the couch or the wall and forget. Thrust up into the slick heat he knew waited for him. Lose himself inside her soft body.

She sucked in a breath when he nipped at her earlobe, but she whispered, "It's my turn to pry. Tell me."

Bryan sighed, seeing he wasn't going to sway her this time. "All right. Come here. At least we can be comfortable." He pulled her to the couch and sat down, then arranged her spread-legged across his lap, facing him. Yeah, almost perfect, though fewer clothes keeping him from the paradise between her legs would be better. He closed his eyes to picture the fine pink flesh, the silky legs, the lovely belly. The heat and promise of her distracted him.

He rubbed his palms over the dip above her rear end then slid his hands down to squeeze the good handful of her.

"Bryan. It's so good." Under his fingers, her hips rotated against him, and she gasped. "It's-it's not just the pheromones, is it?"

He sighed and let his hands go limp and rest on her lower back.

"Maybe. I don't know anything. Except I want you." He arched up to demonstrate, and swore he could feel the heat and dampness of her through the layers of cloth. "Allie. I want you so much I'm in pain."

Her fingers rubbed across his cheek, and he sucked at her forefinger as it dipped into his mouth. Her sigh brought him shoving up against her, demanding entrance, but she was pulling her tasty little finger from his mouth and saying, "Tell me why you had to run."

He nibbled lightly at her neck, frustrated and relieved—she wouldn't let him get away with avoidance. "You're a stubborn woman."

"I've heard." She tilted to one side and started to climb off his lap.

He gripped her wonderful derriere. "No, no, don't stop the torture, Ms. Interrogator. Stay. I'll talk."

He closed his eyes and adjusted her warmth to fit over his throbbing cock. Might as well be blissfully uncomfortable—he only hoped he could still form sentences.

Apparently he didn't start soon enough because she

pushed away from their embrace. She inched away to straddle his thighs, and look steadily into his face.

He sighed and, reaching up, tucked a loose curl behind her ear. "Right. When the pheromones first showed up, I thought I had it made. I loved it for three whole days. Oh, shit, yeah, when the first woman grabbed me I thought I'd gone to some kind of heaven. She was a neighbor in my apartment building who hadn't given me the time of day before. And then, after I managed to get away from her apartment while she was asleep, another one stopped me in the elevator. Who knew so many women walked around with condoms in their handbags? I sure didn't."

She rolled her eyes.

He chuckled and said, "Now don't get your optic nerve in a bunch."

She grinned at him. "Good one, your own?"

"My friend Eric's." He paused. "My ex-friend."

She gently touched his brow and again smoothed the frown. "Why ex?"

"I went to their house for dinner that first week. His wife pushed me into a closet and stripped off her clothes."

"Oh, I think I understand."

He nodded and absently ran his fingertips over the silk of the backs of her knees. His hunger for her still jangled through him, only slightly quieted by the memories.

"By then I knew it was more trouble than I'd bargained for. I had to stop going into crowds. Had to stay away from places women go so I usually only went out at night. More men than women are out really late."

"Any men want you too?"

He closed his eyes and nodded. "But for some reason it doesn't hit gay guys as hard. Females tend to focus more on that particular chemical response, I guess. Some of them couldn't take no for an answer."

Did Bryan sound angry?

Allie felt too muzzy with lust to explain why she needed to make him talk about the whole thing. Couldn't exactly recall why—something to do with sleeping with strangers. She was too befuddled to keep on urging him, at least with something other than her body.

His mouth twisted into a sardonic smile. "One woman pulled a gun on me. Another hired a guy to kidnap me for her."

Ah, it was the memory of the past that brought the shadows to his face and made him angry.

Allie whistled under her breath. "Holy crap."

"Yeah, well I got away from them both. They and the neighbor showed up at my door, naked. Twice." He snorted. "Some of it's pretty damn funny. Wasn't at the time. Anyway, when I came into the lab on the fifth day beaten up and looking like shit, Metcher offered to put me up in their facilities. Temporarily, they said.

"They would have loved access to me twenty-four seven. After the first few weeks, the contract said they could only demand a couple hours now and then. I was sick of that, too. Sick of the lab, the poking, and tests. Huh. I'd heard the amount they'd offered and signed before I knew what the hell I'd sold to them. I thought it was my time. Didn't know it would be my life." He heard his bitterness and shook his head. "Okay. Right. Enough self-pitying bullshit."

Easily distracting himself, Bryan opened his eyes to watch his fingers skim the softest, finest skin he'd sampled. He shoved up her skirt so he could get better access.

She shivered. "Amazing you'd ever want to . . . well, you know . . . ahhh, be with a woman again."

"Mmm, yeah," he murmured, "amazing." He traced the lovely crook at the top of her inner thigh as it angled into her body. He followed it down and pressed his thumb to the thoroughly hot, damp panties. She shivered again.

He gathered her up and pulled her back to where she belonged, hard up against his hardness. She groaned in response.

"The thing is." He swallowed and grimaced. There wasn't a good way to explain. "I can't come if you're really excited."

"Why not?"

"I think it could be bad if you were close to orgasm at the same time as me. It might do one of us damage." He frowned. "Nathan warned me about it. He didn't know for certain, and I sure as hell don't want to find out."

He thought back to the women. It had been a problem at first. He'd had to hold himself back. More than once he'd had to roll away from a bucking, excited woman.

"Not a problem lately since I haven't wanted sex," he whispered in her ear. "But I want you so much. You think we should push this?"

Oh my. Allie's body could just about take some good pushes now. Right up and into her. Hard thrusts that would hit her center. She twisted against him. "Yeah. We can manage it. And later. We'll talk later."

"Ah, so now we dine?" He kissed her neck, her face, as his fingers worked the buttons of the brown dress.

She rose to her feet and he followed her. She intended to go to the bedroom, but he stopped her and tugged gently at the dress.

"This has got to go," he announced.

Standing in the middle of the small living room, she let him pull the uniform up and off her. A brief thought skimmed her consciousness—if only she'd known she was going to indulge in sex for the first time in years, she would have worn her good black lace bra. But at least he didn't get a good look at what she was wearing. It was unclipped and tossed away before she'd even reached behind for the hooks. The man knew his way around feminine garments.

Then he lowered his head to her breast.

A scrape of his teeth and then a tug of his sucking mouth on her nipple. The piercing awakening churned through her body again. She sobbed encouragement, not entirely certain which words she used.

His touch brought such a powerful response it bordered on pain. Expertly, he yanked down her panties. Dazed by the sensations caused by his fingers circling over her sensitive flesh, she stepped out of the last of her clothes. She gasped and pressed against him, rolling her hips impatiently. Her body was too demanding, the excitement coming on too fast. She wanted to enjoy the swelling sensation—but her body's prickling awareness built, rose to thick need, and then, without warning, tumbled into a full orgasm that washed over her in uncontrollable waves. She panted, marveling. Three times. In one day. Huge, mind-blowing orgasms.

"Holy shit." Not exactly poetry, but all her blood had drained from her brain. Didn't just happen to men after all. She leaned against his chest, her legs slightly bent and trembling.

She pressed her face to his neck and kissed the rapid pulse at his throat, delighted by his harsh excited inhalation. He didn't seize her, though. Instead he wrapped his arm around her, and solicitously walked her to the couch. She collapsed flat on her back. Resting for a moment, she sighed with the happy afterglow.

"You're all right, aren't you?" He gave a low breathy laugh. "No wait, I can see you're way better than all right. I meant how do you feel?" He stood over her, fully dressed, looking down at her naked body. The look on his face, pure, heavy-lidded sexual avarice, made her want to whoop with joy. She swallowed and knew she wanted even more. Greedy, greedy woman. Only next time those spasms rolled through her, she wanted to feel her muscles squeeze tight around him, large and hard and inside her.

"I feel wonderful. But now," she croaked, and reaching up, hooked her finger through his belt loop and yanked. "Right now. Take off your clothes."

He didn't move and the tiny furrow appeared between his brows. Oh, she'd forgotten. She pushed herself up and steadied her own rasping breath. "Please, take them off. I won't

get too turned on. I won't touch you until you tell me to."
She swallowed, thinking of how difficult it would be to keep
her hands off him. "I promise."

He snorted. "You make it sound like I'm some sort of shy
virgin."

That seemed about right to her. From what he'd told her,
that's how he ought to be treated, with care. Did it insult
him somehow? Perhaps her suggestion was somehow de-
meaning to his masculinity. Such peculiar creatures, men,
but she realized she must have said the right thing because
he was unbuttoning his shirt, ripping it off and tossing it
aside.

"Oh, you are wonderful," she whispered, trying not to
sound too aroused.

She hoped he'd let her taste the skin on his shoulders, the
flat nipples. She wanted to know if she was right in guessing
the hair swirling over his chest down to the vee in his jeans
was soft rather than crisp.

He pulled off his shoes, climbed out of his jeans and underwear; she gave an involuntary breathy moan of appreciation. She had trouble looking up from those sturdy long
legs, flat belly, and very erect cock.

He took a step closer. She wedged her hands tight between her thighs to keep from grabbing him. He dropped to
a crouch by the sofa so their faces were level.

"It will be fine," she whispered staring into the ocean of
his eyes.

His eyes sparkled with boyish mischief—no, that was definitely something more adult. "Yeah, I'm glad I told you and, hell, you actually paid attention. It's gonna be better than fine, I think."

He rose to his feet and held out a hand. "Show me the bed."

Chapter Five

As they walked hand in hand to the bedroom, Allie marveled at the enfolding grasp of his fingers. Talented fingers. Strong hand—the hands of a dexterous man who worked with his body.

She pulled up their intertwined fingers and kissed each of his knuckles, gently.

He growled and without warning, turned and pressed her against a wall for a long mind-blowing kiss. His tongue sought hers, glided over her lips the way she knew he would circle and tease her swelling clit. She craved sex . . . but oh, this was so nice, too. When he stepped away, she tried to hold him to her for more kisses, but he put his hands firmly on her waist and guided her toward the bed.

"A traditionalist," she laughed over her shoulder. Maybe if she talked, she wouldn't pant and moan like a hungry animal and scare him away. "Probably never did it in outrageous places. Like in public."

"Have you?"

"Naw. Unless you count some, um, oral sex in a diner booth." She shivered at the memory.

He kissed the back of her neck. "Mmm. I certainly do count that."

The fine hairs on her nape rose at the sensation of his solid presence just behind her. Naked presence. With a tentative step backward, she brushed against him—his cock—with the small of her back.

"Allie," he breathed, and pressed the rest of himself to her. So much bare warm flesh sliding on her skin.

Her legs bumped the edge of the bed, and she landed face-first with a happy groan. His hands stroked her rear, the insides of her thighs then pressed her knees open. She didn't need any urging to expose herself to the cool air and his molten touch.

"Yes," she encouraged him trying for a casual voice. "Fine. Good." She gave her rear a wiggle in case he didn't understand.

He bent and pressed his warm mouth to her left cheek. He nuzzled it, and his large hands kneaded her rear end. *Now, now, more, more,* she chanted silently.

"Protection," he growled.

The drawer. She crawled up the bed and yanked it open. Sure enough Kim had some condoms, bless her, even though they were neon colors.

Allie resisted the urge to help roll the fluorescent orange rubber over him. Only what he asked, she reminded herself. Let him be the aggressor. Tamping down her impatience, she tossed him the condom and lay down on her back to watch. She concentrated on the feel of the cool sheets against her back and shoulders to keep from grabbing at him.

166

At last he was next to her, kissing her, his hands on her already tender breasts, again coaxing her sensitive pussy to swelling tension. She lay as still as she could, hoping he'd at last press inside her before she let loose with a howl and jumped on top of him.

"Allie," he murmured and knelt between her legs. His hot blunt head nudged at her opening, and she couldn't contain her moan.

He drew back slightly and brushed his lips across her throat. "We shouldn't do this if you think you might come," he whispered. "Because I'm gonna. I might just looking at you." He drew a knuckle between her breasts. "Jesus, you're wonderful."

"I'm not close," she told him. "I won't. I swear. It's your turn."

He slowly pushed into her, then, and she gasped, unsure if that was discomfort at such a large and hard man filling her after so much time. Propped on his elbows, he eased in, watching her face. Just when she arched away, instinctively protecting herself from pain, he stopped. He kissed the side of her face. "You're hot. Such tight heat around me."

Oh, he was all the way inside her. A perfect fit after all.

She gave an experimental squirm, and the near discomfort of too much gave way to something more astounding.

She arched up again, now unable to keep motionless, she wanted to feel that thick hard heat invade her again.

Bryan sucked in a long, shallow breath. He pulled out and drove into her. The intoxication of her body drove him close to the edge. He gritted his teeth and tried to get himself under control. "Damn."

"Don't worry about me," she gasped.

He kissed the sweet hollow of her neck again and shifted. She ran her hands over his back.

It had been too long and she felt too damn good. Bryan groaned as his testicles tightened, ready. "No, God no. Don't wiggle like that. Talk to me, ahhhh, talk about sports."

"Red Sox. Yankees. Dodgers." With each team name, she twisted around him, swirling up. He was going to come without moving a muscle if she didn't stop.

"Shhh." He grabbed her lovely rear end and held her still. Skin to skin—close to inhabiting another body—he could feel her heart pounding, her breath coming fast, and taste the remnants of old arousal, the sweet scent of her body's fresh excitement.

"Thank you," he whispered.

Her deep laugh shook them both. "Thank *you*."

He waited until he could move again without exploding. Smooth, slow pumping at first, feeling her body squirm to accommodate him.

She raised her legs around his waist and moaned deep in her throat, an animal sound, but it only made him push harder in response. She wanted more and he could give it without fear for them both. Yet. Her breath came in faster pants, and her hands pressed him, demanding deeper thrusts.

Triumphant lust without a trace of fear filled him as he pounded hard into the sweet, ravenous Allie.

"Oh, God, I lied." She pressed her face to his neck, muffling her astonished shout. "I-I'm coming. Again?"

Her hands clenched at him, her slick body squeezed him.

Shit. When her body spasmed and clutched his cock, he had to force himself to go completely still.

Not at the same time. Her body grew less rigid, he could feel the waves of her orgasm ebbing.

Now. Fast, before her excitement returned. Before he exploded with frustrated need. *Now.* He increased his rhythm, pounding, sliding, until his own release rolled over and through him as fierce and out of control as a thunderstorm. He muffled his shout in the wild mass of Allie's curling, damp hair.

Her cool fingers trailed over his back and brought him back to full awareness. Would she be all right? Had he done something stupid allowing himself to come at all?

Carefully withdrawing, he settled beside her. He got rid of the condom all the while keeping watch on her half-closed eyes and the quick rise and fall of her breasts. She turned her head and smiled at him. Relief flooded him. What had he imagined? She'd die of some kind of sexual seizure if he let himself go? The others had all survived after the temporary frenzy of sexual insanity. Maybe Nathan meant he was the one who was in danger.

Bryan sucked in a deep breath of relief. The air was musky with scent of sex.

Damned if that rich aroma and the sight of Allie, sprawled flat on her back with flushed skin and fluffy hair, didn't begin to rouse him.

She lifted her hand a few inches and let it flop back to the bed. "See? I have no bones left."

He lay down behind her and gathered her into his arms.

Fantastically, instead of crawling all over him, she let him spoon, another forgotten time with a woman. Calm, with the leftover twinges of a first-class bout of sex buzzing through him. He nuzzled her hair trying to memorize the details. Another moment he'd store, an image of tenderness.

She stirred slightly, twisting toward him. Now she'd be at him. He froze then almost fearfully asked, "What are you thinking about?"

She didn't give the answer he dreaded. Instead she burst into laughter. "I'm the woman. I'm supposed to ask that. And then you answer something about sports like 'I'm thinking of how much I still hate that instant replay review in football'."

He joined in her laughter then said, "I notice you didn't answer the question."

Allie hesitated. "Okay. Yeah, I was thinking about you and I guess it won't hurt to ask."

Hey, she was actually nice about it, and he might even be able to accommodate her, too, he reflected, as he waited for her hand to grab at him and demand more. His cock twitched with interest at the thought.

Instead she said, "Tell me about your plan. Can I help?"

Allie tried to keep her tone casual. She didn't want to pressure Bryan, but the thought of him walking away in less than twenty-four hours made her open her mouth. Just another day. Long enough to build up some memories of passion inside her for the future that might include another long winter's sleep.

"That's your question?" He sounded almost shocked.

"Okay, so you don't like that one. Um . . . okay. So what's your sign?"

He laughed. "Aquarius. I was surprised but not annoyed by the question."

She pushed up onto one elbow. "What did you think I'd ask?"

He traced the line of her breast with his forefinger. "I thought you'd want more."

"More?" She gave a hoot of laughter. "Sex? You mean?"

He grimaced. "Women usually do."

"Sure, I'd love to." In fact, the suggestion seemed like a fascinating proposition. "But right away? Those-the women want it right away?"

He kissed her puckering nipple. "Yep. Some kind of craziness, huh." He sounded almost amused. "Until they pass out."

She whistled. "You make one heck of a pheromone."

He didn't answer at once, and all trace of amusement had vanished when he spoke again, low and determined. "I have to get rid of it."

"I'll say," she retorted. "I'd hate to be, well . . ." She clamped her mouth shut. She'd been about to say something stupid, like *I'd hate to be with a guy that had other women crawling all over him.*

For a second or two, she'd let herself daydream. Bye diner, hello front seat of a blue sedan. Sure, chuck it all to run away with a stranger. A man she knew nothing about, other than he was wanted by some set of authorities—didn't drug companies have deep pockets? It would be hard to get away from that bunch of corporate goons.

All for a stranger who has to fight off women. Not such a hot plan, perhaps.

He had a very peculiar plan of his own, as it turned out. He was talking, describing a way he could turn off the chemical signals. The method he described involved sleeping with Miss America or some female like her. A perfect woman? Did such a person exist?

Allie stopped daydreaming and fretting so she could concentrate on his explanation.

"Dr. Nathan was the one who talked the most," Bryan said. "So one night I brought some Coronas to the lab. I figured the good doctor drunk would be even chattier. And that's when he told me that a roll in the hay with the flawless female would do it. 'You've already demonstrated that normal females don't have an effect on your generation of the pheromones,' he told me. So she'd have to be a pinup or something. He told me that they already figured out from other experiments that the perfect female would kind of act like a light switch turning the production off, it'd be that fast. That was a week ago. I hightailed it outta there."

She chewed on her lower lip and stared at her hands, trying to hide her dismay. So that was why he'd been heading south. He wasn't just driving aimlessly. He was on his way to the Miss North America competition. "Sure," she managed to croak, "you have to do it. I understand."

She did, too. She just didn't like it.

He moved closer, smoothed the tips of his fingers over

her hip, and her skin still seemed charged by his touch, as if every inch of her was permanently responsive to Bryan.

He watched her—unnerving to have those eyes focused on her. That intent gaze as if nothing else mattered to this gorgeous man, nothing could be as fascinating as Allie Hamden.

He wore a grave frown. Maybe he wanted to tell her it was time for him to leave. "Go on," she said. "You want to say something else. I can tell."

The brooding expression diminished as he shook his head. "I was just wondering if you'd give me the time of day once the stupid curse is lifted."

She wanted to laugh at the absurd thought. Funny to hear that from the sexiest man she'd ever seen—the only man she'd ever met who could drive her to maddening arousal and over the brink again and again—and rarest of all, a man who seemed to give a damn about what she was thinking. He was worried about her attraction to him?

"Hey, you'll have Ms. Perfection. You won't need me."

"Oh hell, she'll probably hate me the moment the curse ends. Probably boot me out of bed." He traced a loop over her shoulder and followed it with a kiss.

"Damn." He briefly rubbed his forehead on her upper arm and sighed. "I justified it to myself, saying I'd stay grateful to her, whoever she was. Told myself it was my turn to use someone else."

"Yeah? What's changed?"

"Now I remember what sex is supposed to be like."

Oh, the warmth that rushed through her at those words.

And then he worried that she might hate him—well, now, that could mean something important.

Something along the lines of . . . he wanted more than a day with her. He wanted to see her again. She rolled over and hugged him. He responded with only a tiny flinch this time and he pulled her close rather than holding her off.

She whispered reassurance. "I'm happy, that's all. I'm not gonna try to start anything."

"Hey, but maybe I am."

She realized that her belly pressed against his hardening cock.

"Whoa." She kissed his shoulder and tasted her way along the impressive line of his collarbone. Her cunt throbbed with overuse; the delicate skin seemed far too sensitive. When he shifted so that his leg pressed between hers, the light touch on her swollen flesh made her jump.

He forked his fingers through her hair, and gently tilted her head back. "You okay?"

"Mmm." Those ocean-colored eyes—a woman could drown in them. She leaned forward and kissed the skin below his ear, and gave in to his silent urging for a lovely rich kiss on the mouth.

She broke away. "You taste wonderful," she whispered. It occurred to her that all of him would be yummy and though she'd never particularly enjoyed fellatio, she had a serious craving now. Developed a yen to taste him everywhere.

She disentangled her limbs from his and sat up.

"Do you mind if I ah . . ." She licked her lips and examined his impressive cock.

"Nope. No." He rolled onto his back. "Be my guest."

His skin was delicious salty satin. She loved the solid heaviness in her mouth. He didn't grab her head and try to ram her down farther, and so for the first time with a man, she indulged in playtime. She sucked and experimented with her tongue and lightly drew her teeth along the length of him.

He gave a deep guttural moan.

She pulled away and frowned up at him. "Oops, sorry."

"That was. Not. Pain."

She gave a happy evil chuckle and went back to play. He'd lain still, but now he pushed up into her hands and mouth and he tangled his hands in her hair. Instead of worrying about being suffocated, she caught his excitement.

She pulled away, out of breath. "Bryan, do you mind if we—"

"Yes, yes, please." He'd ripped open a condom package and rolled it onto himself before she even finished her sentence.

Allie slid slowly up his body, her breasts brushing along his legs, his cock. She was about to climb onto him but she feared that haunted look of his. A man under attack. She cleared her throat. "Do you mind if I'm on top?"

He gripped her bottom and dragged her up. "Honey, we'll do whatever you want. I just want to do it. Now."

So much for his worry about sex, she thought, smug and delighted.

She positioned herself and began to gingerly sink down on him—but the slow motion ended when he gave a firm thrust up, all the way into her. The feel of him was more exciting and less painful than she'd feared. Oh, especially when he twisted deep inside her.

She'd planned to do all the work, but he put his hands on her hips to hold her steady. As he pressed up into her again and again, she didn't mind. She went along for the ride and what a ride he was.

Sliding into pure sensation she left thought and words behind; never before had she allowed herself to travel so far. The raw uncontrolled sensation whipped through her.

A few moments later someone screamed.

"Omigod," she whispered as she collapsed on him. "I made a lot of noise, didn't I?"

"Oh. Yes."

"I'm sorry. I never scream." Maybe the pheromones had caused her to lose control. Sex had never pushed her to abandon herself. She felt transformed, like she was one of those snow globes turned upside down and shaken and slowly settled back into place, only she was all rearranged.

His hands made circles from her shoulder blades to her lower back. "You screamed my name. I like that."

"But I thought you . . . hate that kind of thing. You said it made you feel like an animal."

He shrugged, causing her to slide against his sweaty skin. "Oh, I liked everything about that, Allie."

He gathered her hair into his hands. "Abandon fear, all who enter here." He gave a thrust of his pelvis at the word "enter."

She snorted. "I think I remember that from high school

and it goes, 'abandon hope, all ye who enter here.' *Dante's In-ferno.*"

He swept his hands over her body as if marking her as his territory and then gripped her upper thighs with both hands. "This is not hell. I don't mind being an animal with you."

We're both animals abandoning fear together. She noticed the tension in his hands and the greedy way he eyed her. When he pushed up into her a few times, and groaned, she got the picture. "You're not done, are you."

He shook his head. "Remember? I have to be careful."

"Ah, well then." She chuckled at his indignant yelp when she pulled off and rolled to the side.

"Come on." She held her arms wide. "Inside, now."

He must have been controlling himself up until then, for his arms trembled as he supported himself above her and pressed into her. He groaned "Allie," and her name was a plea that stirred her like a caress. His turn. But even as she decided to hold still, she wiggled, excited by his wild eagerness.

His control must have snapped. She saw the change as his eyes widened. He was like a wild animal as he drove into her body. He clutched her as if she were the food and he a starved man. If it hadn't been such a turn-on, she might have been frightened by the ferocity of his passion. His intent eyes bored into her, even as he did, going so deep inside her she wondered if anyone had touched the places his rock-hard cock reached.

His hoarse wordless cry shook her.

She wrapped her arms around him and their bodies twined. He touched his forehead to hers.

"Jesus," he panted. "I'm sorry. Did I hurt you? I . . ." He shifted, rested on his elbows, still firmly embedded inside her. "I lost control."

She gave a breathless laugh. "You let yourself go all right. Impressive."

She didn't want to pull away, wishing they could remain joined for hours.

He rolled onto his back, dropped the condom into the trash, then urged her onto his chest. For a while she felt and heard the steady thump of his heart, waiting, wondering if she were brave enough to take the risk. Worth a try, at any rate.

She climbed onto him, as if she could pin him down and get him to agree. "Here's a plan. At noon, we'll go get my car," Allie said at last. "And I'll drive you to the competition."

His deep, even breaths pushed her relaxed body up and down. She wondered if he had fallen asleep.

Apparently not, for he answered after a few seconds. "Thanks, but I'd be grateful if you just dropped me at a used car dealer or rental place. I don't want to risk you losing your job."

But she didn't want to risk losing him. "That's okay. If Tagge tells me to take a hike, I can always get a job at Ducky and Elsie's Diner in town."

"Huh." He sounded wary. "Is that what you want?"

She blew a wisp of hair from her face and considered his question. Maybe he'd only been polite before when he implied he wanted to spend time with her. She knew she had to ask. "Sure, I hope you don't mind if I go with you?"

"Hell, I admit it, I'd love your company. But that's not what I was asking. I meant would you want to get another job as a waitress?"

She rested her head on his chest, relieved, but also ready to be defensive. "I like working with people."

"Yeah, I watched you in the diner. You're great. Do you suppose you want to do that with your life?"

She burrowed down and pressed her face against his firm belly. Her life. When was the last time she'd thought further than her next paycheck? He'd awakened more than her libido.

She wouldn't lie to try to pass herself off as a go-getter, so she answered slowly and examined the truth of the words as she said them. "I guess maybe I'd like my own little restaurant some day. I'm not ambitious. I'm pretty ordinary."

"Excuse me? You're something special."

She snorted and mumbled a polite, though nearly incoherent thank you, her lips pressed his skin.

Bryan pulled her tight against him, waiting for the moment he knew was coming too soon. She might think that she wanted to stay with him, but this might be the last time he'd get to hold her strong, round little body. He couldn't guess what she'd do or feel about him when he managed to turn back to a regular guy. Ordinary, again—that word, again.

Allie had seemed such an ordinary woman when he first caught sight of her. Had he ever been so blind before? He saw nothing commonplace about the delectable Allie Hamden.

At last another sort of hunger drove them to abandon the rumpled sheets. Allie found a package of crackers, and he rummaged in the refrigerator, emerging with a chunk of cheddar cheese. Plain cheese and slightly stale crackers washed down by water, the meal tasted rich—better than any restaurant's haute cuisine.

Allie borrowed one of Kim's dresses, a plain flowered cotton number that ended above her knees. It must have been loose on Kim because it clung to Allie's larger frame. When was the last time she'd worn a dress without pantyhose? Usually she wore jeans when she wasn't at work. The openness of her naked legs made her self-conscious. She pressed them together and resisted the urge to rub her hands over her own raw skin. As she moved around the kitchen, she could feel the dampness between her legs. He hadn't come in her so all the moisture was hers alone. From her and his mouth. Oh, my. The memory was strong enough to halt her hand as she rummaged through a junk drawer for a pen.

She found a pen and paper and wrote an apologetic note.

"Ready to go?" he said, and shoved the last of the cheese back in a drawer.

"I hope I can get back here before Kim does," she said, putting a magnet on the note to the fridge. "I'll replace the food."

"We'll leave the woman a lobster dinner."

She liked the sound of that "we". "Yeah, good idea."

At the front door she paused to look around. Her friend's plain little cabin had been transformed. The couch was comfortable, not shabby. The dark walls that had seemed gloomy now made the room cozy. Bryan had a dramatic influence on her perception.

The garage was close to the hotel, but they skirted the area so the walk took twice as long. They might have been on a stroll through a park rather than the no-man's-land of junkyards and industrial parks near the auto shop.

Gino's was a gas station that had seen better days, but Bryan could see that the garage bays were well maintained and the three mechanics looked like men who cared about cars.

"Here." He pulled a roll of money from his pocket and peeled some off. "Pay with cash. Let me."

She stared at the thick wad he jammed back into his jeans. "How much do you have?"

"Not sure. Enough I hope." He'd withdrawn over ten thousand in cash and had been reasonably careful with the money. "Don't want to use credit cards," he explained.

She wrinkled her nose but took the money. "Yeah, makes sense." With a distasteful glance at the cash in her hand, she strode into the mechanic's office.

Bryan stayed outside and watched her laugh with the lanky dark man who gave her a wink. Bryan felt a flash of jealousy—something he hadn't experienced since high school. Stupid. He jammed his hands into his jeans and told himself he just wanted to be on the road, and his impatience had nothing to do with Allie's glowing smile at the other man.

At last she came out waving over her shoulder and jingling keys.

She tried to give him the wad of dough. "Don't worry, Gino won't tell anyone I had my car here. I used my credit card."

Bryan scowled and gently pushed her hand away. "Hey, you're saving my ass. Let me pay for the car."

She returned his frown with interest. "Nope. I had to get the tune-up anyway, and do something about the brakes. You don't owe me a cent."

He shoved his hands into his pockets. "Save it for later then. You're doing me a favor; I'm not letting you pay expenses."

He had no intention of losing that fight. She grumbled something about stubborn men, and located her Neon in a far corner of the parking lot.

They set off on small back roads that curved through the edges of towns. Stopping only for gas, they ate at a drive-through.

"I know a great seafood shack just outside Ocean Springs," she said. "Maybe we can get supper there." Supper, such a banal word. Would they be eating together once he'd finished screwing another woman?

He took a bite of his burger and deftly steered the car back into the heavy traffic. He must have had a lot of practice eating and driving. "Don't need to attract attention to ourselves."

"Yeah, I bet women remember you when you pass through town," she teased.

His grimace quickly turned into a crooked smile so she

risked pushing some more. "Don't they know where you're going? Wouldn't that Dr. Nathan tell them what he told you about the perfect woman?"

He shrugged his strong shoulders. "I guess he hasn't said anything. Anyway, they can't *legally* stop me."

She missed the feel of him and reached to rest her hand on his warm solid thigh. Under her fingers he flinched. The car seat squeaked under his tensing body. He relaxed almost at once and shook his head ruefully. "Sorry. I'm still jumpy."

"Jeez, Bryan, they've done a number on you. But why are they after you if they can't stop you? Why are you running like a fugitive?"

"They're going to keep offering me more and more money." He swallowed the last bite of his sandwich before adding, "Okay, yeah, they don't always stick to the strictly legal. They tried to get me arrested a couple of days ago. Idiots."

He glanced over and must have seen the horror on her face. "Nah, they're not going to deliberately kill the golden goose."

"They don't seem to mind the fact that you're pretty hostile." She sighed and glanced out the window and realized they'd covered more than one hundred fifty miles. "We'll make it to Ocean Springs by four. Amazing."

"How's that?"

All of it, she wanted to say. The way he'd taken her plain existence and turned it into an adventure. "This whole thing, like those guys chasing you."

He chuckled and crumpled the bag that had held his

food. "Amazing? More like a pain in the ass. Until you." He painstakingly licked his fingers, glancing over at her with a lively spark in his eyes.

She gave his leg a squeeze of appreciation. The set of his broad shoulders had relaxed—maybe it was safe to ask the question that had been nagging at her. "And when you're done with this? When it's over?"

"I'm gonna have more than enough money to start my own business," he said.

"What do you have in mind?"

He scratched at his bristly chin. "I've been building cabinets for years. I like doing that. I'm good at it, too. Maybe that. Maybe something more . . ." He looked at her sideways. "More for people."

"What does that mean?" she asked.

He made a rude noise. "Anything but deodorant?" He waved a hand at the green highway sign. "I take this exit, don't I?"

"I think so . . . Listen, that reminds me. Now that we're almost to the city we're going to need to keep better track of the streets and I'm a really rotten navigator. Mind letting me drive?"

He glanced at her, bemused. "Yeah, well, last time I checked it was your car."

A man who didn't feel threatened by a woman who drove. She didn't know many of that rare species.

He pulled into a parking lot so they could get out, stretch, exchange a few lazy kisses which threatened to grow heavier.

Back in the car, they soon drove through the ramshackle

suburb that turned into a line of posh hotels pressed up against the beaches. The edge of Ocean Springs, the resort town that had died, come back, and was fading again.

He yawned and stretched, taking up even more space—he filled the small car with his presence. "Any particular hotel you like?"

"I've always been partial to that famous place that's supposed to be so posh. What's it called? The Springleaf maybe?" she joked.

He flipped open a guide to Ocean Springs she'd grabbed at a gas station.

"Okay, it's on Fourth Avenue."

She slapped the steering wheel. "Come on. I was kidding. That place is way too expensive. Where should we go? Really."

"The Springleaf. Really."

"Jeez, I've heard it's got a whole arboretum in the lobby complete with a pond and exotic birds. It's way too much money—" she started.

He ran a finger along her jaw to her mouth. "What do you care? I'm paying. It's near The Beachway where I, um . . . where the beauty pageant is. The place you like is only a couple of high-rises away. Turn left here."

She nipped at his finger, but didn't argue.

"I bet they won't like cash. Here." He pulled out the stash of money and shoved a few bills into the ashtray. "That should take care of it. Mind using your credit card again?"

She shook her head.

"I'm grateful, Allie." He brushed her hand. "With you

185

along this is more like a vacation. You're a fine surprise. A treat in a a a box of Crackerjacks. A diamond in the ashes."

"A snake in the can."

"Speaking of snakes, ask for the Jungle room." He waved a brochure. "This says it's a once in a lifetime experience that can't be missed."

Once in a lifetime sounded like this whole weird day. "But what if they can trace my credit card."

"They will but by the time Metcher catch up with us, I should be . . . cured."

Cured. Funny how they both danced around the reason they were in this city.

They pulled into the wide arches of the Springleaf. Her faded sundress got a look from the clerk but her card went through.

Back at the car he rested in the passenger seat, head tilted back, eyes closed. Her heart tightened—that's how he'd look asleep next to her in bed.

"We're in," she said and handed him the small magnetic key. "Room 302."

He nodded and stared through the plate glass windows. "I guess the stairs are off the lobby. Yeah, they're gonna be easy to find."

He got out of the car.

"Stairs? You claustrophobic about elevators?"

He adjusted his sunglasses and scanned the area. "Naw, just don't want to risk getting trapped with women."

"Huh. So what are you going to do? Run through the place?"

He gave her a quick kiss on the forehead that made her toes curl.

"Exactly. I'll meet you up there."

He took off at a jog, looking unperturbed but moving fast.

She wanted to laugh, but noticed through the plate glass windows how the women in the lobby stared after him. One or two even took a step in his direction.

She followed slowly and took the gleaming elevator, feeling frumpy and out of place compared to the other passengers. The three silent, well-dressed businesswomen on the elevator looked incapable of sexual frenzy. What would it have been like if Bryan had been aboard? Would the women have clustered around him, howling and groaning, stripping off their clothes and his? Hard to imagine the polished gray-haired woman with the pinstriped suit launching herself at Bryan, but she remembered Dawn in the diner. And herself, oh, just about every moment she'd been in his presence.

Chapter Six

Allie knocked on the door before she slipped the cardkey into the slot. Thick pale green carpeting muffled her steps and even muted her startled exclamation. Every inch of the Jungle room had been painted with huge plants that had animals lurking in their shadows. Fiberglass trunks rose from the floor, and fake vines hung from the tall ceiling; all formed into swings. A fake zebra skin covered the round bed.

Bryan chuckled at her surprise. "Pretty amazing." He leaned against a huge pot of bromeliads and ferns.

"I have never seen anything this awesomely tacky in my whole life."

She turned away from examining a leopard carving and her eyes widened. Now that was definitely not a tacky sight. He was unbuttoning his shirt.

"I'm going to take a shower," he said. "The concierge is sending someone out to get some new clothes for me. You're going to have to add that to my tab."

She'd skirted the huge toadstool chair to get to him but at those words she collapsed on the bed, getting the hint. He wasn't shedding his clothes to get her to jump him. Oh, but she longed to. She'd gone too many hours without touching that delicious skin.

"So you're going to stay naked until you get the new clothes?

He shot her an evil grin. "They said they'd hurry."

She managed to keep her voice casual. "It would never occur to me to call out for clothes."

He grunted. "Yeah, I'm too used to throwing around money, aren't I? I'll stop soon."

He tossed his flannel shirt on a toadstool, turned and headed through the flower-painted doorway.

She couldn't help calling after him, "So, you want company for the shower?"

He reappeared in the doorway. "Yeah. Please. I was hoping you'd ask."

Hot damn. She jumped off the bed.

A fountain stood in the middle of the bathroom. Glass bricks semi-enclosed a walk-in shower that was painted with hippos and—"Hey, is that an alligator?" she squeaked. "Why would anyone want to share a shower with one of those?"

He'd shucked his jeans and she forgot the alligator.

Within minutes the three showerheads splashed over their entangled bodies.

"Ever made it up against an alligator?" he growled in her ear.

Her giggles turned to groans as he pressed her back to the cool tiles.

Afterward they moved to the round bed. Exhausted, she fell asleep while her hair was still damp.

* * *

He dozed for a time and woke at six.

Time to get the show on the road before the Metcher bunch caught up with them. He yanked on a bathrobe to fetch the neatly piled new clothes, a stiff pair of brand-new jeans, underwear, and a red plain T-shirt just outside the door. Dressed and ready as he'd ever be, he went to the bed to say goodbye.

"I'm off," he whispered.

"Oh." She rolled over and sat up. "I want to come, too. I don't mean a threesome . . ." She blushed. "Well. I mean. I . . ."

A heavy weight of fear rolled off his stomach. She didn't despise him for leaving a bed they'd shared so he could look for some other female.

"No. Bad idea."

"But I—"

He leaned over and kissed her into silence. He straightened and looked down into her sleepy face. "I'll be back the moment I can."

What if she came to her senses when the chemicals were gone? Just in case she wouldn't let him back in when he was through, he hauled out his roll of money. He left a few hundred dollars on top of the polished sawed-off tree trunk that served as a table.

The Beachway might have been a luxury hotel years ago. In the lobby the carpet edges peeled back where duct tape didn't hold it down, and dust coated the fake plants.

But gorgeous young women milled around the lobby like

exotic flowers and with beauties like them adorning the place, few people would notice the shabby atmosphere.

Bryan noticed and he felt as seedy as the hotel. Seedier. He paused at the entrance, looking over the women—girls, really. They had to be at least ten years younger than his thirty. Damn.

And they were perky.

Why the hell would anyone want perky?

Was any one of the girls more gorgeous than the others? Not that he could see. They might have all been cast from the same lovely mold.

Pick one, he reminded himself and tried to guess which of the women wouldn't let anything get in her way. He had to do this, but he sure as hell didn't want to hurt anyone.

He shoved his hands into his pockets and walked over to the group.

They faced him expectantly with automatic smiles in place.

"Hi," a redhead said. She tossed back her hair, thrust out her breasts, and aimed a thousand-watt smile at him. "I'm Melanie," she told him in what sounded like a deliberately husky voice. Okay, he didn't care. She'd be fine. He braced himself.

But to his amazement, instead of pushing away from the other women to claim him, she gestured to the blonde at her side and said, "This is Tiffany." Melanie went around the circle and introduced her smiling friends.

He stepped closer to Melanie and waited. And nothing happened. Ten seconds. Thirty seconds. He moved even closer, his arm almost brushing against hers. She tossed back her hair again and gave him a sultry tip of the chin. Yet her hands remained at her side, and her breasts didn't heave with panting desperation.

He tested the air, drawing in a long, slow breath. No trace of the female hunger reached him. Just perfume and hairspray, tinged with sweat. Not one of them was switched on by him. In a group of five women, not one?

His heart swooped with joy. He was the one to gasp with pleasure.

These women liked the look of him. They'd flirt with him, let him buy them drinks. Maybe Melanie would even go further, but he wasn't going to stick around to find out.

He breathed in one last sample and still smelled nothing. No tendrils of desire curled up from their bodies.

His little pheromone factory had been shut down.

He grinned so maniacally that even Melanie's smile wavered uncertainly.

"Ladies, you are the most perfect women I have ever seen in my life. It's a privilege to meet you, but I must be going. Goodbye."

Tiffany rolled her eyes and directed an exaggerated pout at him. "Come on, girls," she said, and walked off in the direction of the bar.

The other women followed. Melanie stopped to look back. He spread his hands and shrugged his regret. She giggled, winked, and to his delighted relief, followed her friends to the bar.

Whistling, he pushed through the big glass doors into the

sultry summer night. When had it happened? Maybe that first time they'd made love? Actually he didn't give a shit when she broke the spell for him. The nightmare was over, and he got to wake up with some fine company at his side. Did she still want him?

He broke into a jog. Allie, the perfect woman, waited for him. He hoped.

Chapter Seven

Allie lay in the bed, too paralyzed to move. Bryan said he'd come back, but when he walked out the door, the silence filled the room and her heart.

She had never avoided hard facts and now examined this one. The strange journey had come to an end.

Mortification flooded her. No, she wouldn't let herself feel bad. Dagnabit, it had been a good ride, the best she'd ever had.

No matter what happened, however long it took her to recover from this wild day, she would not feel regret. Her crotch—actually her entire body—was happily achy from overuse.

She reckoned the external damage wasn't severe. She probably hadn't even lost her job. Which was too bad, because one of the gifts she'd gotten from Bryan was that it might be time to move on. Time to stop creeping through life at a night job. She'd feel sun on her face again. She ran her hands over her hips, tired from a long night of work and a long day of pleasure.

No, she didn't really have any real internal damage either,

unless she counted getting a taste of something she might starve for in the future.

She climbed out of bed and found the shabby sundress. No underwear, no bra, so the sea breeze would flow against her skin. Now that her body was alive she'd be damned if she'd miss a single sensation again.

She found a pad and pen in a drawer embedded in the carved python climbing the wall next to the bed. What could she write that didn't sound defensive or needy?

She settled on, "Gone to the beach. Be back soon," and left the note on the pillow.

When she opened the door, she gave a startled gasp. Bryan filled the doorway, towering over her.

Without a word, he folded his arms around her and surged forward, forcing her to walk backwards until they reached the bed.

She squawked in surprise but any protest died away as he tilted his head and his eager mouth found hers. He ran his hands down her spine. Oh, no. The way her sensitive pussy immediately swelled and her whole body tingled told her he hadn't been successful. The pheromones trapped her.

Besides, he hadn't been gone long enough.

The image of him thrusting into another woman once again made her stomach flip and sink.

"You're back so soon," she croaked.

He kissed her face, nuzzled her neck, and whispered, "You did it. We did it."

In a dramatic gesture, he spun away and sprawled backward on the bed, arms and legs outstretched. "I'm cured."

"But . . . No, no. I'm still . . ." She examined him. A delicious buffet laid out just for her. Just looking at him made her weak with excitement. She climbed on top of him and, kneeling over him, found his mouth again. As she kissed him, she moaned with pleasure and dismay. "No. I want you too much. How can that be unless you're filled with that stuff?"

He brushed her hair from her face and explored her mouth with a thorough kiss. "Shit, and I can still taste your desire." He heaved a sigh that she felt shiver through him. "You saying you don't feel any difference?"

"None. I'm ready for you just thinking about you. And then when you touch me . . ." She felt close to tears. The hours of excitement were breaking her down, driving her just a tad crazy. Maybe this is what happened to those other women, the ones who'd tied him to their beds.

"Shh." He wrapped his arms around her torso, drawing her into a comforting hug. Too bad the feel of his heat seemed to reach in and twist her—until his words distracted her at last.

"Dammit! There has to be a change, I'm telling you. I went out in public, went near a group of women. Nothing happened. Nada."

She at last allowed herself to collapse her weight on him and lay very still. "What does it mean?"

"Honey, you're perfect. That's what I think it means."

She groaned. "No, really."

His hands went to her bottom and he rubbed her in slow circles. "Yes, really. Oh, my. Better than perfect—you forgot your panties."

He pressed up and his erection nudged her tender clitoris. She shivered, her nerve endings melting into desire. "Bryan, I'm out of control. Again. I can't believe it's gone. But, God, I hope you're right."

She shifted so her fingers could stroke the length of his cock through the blue jeans. Realizing his reaction was genuine and that her tumult of need wasn't a byproduct of pheromones added a new dimension to her desire. She needed more than Bryan's body. She needed *him*, his smile, his playful gaze, his strength beside her.

Husky and breathless, he asked. "Aren't you sore?"

She nodded, her hair rustling against his neck. She drew in a deep breath of his already familiar scent. "Yeah, oh yes but not impossibly."

"Impossibly?"

She touched her fingertips to his cheek, feeling suddenly, oddly shy. Easy enough to hide with a bit of humor. "Well, we have to make sure you're really cured."

They set out to love carefully.

"Let's go back to kissing," he said. "Only kisses, everywhere."

He licked his way to her stomach and then the inside of her thighs. One moment tender, the next relentless, his tongue quickened her anticipation. Clearly he enjoyed teasing her as much as she relished his talents. They were good together, so good. Spearing her fingers through his thick hair, she dared imagine weeks of this, months, years . . .

Lovely, but within minutes, she knew she'd want more. All of her skin was tenderized, charged with awareness, as if she had a fever. She burned from the inside out for him. "Now." She arched up.

"Not yet." He suckled one breast and lightly stroked her between her legs. Sensation jangled through her overly aroused body. A slight intimation of pain only intensified the growing fever that took over her body again. Goose bumps rose on her skin.

"Damn it! I need you inside me," she informed him. "Now!"

He gently nipped her nipple and licked it, the warmth of his marvelous mouth replaced by cool air. "What a nice invitation. Yep, I accept."

She lay as still as possible, watching as he rolled on a condom. He knelt above her and nudged her swollen slit with his cock.

"Go on," she gasped.

He teased her with careful slow and shallow strokes.

"Allie," he whispered. "I need this. God, I need to make love. Do you understand?"

She almost sobbed with the tenderness of his kiss.

Oh, but even as she raised her legs higher, she yearned for more heat.

She planted her heels on the sheets and pushed up. "I can take more," she gasped. "If you can. Give it to me."

"Yes." He thrust into her, hitting that sweet center no one else had ever touched. Yet he moved carefully, until she impatiently wriggled up. *Harder.* He got the message.

As gentleness gave way to pounding passion she writhed and twisted beneath him, aching for more, getting lost in sensation but not letting her gaze leave his face. He wanted to make love, not fuck mindlessly. But oh . . .

"It's okay," she said, hoping that he knew what she meant. "You can. I'm not going to lose it."

"Yes. You will. I'm gonna make you lose control." He was demanding more now, more heated kisses, deeper thrusts. He licked the inside of her mouth. "Together. Both."

She hazily wondered which both. Fucking and making love? Or both of them coming at once?

It couldn't be true that he was cured. They were thoroughly entangled, and her body screamed for him to pound harder, faster. Oh, the thick heaviness tightened in her until she had to press her mouth to his shoulder to muffle the cry of surprised joy as jolts of pleasure shuddered through her.

"Yes, oh, thank you," she babbled. "Oh please you, too. I don't care."

Bryan knew that he had no need to think. He could let himself fly out and meet Allie, go as deep as each thrust would let him and lose himself in their lovemaking. He let go even as the first of her spasms gripped him. The powerful orgasm hit him at the same moment as hers; the explosion of pleasure ripped through his whole body.

They both survived.

Maybe.

They panted into the silence for a few moments until she scooted her legs into a more comfortable position and allowed herself to settle on him.

"That's it. I'm dead," she informed his shoulder.

The phone perched on the python trilled.

They looked at it. It stopped, and then a minute later, began chirping again.

Bryan sighed. He eased out of Allie and rolled over. God, even the backs of his legs felt as if they'd melted in the heat of their passion.

"Yeah?" he barked.

He'd suspected Metcher, and yet was surprised to hear a familiar, nervous voice. "Ah, Bryan? This is Dr. Nathan. They, um, had me get a plane . . . And now. We're downstairs."

Before Bryan could speak there was a thud, some rustling and angry voices as another man grabbed the phone. Someone, probably the one he called the enforcer, bellowed into Bryan's ear. "We're coming up if you if you don't come down here." Another muffled angry exchange followed and Nathan was back on the line.

Nathan sounded even more nervous. "We, um, we don't mean to intrude, Bryan, but I'm sure you understand that Metcher is rather eager for your cooperation."

Bryan held back a groan. He rested a hand on Allie's hip and slid closer to her. There. That was better. He could manage a light tone. "You must have finally spilled the beans about spilling the beans to me."

"Listen, Bryan, you have to—"

He interrupted. "I don't have to do a damn thing, Nathan, but I will. Ten minutes. I'll meet you in the bar."

He slammed the phone back on the python.

Allie was propped on an elbow and blew a ringlet of hair from her forehead.

He reached over and pushed her hair from her face with

the side of his thumb. "I've always liked women with wild hair."

She wouldn't be distracted. "That doctor is here? With those men?"

"Yeah, those men."

"Oh no! What will we do?"

He kissed the side of her chin. "No sweat. I'm going to go meet them. Make them buy me a beer even. They found me, but there isn't a damned thing they could do anymore."

"Oh. Right." Not convinced, but not willing to argue, Allie brushed her lips across to Bryan's mouth in search of a succulent kiss.

At last he got out of bed to get dressed. He was tucking the T-shirt into the jeans when she decided.

"I'm coming too."

He looked up sharply. "I want to talk to them alone."

She considered feeling hurt, but was too exhausted and too worried about what might happen. "How about a compromise? I'll stay out of sight for ten minutes."

Bryan squinted at her. "You always this bossy?"

She pursed her lips. "Probably."

"I'd better get used to it then."

Allie thought about doing a cartwheel or bursting into song. Instead she nodded vigorously. "Yeah, you better."

He kissed her forehead and left, strutting like a man who'd won the lottery. She sighed with joy and fear. After the door closed she jumped out of bed, determined to make it five minutes instead of ten.

Chapter Eight

Bryan took the elevator just like any other regular slob. His heart pounded as he covertly watched the only other passenger, a thin woman with a Red Sox T-shirt. She must have noticed his examination, for she gave him a tentative smile. And then—hallelujah—she got off on the next floor.

He wanted to go after her to thank her, shake her hand, invite her out for pizza and beer. A fellow human.

He was humming as he walked into the wide marble-floored lobby and caught sight of the four men huddled under a banana tree. The desk clerk watched them with a malignant eye. Perhaps they'd tried to slip past and he'd proved too honest to bribe because the hotel provided actual security for its guests. Damn, he should have bypassed the rat holes and gone for first-class accommodations before now. He might have actually gotten some sleep during his week on the road. But then he wouldn't have Allie. Did he have her? Just watch her try to get away.

Smiling, Bryan sauntered over to the disheveled group of Metcher men.

"You," snarled the large one. "What the hell do you think you're doing?"

"Hello." He waggled his fingers at them cheerily. "Bad news. You're wasting your time. I'm not worth a thing to you anymore."

They gaped at him. "What?"

Bryan jerked his head to point out two middle-aged women—cosmetic saleswomen, judging from the cases they carried—waiting in a corner of the lobby. "Come on. I'll demonstrate."

He walked toward the two women, who watched curiously as the group of Metcher men stalked after Bryan. They must have made a strange sight.

"Hello, ladies," Bryan said. "How are you this evening? May my friends and I buy you a drink?"

"Well, I don't know." One of the women touched the elaborate curls of her hairdo and giggled uncertainly.

Bryan sauntered over. He stood right next to her. The Metchers tensed, probably ready to jump in, the way guards once had to in the lab when Bryan accidentally walked too near an unsuspecting lab technician and she'd tackled him.

The other woman clicked her tongue impatiently, and nudged her friend with an elbow. "No, thanks anyway gentlemen. We have to get going. Thanks, anyway."

The pair strolled away, leaving Bryan grinning and the Metchers slack-jawed.

"Shit. You did it." The pale one breathed.

"Get the dog to make sure," the enforcer ordered. The

dog handler almost saluted before he took off across the lobby.

Bryan had had enough. He strolled around the knot of men and headed to the elevator.

"See you later," he said.

At that moment Allie in her faded little sundress stepped out of the little café next to the lobby. She showed way too much of her silky bare legs to the Metcher idiots.

"The waitress," the enforcer snarled. "Miss Hamden, what do you think you're doing?"

"Taking a vacation," she said. "I was tired of smart-ass customers bothering me after hours."

Bryan relaxed and considered applauding. He'd wondered if she was going to be cowed by the Metchers. Nope, she might be vulnerable in bed, but he should have expected courage from the woman who could face down grouchy truck drivers all night long.

From the front desk someone shouted, "Excuse me sir, dogs are not allowed."

Elsie's claws clicked across the marble floor as she yanked her handler towards them. Bryan braced himself for the happy onslaught, but she bypassed him and went straight for Allie.

The dog panted and rubbed her head against Allie's legs. Bryan's heart plummeted.

"Hey, pup," Allie leaned over and scratched Elsie's ears.

Bryan tensed. Could he have somehow transferred the pheromones to her? Would men be all over her? He glanced at the Metcher men who inched toward Allie. If any of them so much as touched her . . . Bryan reached for the huge brass vase on the display, ready to brain the first who laid a finger on Allie.

But Elsie moved on and the handler didn't give the signal that Elsie had found anything. The dog strolled past each person, sniffing. She got to Bryan where he stood still not allowing himself to show so much as a twitch. He forgot to breathe.

Nothing. No pawing or barking.

Bryan crowed and dropped to a crouch to rub the ecstatic dog's ears. "Oh, Elsie," he intoned with mock sorrow. "You're yet another female who's lost interest in me."

The frowning desk clerk hurried over, protesting. "The dog must go." No one paid any attention.

The dog handler clicked his tongue, and Elsie gave Bryan's hand an apologetic lick and left.

The handler fed Elsie a treat and eyed Bryan who'd straightened up. "So I'm betting we've been wasting our time for a while. You must have stopped production of the pheromones back at that diner," the handler remarked conversationally as he stroked Elsie. He yawned and checked his watch.

Bryan shook his head. "Naw. I used cayenne pepper to throw poor Elsie off."

The thin dog handler scowled and at last looked upset. "You kidding me? That wouldn't put a dog like her off. She can handle anything."

Interesting. Bryan considered the implications until he was distracted by the enforcer. Unlike the dog handler, he

205

seemed a trifle annoyed that Bryan had lost the curse. Bryan wondered if he would actually have a fit there in the lobby. The big guy spun around to Nathan. "This is your fault."

Under his scraggly beard, Nathan paled and took a step backward.

The enforcer followed, and stabbed a finger into Nathan's skinny chest. "If you hadn't been such a—"

"Hey, it had to happen sometime." Bryan gently shoved Nathan out of the way and stepped between them. He was at least six inches taller than the enforcer, and he'd had more than enough of these Metcher fools. "I wasn't going to put up with being your pheromone factory forever. What the hell did you plan to do? Shove me in a lab cage?"

The Enforcer's hand dropped to his side. "You had a contract and—"

"Get over it, huh? It's not so bad. Metcher's got baskets of my dirty laundry to play with."

The enforcer lapsed into an angry silence.

Bryan glanced at Allie. She flushed with embarrassment, but she wore a thoroughly pleased smirk. Yeah, that smirk told him she knew what the dog handler's words meant— she was so perfect it hadn't taken a full session in bed.

Maybe he'd lost the "hunting for a mate" pheromones the moment he'd kissed her mouth or perhaps when he'd kissed her body and tasted her delicious essence.

The Metchers didn't hang around long after that. Negotiations went quickly. Bryan agreed to another, final battery of tests in exchange for a last, obscenely high sum.

They cleared out. Nathan stayed behind and followed Bryan and Allie into the bar to moan over his lost career at Metcher. "I was sick of the corporate life," he admitted. "But I don't have any interest in switching to academia."

Bryan drank his Corona, most of his attention focused on Allie as she dipped her finger into the exotic strawberry thing she'd ordered and daintily licked the pink droplet off her finger. Clueless Nathan didn't appear to notice—how the hell could the man ignore an erotic demonstration like that?

Nathan rambled on about the research he wanted to do, something about nasal receptors and pheromones again.

Allie put down her drink and wiped her mouth. She interrupted Nathan's lecture. "Hey, if the receptors are here—" she tapped her nose, "—how come I could pick up these pheromones? I'd pretty well blasted my nose with cleanser. I still don't have much of a sense of smell back yet."

Nathan swirled the ice in his Coke. "If the receptors are damaged you would have less response, perhaps even no arousal."

"Must be why you could resist me long enough to be rude," Bryan said.

She apparently ignored him, though the corner of her mouth twitched up. "So if my receptors were blasted, there were other reasons I was so interested in Bryan?"

Bryan leaned over and inhaled her sweet mix of sex and Allie. "Was?" he whispered. "You got that wrong. You are interested."

She leaned her cheek against his. "I am. Still so . . .

very . . ." She flicked and nibbled the edge of his ear. "Very interested."

He tried without success to hold back the answering shudder and groan.

Nathan didn't notice. He rubbed at his beard and stared absently into space. "Intriguing question. If your receptors were damaged would you be drawn to him? In most cases of arousal there are more than pheromones involved. For instance if you were not attracted to men, even if you'd inhaled a pure concentration of PGH3, you would have experienced a far milder response. And the fact is that once he stopped producing PGH3, your own response is what carries the day in terms of—"

Bryan couldn't resist the outline of Allie's hip under the skimpy sundress. He traced her from the dip of her waist to the top of her thigh with his fingers, then decided to squeeze the delectable firm flesh. She gave a breathless gasp and twisted her chair to face him.

Nathan's voice faded. Even a man as dense as Nathan must have seen their attention lay elsewhere.

He cleared his throat and the barstool groaned as he got to his feet. "You know you two ought to go somewhere else. Somewhere private."

"You're right." Bryan reached into his back pocket, pulled out a clip of cash. "I'll get this."

Nathan tugged at his beard. "Seems like I ought to pay. I helped make your life miserable."

"Nah, thanks to Metcher . . ." He didn't finish the sentence but slid his hand over Allie's thigh. She stood and leaned against him. He had trouble concentrating enough to wedge out a bill.

"Well," Nathan began again.

Bryan slapped a fifty onto the bar. "I can afford this place. Hell, because of those pheromones I'm rich enough to invest in a restaurant. A chain of restaurants."

Allie, who had been trying to burrow under his arm, froze.

"A restaurant?" she asked faintly.

"Hmmm." He nuzzled her mouth with his lips and settled in for another delicious kiss. She pulled back and studied him, her face aglow. She had the delighted smile of a woman up for immediate fun and the glow of someone looking forward to longer-term plans, too.

"Restaurant?" Nathan perked up. "An interesting investment if you have the right—"

"We'll talk." Bryan didn't even glance at him as he tucked away the rest of the money and reached for Allie. "Right now, I'm busy. Yeah. Now. And for a very, very long time." He tightened his arm around Allie's torso so she couldn't escape, and they waved goodbye to Nathan.

Epilogue

Cupping the glass holder, Allie leaned over the flame and blew. One candle down, six to go. She straightened and, stretching her arms over her head, took a moment to let the breeze touch her skin and listen to the quiet *shush* of the surf. They'd had a good crowd that evening and she loved the chatter of people having fun, but after the restaurant closed the silence was heaven. So far, so good. A month after opening, The Genuine Article was thriving under Bryan's management and her culinary skills.

"Kind of dark out here."

She gasped. "You startled me."

The sea breeze ruffled his hair, and she itched to brush the locks back into place. Bryan chuckled. "I've been watching you for a while. Good thing my intentions are honorable."

"Are they?"

"Depends. Are you done?"

The kitchen and dining room had already been cleaned and readied for the next day. Their staff had gone home.

She lowered her arms and crossed them over her breasts, which already tingled in anticipation. "Yeah, I'm done."

His smile glinted in the light of the remaining candles as he ambled toward her. "Okay, I've changed my mind about the honorable bit. We haven't done anything out here yet, have we?"

"But we're outside. Anyone walking by on the beach could see us."

He leaned down and blew out one of the remaining candles. "The gazebo."

"Oh." He'd put cushions on the benches that morning and now she knew why. Clever man. One more reason to love him.

She considered going to him, winding her arm around his waist as they walked across the flagstone patio to the small garden and the gazebo. No, she wanted the first contact to be in the sheltering darkness so she could lose herself the instant they touched.

"Anticipation is wonderful," she informed him as he reached for her shoulders and drew her to him.

He bent and thoroughly kissed her. "I can think of better things."

Their long, lazy kiss grew more passionate. He pulled away, and she gave a complaining little whimper.

"Wait," he said.

Her eyes had adjusted to the darkness, and she saw a wine bucket with a bottle of champagne resting in ice. Two flutes stood on the flagstones next to it.

"What's that for?"

He poured and handed her a glass. "We're celebrating."

She sipped. The cold crisp wine tasted perfect. "Great. I

love parties." Stepping closer she trailed her fingers down the row of buttons on his crisp white shirt. She whispered, "Is this going to be one of those wild get naked blowouts? Those are my favorites."

"Don't you want to know why we're celebrating?"

"You mean we have to have a reason?"

He laughed. "Metcher."

"Ha. Those ingrates. Corporate headquarters didn't even RSVP the invitation to the restaurant's opening I sent."

He swallowed his champagne, put down the glass, and enfolded her in his arms. She pressed her face to his shoulder and breathed in his sweet scent of fresh wood and pure Bryan. At last. She'd been waiting for this moment for hours.

He kissed her hair. "Maybe you shouldn't have included the special invitation to their 'goon squad, intimidators, and Elsie'."

"Picky, picky. So why are we celebrating Metcher?"

"You remember the lawyer that contacted me? He said he represented the auditors."

She snuggled closer. "You get mail from those bozos every few days. What's new?"

"What's new is another five million. According to the terms of their own contract, they underestimated my extra payment by a bit."

She didn't drop her glass but some wine spilled. "Five million? Dollars?"

"Yep. And from what the lawyer says, Metcher is so worried I'll sue them, they're going out of their way to make sure I get the money as soon as possible." He laughed. "If only they knew how grateful I am to them."

"Those fools? They hounded you and put you in danger. I don't know why you're not—"

He interrupted. "They chased me straight into your arms. How could I not be grateful?"

A remark like that deserved a reward. She began by unbuttoning his shirt.

Taming Him

MICHELLE M. PILLOW

To Mandy for your support and humor,
no matter what I do. Actually, thanks for making me
pasta and . . . for making me pasta . . . Oh yea, and for
the support thing, but mostly for the pasta.

Author's Note

The world of the Dragoonas, while captivating and erotic, is quite a departure from my normal fictitious endeavors. I hope that you enjoy reading it as much as I've enjoyed writing it.

Chapter One

Alien abduction.

Maggie Stewart shook her head in disbelief as she tried to rationalize the sight before her. Things like that just did not happen in the real world, or if they did, they happened to strange, uneducated people who just wanted attention. Come on. A bunch of intelligent life forms flying around space just bent on sticking things up other aliens' asses? Hum, *yeah*. Sure. Whatever. Aliens come to Earth to probe the human anus. Not bloody likely.

Nope. There is no such thing as an alien abduction.

No such thing as extraterrestrials.

No such thing as this flying saucer landing right in front of my suddenly dead car in the middle of nowhere.

Maggie gripped the wheel tighter, her knuckles white. She was a sane, logical person. Things like this didn't happen to sane, logical people. If she just reasoned it out enough, the flying saucer would just go away.

Just wait . . .

Waiting . . .

Waiting . . .

It didn't go away.

Her headlights dimmed, flickering until they turned off completely. There were no streetlights on the mountain pass road and she should've been left in utter darkness. However, the light shining down from the ship lit up the entire country road and she could see just fine. This was insane. In a second she'd wake up and it would just disappear.

Wake up, Maggie. Wake up.

Maggie couldn't force herself to move. She was too stunned. It was like a bad fifties movie. The bright lights flashed around the center base of the oval ship. All was silent, except the sound of her heartbeat reverberating in her head. She expected to see dirt and debris flying around her as the craft kicked out its exhaust—or whatever it was these things did. How was she supposed to know what it was called? It wasn't like she worked for NASA. She was just a writer.

Oh, that's it. It's not an alien craft. My imagination is getting away with me. It's just some government ship. Some secret testing thing I've stumbled upon, and soon the military is going to come marching out.

The idea that she'd driven in on some government test facility did little to calm her nerves. She wasn't sure what was worse—aliens or government military. Both could be dangerous. The ship finally stopped moving, and a bright light illuminated in an arch around the section facing her car.

Oh, great, they're coming out to say hi.

Maggie tried to move, but she was still petrified. It was like the simple task of breathing was taking all her energy.

Even with her body numbed with fear, her mind was coherent, still trying to rationalize the impossible.

There is no such thing as aliens. There is no such thing as extraterrestrials. There is no such thing as that incredibly built giant humanoid creature walking down the metal docking plank thingy surrounded by bright lights.

She found enough strength to hit the power lock button and was slightly amazed when it worked. The locks slid down and she felt an insane moment of relief—like when she was a kid and was sure a blanket would protect her from the bogey man. The relief was short-lived. The locks only popped back up. She hit them again, glancing to the man as he made his way slowly down from the ship.

The sound of the locks latching only to immediately unlatch seemed to echo in the car. Hitting the button repeatedly, she finally gave up and slammed her hand down on the lock to manually set it. Again, it popped up.

Okay, the locks could easily be attributed to a faulty electrical system in her brand-new rental car. That she could accept. It didn't mean alien forces were at play or anything.

Great. One mystery solved. Now, about this man coming at her.

Could you call an alien a man?

Light silhouetted the stranger as he walked closer to her car. A whimper passed her lips. There was something seductive to the sway of his hips, the way the light caressed him as he moved. His arms hung at his sides, as he walked with authority. Maggie wasn't sure if it was just her impressions of him, but somehow she knew this man had some sort of power in whatever he did. He was powerful, strong, in charge. She was so frightened that she couldn't even tremble in fear.

I didn't even want to come to the Ozarks anyway. Oh, wait, yes I did. I wanted to get away from the latest cheating boyfriend. Damned bastard was having sex with everything but me.

Think, Maggie. Reason it out.

Maybe this man wasn't an alien at all. He looked human in form—two muscular legs, two strong arms. Perhaps he was military. Some secret project she just happened to run across. His body was definitely male and in splendid shape. She saw the tapered outline of his waist, the large breadth of his shoulders. He even moved in that authoritative way those types of guys had.

Yeah, this guy could definitely be military. Special Ops.

The man came closer. Maggie gripped the wheel, as if that simple action could stop him from coming closer, as if her sheer will would keep him at bay. What did the military want with her? She was just passing through. Maybe if she closed her eyes tight, they would think she didn't see them.

Not likely.

Wake up, Maggie. Wake up.

A hand touched the hood of her car, rubbing over it as he walked closer to her window. She watched his fingers as he petted the rental as if it were a wild beast. A chill worked over her body, making her nipples so hard she thought they would burst. There was something soothing yet frightening about the gliding motion of his hand. Her body tingled with desire so hot her panties became instantly moist.

This was just like her dreams, only it felt more real. Maybe if she just stayed still, she'd wake up. If this was her dream, she knew what this man wanted. He wanted her—all of her. And he wouldn't stop until he got it.

No, the dreams were just a psychological reaction to being cheated on by a supposedly impotent boyfriend. They stemmed from the self-worth issues she'd been having lately. If a man didn't want her, her mind gave her an alien who did—one with a hard cock and boundless desire. That's what the shrink had said anyway before suggesting she take this trip to clear her head. Maggie was a rational, smart person. The old shrink was right, wasn't he?

This was *not* an alien.

This was *not* happening!

Her foot twitched, the first sign of movement in her body since she first saw the hand gliding over her hood. She pressed down on the gas pedal, hard. Nothing happened. The car didn't even sputter in response. Regardless, she tried again and again, pumping the gas pedal by frantically jerking her leg.

The man's fingers skimmed along her window, gliding up to the roof. The ship's light momentarily blinded her and she couldn't see his face as he passed by. His clothes were tight, dark. Slowly she turned her head to watch him. His hips and stomach were next to the car window. She gripped the wheel tighter. Her mouth gaped open, sucking in long, hard breaths. A tap sounded on the roof, as if he were drumming his fingers in thought.

Go away. Go away. Wake up, Maggie.

His movements were leisurely as he bent over to the side. Maggie stared at the window, watching, tense, breathing so hard she felt faint. Time slowed in the agony of waiting for the unknown. What did he want? What would he do? Who? Why?

It's just a man. A Special Ops, military man. Just a man. Just a man. Just a . . .

His face came into view. The darkness hid him, but then he turned, looking into her window. For the most part his features were human-like in placement, but a narrow, hard ridge came down over his forehead, blending into his nose. His eyes glinted silver, completely filled in with the almost liquid silver color. She saw her pale reflection in those eyes.

That is not *just a man.*

A weak scream left her, so soft it would do no good. A tear fell over her cheek. She shook with fright as she slapped her hand over the door lock, forcing it down. It popped right back up. She hit it again and again and each time it unlocked.

Stupid locks. Stupid locks!

He easily shifted his weight, and his muscles rippled beneath his clothing. The man tilted his head. With his eyes so strange a color, she couldn't see what he looked at. Before she knew it, the door was opening and he reached inside. The hand came for her, and she screamed, loud and long, finally finding her voice. It was too late. Besides, she was sure there would be no one to hear her cries, no one to come to her rescue.

The alien man didn't flinch. Maggie tried to move, but

fear kept her immobile for the most part. His hand came for her. She screamed louder, weakly hitting at his arm, a feeble defense to his obviously superior strength.

Then he touched her and a euphoric pleasure shot through her at the contact. All fear left her, replaced by longing and hope. She basked in the feelings, wanting them, needing them. Everything was going to be just fine. She was happy, at peace. Growing weak, she moaned softly right before her whole world went black.

She was in the dream again. The mist, the voice, the feelings inside her—they were all part of the dream. Maggie couldn't make out everything around her, but she knew she was safe in her bedroom and her thoughts were lucid. In the morning she wouldn't remember what happened, at least not all of it, but when she was dreaming, it was all so clear to her.

She was waiting.

Seeing a shadowed figure towering over her bed, Maggie smiled. This was what she was waiting for and this was what she wanted.

Maggie's skin tingled, and she looked down. Her clothes dissolved from her body, leaving her naked. It was as if hands undressed her, yet she didn't see them. Maybe it was the-man-at-the-end-of-the-bed's will.

Her flushed skin glowed with an eerie blue light, caressing her in a way that made her appreciate her own body. She'd never been one to stare at herself naked as she hurriedly dressed each morning, but in the dreams she was empowered by her own naked allure. It was as if her being naked controlled the man waiting to be called forward.

It was up to her whether he'd come to her or not. At first, when the dreams came, she'd just lay there night after night, keeping him away. Then, unable to take just staring at him, she beckoned him closer. He knew, without her speaking, that she allowed him that much. Maggie somehow just understood him, what he thought, what he wanted. The following night, she'd allowed him to sit on the bed. Things progressed like that for about a week, and each night, the more pieces of his clothing were stripped from him, the closer he got, until he was naked and ready to please her.

Maggie shivered, her body rippling with pleasure as he looked at her dream man now. The man was hot. No, not just hot, but H-O-T hot. He was the kind of man women only imagined in their best fantasies.

By the time he sat on the bed, his boots were gone, as was his shirt. She couldn't make out his face, but she saw his chest shadowed by the blue light—his hard nipples, the ridges of endless muscles. When he moved it was with a liquid grace, as if he knew how to work his body, was used to all kinds of physical activity.

Only when she'd been ready did he bring his tight body above hers. His pants melted from him, and suddenly she was on her hands and knees. At that point was when the blurring started in her mind, leaving her with only sensations. She could feel the impression of a thick, hard cock coming up behind her. Her pussy would drip a seemingly impossible amount of cream, and she was ready to be taken.

Maggie was always frustrated that she couldn't turn around to see him when he fucked her. The dream never let her have the pleasure of seeing his face as he slid deep into her wet pussy. She could never see his cock, never touch him, as she kneeled before him, gripping the coverlet on her bed. It didn't matter. The man knew how to work his hips and her body was always ready to receive him with little foreplay.

Deep in her soul, she had the faint impression that he was frustrated as well, as if he wanted to caress her, take his time loving her. She also sensed that he couldn't, not yet. It was as if his time in her dreams was limited to a few moments and he had to take her right then and there or not at all.

Everything was starting the same as before in this particular dream, only as she turned away from him to offer her pussy, the bedroom melted until she was in a cloud of mist and impressions of hard, cold metal. She waited on her hands and knees, her ass thrust out in invitation. Her pussy clenched in anticipation, even as her body yearned for more than just the thrust of his giant cock inside her. She couldn't seem to cry out, as she wanted to.

How pathetic was she that her best sex came from dreaming?

Maggie waited, her body poised, her legs spread. Despite the limitations, the sex always brought her to climax. Her stomach tightened and she gripped the blankets hidden in the cloudy mist. She couldn't see her hands, could barely see her own breasts. Maybe this time he'd touch more than her hips.

Time seemed to hold still, until even her ass was clenching in anticipation of the first thrust. Hands glided onto her flesh, finding hold on her hips. His cock head was hot, practically searing her as it touched her from behind. Her body was immobile. She wanted to touch her breasts, thumb her nipples. She wanted to lean up and feel his muscled chest against her back.

Even without looking, she knew it was him. It was her dream, wasn't it? Why would she let anyone else take her but the man in her dream? Besides, it was his masculine smell that wafted over her. It was his low voice whispering in her head. She couldn't make out the words, just a subtle tone to the way he talked.

He didn't take her right away this time as his cock stroked up and down her wet slit. She trembled. Why was he holding back? Why was he waiting to take her? He never teased her, not like this. Sure, during the day her senses were tormented with the anticipation of going to bed, hoping he'd come, but he never sexually toyed with her.

What was going on?

Before she could question, he gripped her hips and thrust forward. His hard cock impaled her, fitting so deep she thought he'd rip her apart. Damn, she forgot how big he was. It was like he was stretching her more and more, as if his cock grew bigger each time they had sex. Now it was practically ripping her apart.

Maggie knew it was just a dream. Nothing that large would fit in her body. She didn't care that it was a only a dream, she wanted to be fucked. Even as his cock was in her, she wanted more of him. She wanted his hands on her body. She wanted his finger rimming her ass—something no man had ever done for her, but suddenly she wanted it from him. Hell, she wanted his cock in her ass.

Maggie wanted his giant dick in her mouth, choking her with its size as she sucked him off and drank his cum. She wanted his mouth on her clit, his face smothered in her pussy as she straddled his face. She wanted him to fuck her in every position, every way. Every so-called depraved sexual act—that was what she wanted from him.

Maggie felt a prickling and knew that the watchers were back. That's what she called them in her head—the watchers. They hadn't been there at first and she always forgot about them until they were there. She felt their eyes, even as they were hidden in the mist. Her dream lover knew they were there as well. As soon as they appeared, he began to thrust, moving his large cock inside her, pounding her with it.

The sexual energy in the room intensified until the place smelled of sex. Instantly, she got the impression of males stroking their cocks as they watched her. Maggie tensed, the erotic thoughts just too much. Climaxing hard, her whole body jerked, her mouth opening with a silent cry.

That's when she remembered something else as well. The man behind her never came, never was fulfilled. It dampened the sensations of her release slightly to know he hadn't reached his peak. Then suddenly, his hands were gone and she was alone in her room. The dream was over.

Chapter Two

Maggie gasped, sitting up in bed. Her room was dark, just like she liked it. She'd had this strange dream so many times, only now it was more real. She touched her chest, feeling how hard her nipples were beneath her clothing. Her thighs were sticky and a light sheen of sweat glistened over her flesh.

Throwing the covers off her body, she swung her legs around. Her bare feet hit the cool, smooth floor. She started to stand.

Wait. Cold? Smooth? Her room was carpeted. Hotels were carpeted. Where was she?

Maggie screamed at the top of her lungs, drawing her knees toward her chest and hugging them tight. The room instantly lit up at the sound. Everything around her was silver metal, except for the strange, squishy mattress underneath her. It was like a gel pack of some sort. The room looked just like in the science fiction movies she saw on television. With a lump forming in her throat, she remembered the strange ship landing in front of her car.

A ship? An actual alien spaceship? Or was it just a human aircraft landing at a secret military base?

No. No. No. This isn't happening.

"Wake up," she whispered to herself. "Wake up, Maggie."

Maggie rocked on the bed. Her hair was pulled back in a messy bun. She still wore her clothes—the old gray T-shirt, her jeans. Only her sandals were missing. She did a mental examination of her body. Nope. No anal probing. That was something at least.

"Think, Maggie. Think." She bit her lip and closed her eyes, remembering. "Okay. Country road. Car dies. Strange light from above. Military man. He comes for the car. Eyes."

She remembered the most brilliant liquid silver eyes she'd ever seen. Genetic experiment? Government implants? Alien? Somehow, deep inside, she knew it was an alien.

Something deep inside her told her she was on an alien spaceship. She wasn't sure how she knew. It could've been fear wreaking havoc on her mind or it could've been intuition.

After the car, everything was a blur. Darkness. Light. Darkness. Light. She'd been carried. She felt arms on her— euphoria-inducing arms, very muscular euphoria-inducing arms. Feeling her body twitch with desire, she frowned. Great, she needed sex so bad that she was getting aroused just thinking about a kidnapping alien.

So much for the dream being fulfilling.

There was more, but she couldn't decipher between dreams and reality. For all she knew this place was a dream. Had she become so delusional that she was now living inside her mind? Maggie looked around, waiting to see if the dream lover would appear to her.

When he didn't, she tried to figure out what to do next. The thin blanket beside her was so lightweight that she wouldn't draw much comfort from hiding beneath it. Regardless, she pulled it tight to her chest, rocking slightly back and forth. She glanced around the room.

A row of metal drawers lined a wall, at least she thought they were drawers. They didn't have any handles and the surfaces were smooth. Next to the drawers was a small closet door. Maggie leaned over, trying to peek in. Maybe it wasn't a closet but a bathroom of some sort. Across from the bed, on the far side of the room, a closed door was smooth and metal like the rest of the room. A bunch of buttons and sensors were next to it, along with a black computer screen. She could only assume that was the way out. There were no windows so she couldn't look outside, but it didn't feel like the room was moving.

"If you're messing with me, Jeff, so help me I'm going to kill you," she whispered. Jefferson Clarkson III was her ex-boyfriend who had been blessed with money, influence, and a wandering penis. It would be just like him to hire someone to kidnap her. He wasn't happy that she left him.

"You're leaving *me?*" had been his exact words of disbelief. "You are seriously leaving me?"

Maggie could still see the look on his bewildered face. His constant phone calls were one of the reasons she'd been in the Ozarks in the first place. Despite herself, she chuckled weakly and said, "What a jerk wad."

Maggie looked around again, trying to take stock of her situation. She was dressed. She didn't feel violated. Her stomach growled and she frowned. She was starving. The large cappuccino and convenience store hot dog she'd had the day before just wasn't lasting.

It was just the day before right? How long had she been asleep?

"Hello?" she asked. All too vividly she again remembered the man with the liquid silver eyes. If they had merely been mirrored or gray, she would've thought he wore contacts. As it was, they moved and swirled like liquid pools of mercury. She bit her lip, feeling oddly aroused by the memory. It was almost as if she knew him, but that was impossible. He wasn't even human. There was no way Jeff hired a man to look like that. "Can anyone hear me?"

Maggie didn't receive an answer. Slowly, she forced herself to get off the bed. She really needed to use the bathroom. The cool floor made her shiver. She went to the opened door. There was no toilet, just something that looked like a shower stall.

"Hello? Somebody?" she called. "I need some help here."

The door on the far side of the room opened. Maggie gasped. It was him. It was the man who'd taken her from her car.

Except for his face, her kidnapper looked very human. She liked his darker flesh and the way his muscles bulged in all the right places. Thick black hair fell in sexy waves down his shoulders, and she seemed to recall that he'd had it pulled back the night before. In the brighter light his silver eyes didn't seem to glow so eerily, but they were still not human. The brown ridge over his brow was the same and he didn't have eyebrows. It made him look menacing, as if he was glaring at her.

Maggie forgot all about her personal discomforts as she backed up against the wall. The man was positively huge. His broad shoulders stretched the shiny black material of his clothes. Those silver eyes stared at her, making her feel both wanton and scared. He threw off an absolutely intoxicating sexual energy and power, and she couldn't help but feel its effect.

Confident. Strong. Big.

"*U du tah ma de.*" His voice was low, rich, authoritative. The sound surrounded her.

Maggie pulled her arms around her waist, pressing into the wall. If this had been any other situation, she'd have been attracted to him. His firm mouth pulled slightly as he stared at her. He felt familiar, but that didn't make sense. How could an alien feel familiar?

It wasn't like he was her dream lover. He couldn't be. The shrink said that was all in her mind. He said sexual dreams happened to almost everyone.

"*Teanastellen?*"

Maggie realized he was trying to talk to her. She shook her head, having no clue what he was saying.

"*Maakey?*"

Maggie again shook her head. The man stepped forward, and the door automatically closed behind him. She made a weak noise and closed her eyes, willing him to go away.

"*I ni bara?*"

He'd come closer. Maggie opened her eyes. For all his size, his stance wasn't overly aggressive. He lifted a gentle hand to her.

"*G'day?*" He stepped closer and Maggie stiffened. "*Hallo? Bon die? Olá? Konnichi wa? Daw daw? Buon giorno? Salut? Buenos dias? Hello, how are you?*"

Maggie took a deep breath at the last one. He was going through different Earth languages and various greetings. She recognized a few of them.

"You understand this language?" he asked, speaking perfect English though there was a slight bristled accent to his words. It was damned sexy.

Maggie nodded.

"Ah, good." He smiled, letting the side of his lip curl up. "There are over four hundred and eighty Blue Planet languages, not too many, but I was worried I'd have to go through them all."

"You speak them all?" she asked, her voice a whisper.

"They are not so hard," he answered.

Maggie would've laughed if the situation wasn't so surreal. Not so hard? "Why am I here? What do you want?"

"To be my . . . you call it wife," the man said bluntly, as if it was the most normal thing in the world. There was definitely something rigid and militant to the way he was standing, feet braced apart, strong arms hanging stiffly at his sides. This was a warrior, to be sure. With a body like that, he had to be. "Did you not get the images projected from our computers? When you slept just now, you should have seen all this. They are to prepare you."

This strangely handsome piece of flesh was her dream man? Maggie froze. She wanted to die. This was the man she'd acted so wanton with? No, it couldn't be. This was just too humiliating. Great, now she was a cosmic slut. It wasn't fair. Dreams were in her head. Her dreams were hers and hers alone. No one was ever supposed to live them with her.

As she looked at him, Maggie vaguely began to recall him in the fog of her mind, but the memory of it was still too hazy and scattered. She'd never actually seen his face. Though, there was one hazy image that stood out—that of a strange blue and red dragon.

"I have waited a year for this." The man looked at her as if this should all mean something to her. The more she watched him in the light, she saw a subtle color shift in his gaze, a slight purpling that made it easy to see where he looked. More often than not, it was at her. "Let me explain. We are . . . you would call it military. We are on a deep space mission. I wish to have someone in my quarters at all times. Regulation says I have to marry to do so, so I marry. I followed the signs and stopped by your Blue Planet to get you. Do not look so worried. I studied your planet scans and then the . . . you call them gods . . . sent me to you. It is . . . you call it fate."

Stunned, Maggie said a little too sarcastically, "I'd rather you just anal probed me and dropped me back off."

The ridge above his eyes shifted. He glanced down over her body with unmistakable interest. "You wish for me to . . . Already?"

Maggie paled, realizing she'd said the words out loud. "It's just a . . . *oh*."

Okay, talking about anal probing was the last thing she wanted to do with the alien that had kidnapped her—especially when that alien was so wickedly handsome. If anyone was going to be probing her, she really hoped he'd volunteer. He seemed hesitant as he reached for her. Maggie screamed, sliding along the wall out of his reach.

"It's just a saying," she cried. "Crazy people get abducted by aliens and claim to be . . . Oh gawd, I'm insane. That's it. Jeff slipped me some bad acid or something, and now I'm in a loony bin. You're probably my doctor."

"You need medical attention?" he asked.

"I need . . ." Maggie took a deep breath. Her knees weakened. "I need a stiff drink." She looked him over. Damn, he was sexy. Was it wrong to find aliens sexy? "Make that a whole bottle and some kind of pill—lots and lots of pills."

"I will take you to the doctors. They will help you and find you the bottle you need." When he tried to touch her, she jerked away.

"Who are you?" she asked. "What are you?"

"I am Vladei," he answered. "I am a *Dragoona*."

"Dragon," she whispered.

He nodded. "Yes, very much linked to what you knew as dragons. It has been awhile since we have visited the Blue Planet, but the dragons you now know of were our pets, I believe. You called us wizards or dragon tamers."

"I want to go home," Maggie said weakly.

Vladei reached down for her, so quick she couldn't jerk away. His hand was warm on her flesh as he pulled on her arm, forcing her to stand before him. Instantly, her body calmed. Her heart slowed and she felt no fear. His smell surrounded her, drawing her in. His scent was intoxicating, almost like a euphoric drug. Her body stirred where he touched her, as if he injected her blood with a potent ecstasy. Hot desire coursed through her, and her panties became soaked in a way that she'd only read about in erotic novels.

"You are home," he said.

Maggie moaned weakly. If the touch of his hand did this to her, what would the touch of his body be like? Just thinking about it made her nearly orgasm.

"Give me your name, temptress." His mouth drew close to hers, hovering close to her lips.

"Maggie Stewart." Maggie was too far aroused to stop and think.

"Maggie," he repeated, caressing the word with his firm mouth. Then he kissed her. She moaned. His long tongue parted her lips, slipping between her teeth. The euphoria seemed to leak out of him, surging through her from his hand and mouth. Her nipples ached, so hard they seemed to stab at her bra and T-shirt.

When he didn't move to press his delicious body to hers, she moaned louder, wondering how a stranger could turn her on so much. The pleasure was too great and she couldn't force her thoughts to dwell on the fact. If ever she needed to be slammed up against a wall and fucked, now was the time. Alien or not, she wanted this man. It had been too long since she'd been so aroused—not counting the dreams. Jeff had been an adequate lover at best. Vladei, with his thick muscles and strong body would undoubtedly be a fantastic lover. She bet he could lift her off the ground and pound into her with little effort.

She pulled her mouth away, gasping, "What are you doing to me?"

"Joining you to me." He leaned closer, trapping her to the wall with his hand. His voice was low, hoarse. "Is your body enjoying this as much as mine?"

"Ah," she breathed. Her breasts ached. She'd never been so turned on in her life.

"Try to relax. Let my pheromones work inside you. Soon you will know on instinct that which you do not know with your head." Vladei leaned closer, his mouth coming close once more. "You were chosen for me to be my wife. I went to the gods and told them I was ready and they led me to you."

Somehow, she believed his words. They just felt true. She couldn't explain it.

"This is crazy," she whispered. "I can't be your wife."

"No, you are not yet," he agreed. His voice dipped into a sultry growl. "But as soon as you tame the dragon you will be."

At his words, a surge of sexual power and excitement hit her. "Tame the dragon?"

"My cock is hard for you. Will you accept it?"

What? She gasped, climaxing so hard her back arched and she gasped for air. Maggie could speak.

"Ah," Vladei panted. He bit his lip and ripped his hand away. He grabbed his wrist, as if his hand was burnt. Maggie sank to the floor, feeling as if she'd just had a marathon with her vibrator. Her whole body was numb. Breathing heavily, he said, "I did not expect such a connection."

Maggie glanced up over his tight body. A large bulge pressed against his snug fitting pants. She was no untried virgin, but she also wasn't a porn star. The unmistakable girth of his cock, still hard and wanting, caused her to pull back ever so slightly. She could make out its rod-like shape contoured beneath the material. It was a virtual battering ram waiting to break through the barrier of tight clothing. Just like in her dreams, he hadn't gotten release from their contact. She swallowed nervously, staring at the massive weapon he wielded between his thighs. The thing was huge!

"Come." His voice was hoarse. "I will bring you to the doctors. I should not be selfish if you have need of medical attention. We can finish this bonding later."

"I might need a doctor to examine my head, Vladei," Maggie said, "but I really need a drink more."

Chapter Three

M aggie numbly followed Vladei though the halls. After she insisted she was completely fine and didn't want to see a doctor, he agreed to give her a tour of the ship. Several hours passed in his amiable company.

Vladei was kind and acted like a gentleman for the most part, though he didn't say much. Pressing his hand to the door scanners, he let her pass through the doorways first. And when she walked, he would hold her elbow in an automatic, if not unnecessary, gesture of helping.

If not for the reminder of the weakening potency of his touch, she'd have thought the long metal corridors with their intermittent rows of lights belonged on a Hollywood movie set. It was strange but she wasn't scared, not really anymore. Instinctively, she knew she could trust him, that everything would turn out fine, even if she was still a little mentally wary.

The other Dragoonas she met were polite, if not a little distant. All of them were men—strong, large, military type men with the type of physique only reached with years of hard training. It made sense because according to Vladei, they were military. Their tight uniforms pulled against their hard frames, outlining each fine specimen to perfection. It was hard, but she tried not to stare, not wanting to admit that the sight of so much male beauty was stirring her desire for Vladei. She might like looking at the soldiers, but she wanted to touch the man who led her through the halls. She watched the men's faces, wondering if they were the ones who'd watched her sleeping with Vladei in her dreams. If they were, they gave nothing away—no knowing looks, no small smiles.

She was still barefoot, but no one seemed to notice. It amused her to catch a few of them staring at her boobs like they'd never seen a pair before. It was obvious that when it came to breasts men were the same—no matter the species. They bowed low to her, speaking in a language she didn't really understand. Vladei informed her that not everyone on the ship spoke Blue Planet languages, but now that she was on board most of them would willingly learn hers so that they could communicate with her. According to him, it should only take a few days for that to happen.

As they walked, it was hard not to stare at Vladei's perfect body. This was all so surreal. She didn't have family back home, or even a wonderful job—she was a writer, often sending stuff to magazines and publishing houses, hoping to get a decent paying job. But staying on a spaceship with an alien husband didn't really fit into the category of acceptable life plans.

Why wasn't she freaking out right now? Glancing at Vladei's firm ass, she sighed. He'd done something to her.

There was no fear, barely any worry—at least not about where she was. The more she walked around, the more ingrained ideas began to surface. Was she under a spell? Could this be real? Why did she suddenly know what to do with the little box next to a round window?

"Here, look," he said softly. She blinked at the softness of his voice, instantly following his hand. He motioned to the small, round window as he pressed the box. A veil lifted, shimmering away into nothingness so they could look outside. Maggie stepped closer to the window. Stars spread out over the sky. If she doubted any of this, the spectacular view instantly changed her mind.

"Why me?" she asked.

Valdei stopped. "Why not you?"

"What if I were married already?" she asked. "I mean, how do you know anything about me? What makes you think I'm the one?"

He actually looked like she'd slapped him. His large body tensed. "You are . . . already . . . taken?"

Maggie didn't answer.

"I did not feel this when I bonded you," Vladei continued. He looked at his hand, the one he'd touched her with. Slowly he bent his fingers, studying them intently. Maggie felt her body heating anew with the memory of his euphoric touch.

Seeing the weakness, she lied, believing it was the logical thing to do. "Well, I am married, so you should take me back."

Vladei eyed her. He lifted his chin. Very stiffly, he nodded.

"I apologize. I did not mean to offend. I do not know how this happened. The signs were clear. I was called to you, but . . . I am sorry."

Maggie wondered at her disappointment. He must not want her too badly if he was willing to give her up so easily. Maybe the Dragoonas would take her home now. She could go find a hotel, get a good night's sleep, and then spend the rest of her life convinced this was a dream. Looking at Vladei, she wondered if perhaps this could be an erotic dream.

Why was she even contemplating such a thing? Glancing over his tight body, she thought, *Oh, yeah, 'cause he is built like a Greek god.*

"You will be returned, of course," Vladei said, appearing pained by the admission. "It will take five of your days to get back."

"Five days?" she repeated, shocked. "But we just left."

"You slept so that the computer could prepare you for me," he said simply. When he turned it seemed like some of the energy was taken out of his steps. A strange sorrow came over her, as if she could feel it in him. "Come. I will take you back to the room. There you will be fed and your needs attended to."

Vladei turned and led the way down the hall to her room. Pushing a button on the door, he stepped aside to let her pass.

"Where will you be?" she asked, wondering why she suddenly wanted him to share the room with her. She stepped passed him, torn between logic and the desire to invite him in.

"I will report for my punishment." Vladei nodded, ran his hand over the scanner. The door slid down between them.

"Wait. Punishment?" What did he mean by that? Maggie touched the door, wondering why it felt like her heart was being ripped out. Eyeing the sensor, she pushed at it, hoping to open the door. It wasn't like the window control Vladei had showed her and it wasn't like the door sensors she'd seen others using in the hall. She kept pushing at it, hoping to get it to do what she wanted. The lights dimmed and brightened, a tray slid out from the wall, the bed made itself, but the door didn't open. She couldn't instinctively figure it out. Slamming her palm against the metal she yelled, "Vladei, wait! Come back!"

Vladei could not believe he could make such a mistake. He'd been so enraptured with the woman's beauty—her soft brown hair, her round hazel eyes, and her large breasts—that he hadn't felt she was taken. Naturally, he should have seen that she wasn't available and it was his fault that he'd messed up so badly.

Still when he thought of her, his cock was hard with desire. Being out in deep space with the Dragoona military made it difficult to find female companionship. Though they did dock at various humanoid ports to find sexual pleasures with whores, it wasn't often enough to suit his tastes.

Vladei was tired of being alone. He wanted a woman in his bed and in his heart. So, he'd offered his blood to the gods, prayed for a companion, and then waited for a sign.

The gods sent him a vision of the Blue Planet and he knew that his wife would be there. That was a year ago. He'd studied all Dragoona military records on the Blue Planet, learning the languages.

Truthfully, it had only taken a couple months to do all that. His kind had been to the Blue Planet long ago, but there wasn't much in the military records about its modern day culture. It was said some of the humans had called them wizards and witches, accusing the Dragoona of bespelling humankind when in truth they were merely bonding with their mates. That fear was one of the reasons he'd brought Maggie to his ship and not stayed with her on her own ground. He didn't want to cause trouble with the locals and since the Blue Planet did not acknowledge alien races, he couldn't just land his ship in broad daylight. Law forbade it.

Most of the time, he lay awake in bed, fantasizing of the night when the woman would someday be his. Once married, he could take his wife with him wherever he went. Dragoona law made them the same person. They shared everything equally. Though they did different things, all consequences were shared. Her good deeds would be his, her crimes would be his crimes, and vice versa. Her life was his, his life was hers.

He'd have someone in his bed, available for all his sexual fantasies. It had been so long since he'd had sex. Sure he pleasured himself. He was Dragoona, after all. He had to. But, after pleading to the gods for a wife, he had to save himself for her. If he found release with another, the gods would forever deny his request.

Why did the gods allow him to assess her dreams if she was taken? It made no sense. He'd gone to her night after night, giving her pleasure and denying himself. He'd stretched her body to fit him. He'd done everything he was supposed to. Then, why did the gods curse him? Had he done something wrong?

It wasn't just sexual pleasure he craved. There would be more between them. He would be connected to his wife, close. Vladei desired that intimacy with her as well. He would give his life to make her happy, to give her everything she wanted and needed.

Vladei took a deep breath. He'd bonded to a taken woman and the laws were clear. He would have to be punished for it, and Maggie would be the one to do it. The loss he felt was so great it nearly stopped his heart from beating. He took a deep breath. It was time to begin the preparations.

Maggie was fed and given a change of clothes. The tight black outfit was much like Vladei's. He didn't come back to her, but sent others like promised. She was shown how to bathe in a laser shower. The food had a strange texture to it, but tasted like a mixture of oranges and chicken. The men who came to her didn't readily speak, except for the most basic of phrases.

"Hello."

"Good day."

"Nice to meet you."

They wore tight black clothes that molded to their fit bodies and they had, more or less, the same ridge along their brows and the same liquid silver-colored eyes. The only difference she saw in the outfits was in the cut of the neckline. Some were squared, some v-necked, and like Vladei's some were rounded. She wondered if this indicated rank. Vladei had said they were in deep space on a mission.

Maggie couldn't help but smile, as the men practically tripped over themselves to serve her. It was surreal, seeing a bunch of fierce dragonlike warrior men scurrying to pick up the hair tie she dropped while combing her fingers through her hair. The man who handed it up to her did so from his knees. She took it and he actually bowed to her, getting on all fours at her feet.

"Thank you," he said to her before standing.

He was thanking her for allowing him to pick up her hair tie? Maggie suppressed a wide grin. She got the feeling that these men would do anything she asked of them—even if she were to demand they strip from their clothing and stroke each other to completion for her viewing pleasure. In fact, by the way all of their pants bulged at her nearness, she was sure they'd happily comply. But, for some strange reason, even with all their heated stares, she got the impression they would never touch her—at least not without Vladei present.

Okay, being treated like a queen was tempting, especially when her subjects were such hunky specimens of male beauty. It was fun to watch them bend over and pick things up off the floor. Maggie would never admit it, but she'd dropped a few things on purpose.

There was one who especially caught her attention, though it was mostly on a sexual, primitive level. He had stunningly beautiful black hair, thin strands of silk gliding over his shoulders. She didn't ache for him as she did Vladei, but she liked looking at him, liked watching his body move.

But, for all the Dragoonas' gorgeousness, she found herself missing Vladei. He was a stranger—an extraordinary stranger at that—and yet she felt as if she knew him. Her body ached for him in a way it had never ached for anyone. Fear unfurled in her chest—not fear of the ship or the Dragoona people, but fear that she would never feel such desire again once they took her back to Earth.

Maggie lay down in the small bed. The lights turned off almost immediately. She was tired from her long day, but she couldn't fall asleep. Now that she was alone in the dark, wickedly delightful thoughts of Vladei plagued her mind. Her body ached for him.

No matter how horny she was, or how wet her pussy seemed to get with just the thought of his hand touching her, staying was not an option. She knew nothing of Vladei's world. Sure, they appeared like they would treat her nice now and they said they were taking her home—but did she really know any of that for certain? What would happen in a month? After the wedding vows were spoken? She knew nothing of their culture. Well, that wasn't true. She knew a few things—the things they had imbedded in her mind for her to know. But, what were they keeping from her?

"Do you ever know anything for sure?" she asked herself. She'd thought she'd known Jeff. Hell, she'd even put up with him when he claimed to be impotent for those many months. What she couldn't get was how exactly an impotent man could spent the entire time banging his father's secretary and everything else that walked. Now that man had issues. He'd actually told her that the things he wanted in bed were things he could not sully her with—his future bride. Yeah, like she'd ever agree to marry him with a proposal like that. Maggie snorted sarcastically. Somehow, her mouth was just too precious to wrap around Jeff's cock. He'd only ever had sex with her missionary style, and it was mediocre sex at that.

It stank, too, because all her friends were Jeff's friends. Damned, superficial bastards had taken his side. He was the one with the money, after all.

Turning on her side, she sighed. Maggie had always been kind of a loner. She didn't make friends easily and preferred to stay home instead of going out to clubs. She really was pathetic, wasn't she? She had more pleasure reading books than she got in the real world. Maybe that's why she'd become a writer. Maggie wasn't even sure she was a good writer. She wasn't famous, wasn't well known, but she did make a fairly decent living doing it. Hell, she was too timid to be a good fiction writer. Take erotica, for instance. She'd always wanted to try writing it, but had never had the nerve to put pen to paper and start a story.

Sighing, she closed her eyes. If she was going to figure anything out, she needed to get some sleep. Vladei's face came to mind, and she smiled softly. Now there was a man who'd want more than just missionary from her. She wondered if he'd come to her in her dreams. Her body stung, really hoping he would. Maggie couldn't fall asleep fast enough.

The next morning, or what she assumed to be the next morning, the lights turned on as she sat up in bed. She'd slept like a rock, but didn't feel rested. Vladei hadn't come for her, though she'd waited for him. Her body was taut with unfulfilled desires.

Stumbling to the bathroom and into the laser shower, Maggie instantly reached between her thighs to hopefully ease some of the pain of her arousal. The green lights ran all over her body, warming her flesh. Her finger slid along her slick pussy, tweaking the hidden pearl there. She pinched her nipples, thrust at her hand. Nothing worked. When she finally came, it was a mediocre release that left her wanting.

Pulling on the tight black clothing they'd given her, Maggie was surprised to see the dark-haired man waiting in her room when she came out. So surprised, that she stubbed her toe on the door frame. Instantly, the man set his tray down on the bed and moved to grab her foot. Maggie held onto the wall and he began to rub her toe.

Desire shot through her—a completely wicked and carnal sensation. She looked down. The man's cock was hard, thrust against this tight pants. What was wrong with her? She spent all this time dreaming of Vladei and now she was ready to beg this man to fuck her, to end the ache she felt. Maggie trembled. He looked up and his liquid silver eyes narrowed. She wondered if he knew what she was thinking. Vladei popped into her mind. She wanted him there as well. She wanted both of these men at the same time.

Wicked, wicked thoughts!

Maggie shook her head. What was wrong with her? She wasn't wanton or wicked. She was average. She didn't dream of having ménages. Then, thinking of the men who'd watched her fuck Vladei in her dreams, she tensed. The man continued to rub her foot, working up her ankle.

"Ah, really, I'm good, thank you," Maggie said, trying to extract her foot from his very capable hands. He glanced up at her, almost looking disappointed that she pulled away from him. His touch didn't send hot waves of pleasure through her like Vladei's had, but there was a primitive sexual call to his touch.

"Thank you," he said, rising to his feet. His voice was gruff as he nodded. When he walked away, his body was stiff. The man picked the tray off the bed and hit a button on the wall. A small platform came out, and he sat the platter of food on it. Nodding his head, the man left.

Maggie sighed, wondering, if she threw her whole body on the floor, if Vladei would show up and give her a full body massage. Her body pulsed to life at the thought. Great. Just great. She was horny again. Her foot tingled as she made her way to the food.

Standing by the platform, she ate in silence. Afterward, she stuck her head in the laser shower and washed her teeth. Hearing footsteps, she sighed and again went to see who was in the room.

To her disappointment, it wasn't Vladei. The stranger nodded, took her empty tray and left. She caught her eyes drifting to his tight ass as he walked. The man gave her a slight smile as he caught her doing it. She was so aroused, that for a moment she considered pinning him to the bed and having her way with him. The man nodded once as the door closed between them.

What was happening to her? It was like she was suddenly insatiable.

Soon, another man came. He handed her a silver dish with what looked like a small pebble on it. Maggie frowned at it, rolling it between her fingers. Seeing her confusion, he motioned for her to put it back on the tray. She did and he slid it into the sensor panel by the door without touching it and left.

"Okay," Maggie drawled to herself. "That was just weird."

The day passed with more visitors, all of them polite, but none of them were Vladei. They brought her food, more clothes, showed her how to open the drawers. One took her around the ship. His English was broken, but she was able to understand a lot of what he said. He pointed out parts of the ship—the cockpit, mess hall, control rooms. When she asked about Vladei the man paled and said nothing, shaking his head in denial.

Oddly, she became more comfortable with being on the ship. A few times, staring out the round portholes at space, her stomach would lurch and she'd feel a little sick—worried about the atmosphere breaching the hull. The fear was unfounded and basically the influence of too many Hollywood movies.

Later that evening, she was dropped off at her room. She sighed, worried about Vladei. He'd mentioned punishment, and she wondered if something bad had happened to him.

Going to bed, she again dreamed of waiting for him, her body longing for him, wanting him, desiring him.

The next morning, the process started all over again. Still, no Vladei and everyone refused to speak of it to her. By the third night, she couldn't eat. There was no denying it. She missed him.

Chapter Four

Day four on the ship, she got up, ready for much of the same. Someone brought her food and she ate. She took a laser shower and put on the tight black uniform. Hearing the door, she sighed, pretty sure it was the man who came to take the tray away. She came out of the bathroom and froze.

Vladei stood before her. His face was pale, drawn. His hair was pulled back to the nape of his neck. "You are ready?"

"Ready?" she asked, thinking he meant to go back to Earth. Her mind screamed, *No!* How could she go back? Her body was aching for sex, for sex with this handsome alien before her. "Yes, I think so."

"Very well."

Before Maggie could ask for clarification, Vladei turned and ran his hand over the door. It soundlessly slid up. Three Dragoonas stood on the other side. She shivered to see the black-haired man was amongst them. She'd fantasized about him in bed with her and Vladei. In fact, her mind had wandered to such things often. What else was she supposed to do with so much time on her hands and only hot, built men roaming around to serve her? Her body was so tight with longing that not a minute passed when she wasn't thinking of ways to ease the aching in her thighs. Being fucked by several men at once was only one of those many ways.

One man pushed in a cart, distracting her attention. On top of it was a long black whip, a thin knife, and a long rope. She instantly pulled back, wondering what they were going to do to her. Her eyes flew to Vladei. He wouldn't look at her.

"Choose one," the man who pushed the cart ordered. The two others, both with rounded necklines stood behind Vladei.

Maggie lightly touched a whip and drew her hand back. "For what?"

The man picked up the whip and lifted it to her. Maggie cringed.

"Take it," Vladei said, his jaw clenched.

Maggie obeyed, compelled to listen to him. She gripped the leather in her trembling hands. At least they gave her the weapon, instead of taking it for themselves.

Vladei nodded. The man with the cart left the room, taking the rest of his torture devices with him. Maggie gripped the whip, sighing with relief to have them gone.

Vladei lifted up his arms, and the two men stripped him of his shirt. Maggie gasped. Dark flesh covered his chest, every inch of it hard, perfect muscle. The harder texture of his two small nipples matched the ridged flesh of his forehead. Glancing down over his stomach, she saw two small blue points coming up from his pants. It looked like a tattoo of sorts on both hips. When he turned, his back facing her, she saw a small ridge running down the back of his neck, stopping between his shoulder blades. Other than that, he looked completely human.

"For bonding a taken woman," the black-haired man announced. Two shackles came down from the ceiling as he pushed a button. "You will be whipped one hundred times. Each lash to draw blood."

Valdei didn't move as the two men handcuffed his wrists. In fact, he all but helped them. The man with lighter coloring pushed a button, and the shackles drew his arms up.

Muscles rippled beneath Vladei's flesh. His head fell forward and he braced his feet. The two men stepped back, looking expectantly at her.

Maggie watched them as if they put on a strange play. When they motioned for her to come forward to Vladei, she realized they meant for her to whip him.

"Uh," Maggie said, shaking her head in instant denial. "I can't . . . You can't possibly think that I would . . . No."

Vladei glanced over his shoulder at her before turning around to face her. His hands were still trapped over his head. Damn, but he was gorgeous like that. Why in the world had she said she was married? Could she take it back and end this? What would happen? Would she get in trouble for lying to them? Would they still return her to Earth? Did she really want to go home to Earth? Did it matter what happened to her when they were about to whip Vladei for her lie?

She knew she was being selfish, worrying about herself

when Vladei needed her to speak up. Fear made her tremble as she looked at him. Part of her really wanted to stay on the ship, to live the exciting life traveling the stars would bring. A bigger part of her wanted to stay as Vladei's wife, to take the leap of faith and trust in his gods that she would not regret it.

"You must," Vladei said. "I have wronged you, disrespected you. It is our law that I be punished for it."

"I can't whip you," Maggie said, dropping the weapon on the ground. She refused to hold it. "I just can't."

His jaw tightened. "If you refuse, I die."

Maggie didn't move. What did she do? She couldn't beat him. She couldn't hurt him like that.

You have to tell the truth. You have to tell them you're not married. You have to tell them that Vladei didn't dishonor you, that you were just a scaredy cat.

Maggie frowned. Dare she risk it? What would happen if she did? Each day the burden of her lie had welled within her until she almost told the truth. But she hadn't dared. She'd been too scared. Somehow, in her heart, she'd felt Vladei's sadness and knew he was technically all right. Just as now, she felt that he told the truth. If she didn't whip him, he'd be killed for this supposed insult. He'd be unjustly punished.

"I am sorry. I didn't know I offended you so deeply," Vladei said when she didn't speak, didn't move to pick up the whip. The two men beside him looked shocked.

"He did not claim your body," the lighter man said. "You wish death for—"

The black-haired man next to him shook his head, silently telling the other one not to interfere.

"I have no fear of death," Vladei said bravely. He lifted his chin, glaring at her. "If it is your will and the will of the gods, I am ready."

"Okay," Maggie interrupted. She lifted her hand and shook her head. Closing her eyes, she asked, "Don't you think this is all going a little too far?"

When she peeked at them, the three men's looks said otherwise.

"I'm not whipping him for touching my arm and he shouldn't be killed for it either," Maggie said.

"But, the bonding . . . ?" the dark man asked. His firm lips pressed tightly together. "He had disrespected you, a woman, giver of life."

Maggie bit her lip. This was insanity. What was she doing? Weakly, she closed her eyes and said, "He didn't disrespect me. I'm not married. I'm not bonded elsewhere. I lied."

The men gasped at her confession.

"What?" Vladei demanded. "What did you just say?"

"I said I'm not married," Maggie repeated, louder. She pulled her arms protectively around her chest. "I lied to you so you would take me home. I didn't know you'd be whipped and killed for it. I just wanted to go home."

Vladei's body stiffened. The men looked horrified. His voice rose, as he said, "You were given the dreams and surely feel it as I do and yet you lie to me? Why? I feel the connection between us. I was sure of it before I brought you here and yet you—"

"Hey, buddy, back off!" Maggie answered. Vladei's nostrils flared. Before he could yell at her, she said, "This isn't exactly easy for me. Where I come from a man asks you out on a date and, if things go well, maybe you talk marriage after a year or so. You can't expect me to discover there are aliens flying around outer space, that you have some gods who tell you who to marry, and then just accept that I'm that someone, no questions asked, all in one day. What did you expect me to say?"

"The dreams should have come to you. If it is true that you are not taken elsewhere, then you must feel me as I feel you. We bonded," Vladei insisted. His eyes narrowed, and she saw the passion he had for her. She felt it as if it was her own. Still, she was scared.

"Where I come from, dreams are just random thoughts that you have when you're asleep. They don't mean a thing!" Maggie wanted to make him understand, but she also wanted to convince herself of it. Things like this just didn't happen. Logical, sane people were not abducted by handsome aliens and they certainly didn't fall in love with those handsome aliens. It just didn't happen!

"Why are you being so stubborn?" he yelled, straining against his ties.

Me? Stubborn?

"Why are you being so unreasonable?" she countered, her voice just as harsh as his. Maggie was glad his friends didn't release him. She wasn't sure she could handle him if he were free.

The two men glanced at each other. The lighter one nodded and left the room. The dark-haired one said, "We will leave you two to settle this."

He too walked from the room, leaving Vladei tied up. The door slid shut, leaving them alone. Vladei yelled after them in the rough, throaty language she'd heard them use with each other and kicked toward the door. His body swung back and forth a few times before he stood once more.

"You know what?" Maggie growled. She reached down and grabbed the whip. "I may just whip you for this whole mess. What kind of barbaric race flies down to a planet, clubs the woman over the head, and then tells her they're getting married? Hell, when's the last time you visited us? While there were cavemen running around and clubbing was considered romantic?"

Vladei looked mortified. "I did not club you. It is against the law to hurt women—especially those we are to make Dragoona women. The men on this ship are here to serve you and will do so gladly in hopes of a reward. You are special."

"Gee, thanks," she drawled sarcastically, even as she felt some small measure of delight at his words. No one had ever called her special before, not like that, not so passionately. Even so, it was all too much. How could she be expected to absorb it all and not make a mistake along the way? No one was perfect.

"You are welcome," he said, nodding.

Maggie chuckled. These people really had no concept of sarcasm. She tossed the whip aside. She didn't know how to wield it correctly anyway, not even in play. His eyes followed it. Was that disappointment on his face?

"And I swear I never clubbed you. You blacked out and I carried you."

Maggie didn't answer. Her eyes were caught by the way his chest lifted with each breath. Damn, but the man was full of muscles. Why was she protesting being married to him again? As a physical specimen, she could definitely do worse. Her thighs tightened. She was so wet she could barely breathe without feeling the twinges of her desire.

"How could you lie about this?" Vladei asked, his voice rising passionately. "I have spent every second since we were last together repenting for what I had done to you."

"You did?" Maggie couldn't help it. He looked so darned vulnerable. Judging by his body and the way others looked at him with respect, he was all warrior and here he was hanging before her all cute and defenseless. It was just too sexy to resist. Her body quivered with longing for him.

His eyes narrowed and she knew she'd somehow questioned his manhood by asking. "Yes."

"What did you have to do?" She stepped closer. He smelled good, looked even better.

"I pledged to the gods to not pleasure myself for a week," he said. His face was so serious, it took all her willpower not to laugh. No masturbating for a week? That was such a man thing to pick as a punishment. "And I paid a blood offering."

Maggie tensed. Okay, that one wasn't so funny. "You killed something?"

His mouth quirked. "I offered my blood."

"Oh, well, that's different." Maggie looked over his chest and arms, not seeing any wounds.

Seeming to understand her curiosity, he said, "Inner thigh."

Her eyes moved down to his tight pants. They hugged his sculpted waist. She licked her lips. The tight bulge was there again, straining against the black material. "Can I see?"

"You are not my wife," he countered. The expression on his face said he was teasing.

"I'm not?" Maggie asked, surprised. "But, you said . . ."

"No, we have not consummated the bonding."

Maggie shivered all over. This was crazy. Suddenly, she didn't care how insane the situation was. This is what she wanted.

"If you choose to be my wife, you may do as you wish to me," Vladei said. There was a challenge in his eyes. "Otherwise, it is best if we do not consummate the bond and if you do not tame the dragon."

"Tame the dragon?" Maggie asked. He'd said that once before.

"It is how it translates," he answered.

"How do you tame it?"

"Are you saying you will stay as my wife?" he asked.

"No."

"Then you do not need to know," he answered. Leaning back his head, he closed his eyes. "Will you let me down now? If I am not to be punished, I have duties I must attend to."

When Maggie didn't move to try and get him down, Vladei turned to watch her carefully. He couldn't believe she lied to him about something as important as being married. He could care less about the blood offering or swearing off self pleasure, but the torture he'd felt inside his chest had been horrific. For whatever reason, the gods had chosen to test him with this. Though, now that he knew the truth, he wouldn't be letting her go back to the Blue Planet. He only hoped his men had heard his order to turn back around as they left him alone in his room with the temptress.

He couldn't stay mad at her though, not when her features softened and she looked at him like that. Maggie was ravishing in the tight black uniform of the crew. It hugged to her lush curves like a second skin. Seeing that she wasn't about to unshackle him, he proudly lifted his chin.

"So, you think no self pleasuring for a week is sufficient enough punishment for kidnapping me?" she asked, returning his challenging look with one of her own.

Oh, this one was stubborn. She lit a fire in his blood. He liked that.

"Yes, longer than sufficient." Vladei stiffened. His voice a little hard, he asked, "Why? How long can you go without pleasure?"

Her eyes widened as she got his meaning. Shrugging, she said, "Months. Years."

It was his turn to be shocked. In fact, he was a little horrified that she might wish to spend their marriage taking such long breaks in between lovemaking. Most Dragoonas found release *at least* three times a day. He looked her over. It would be the ultimate torture to have to see her lush curves for months on end and not touch her. The temptation alone was likely to drive him mad. However would he survive it? Perhaps once they bonded his pheromones would increase her sex drive to match his. He swallowed nervously. He could only hope it would. "How is this possible? You must have much self control."

She didn't answer.

"Will you stay here?" he asked, not comforted by her silence. "As my wife?"

Maggie still didn't answer. She just stared at him with her wide eyes, letting them roam over his body, taking in his stiff erection beneath his pants. She licked her lips and he felt his body lurch.

"Vladei, I can't stay here," she said shaking her head. "It's just not logical."

"Logical? What does logic have to go with what is meant to be?"

"Everything."

"Give me five good reasons why you cannot stay."

"Five? Okay," Maggie bit her lip. "I'm human. I don't belong here. I'm human. This is crazy. I'm human."

This was too easy.

"I am Dragoona and my kind is highly compatible to humans, not only in the ways of the flesh, but in our life spans and breeding cycles. In fact, some of my ancestors were human from your Middle Ages. There is no reason for this to be a problem between us. You are fated to be my wife. You belong with me as my wife because the gods have willed it. And, nothing willed by the gods is deemed crazy." Vladei grinned, as his answer took care of all her reservations about being his wife.

"You think to have an answer for everything, don't you?"

she grumbled, but he could see the smile she was trying to hide from him.

"Yes," he said, winking audaciously at her. "Any other questions?"

The cream between her thighs stirred when she moved. He caught a whiff of it and nearly broke the metal shackles on his wrists. He forced calmness into his blood. There would be time for that—very soon. He'd let her get comfortable first. It was only fair he answered her questions.

"There is something," she said, cautiously, still unsure about so many of their customs and ways. "One of the men gave me a little pebble and then stuck it in the door. What in the world was that all about?"

Maggie looked so confused that he couldn't help but chuckle. "The ship's computer logs your DNA and other bodily readings—like temperature and biological makeup. You touched it and when you put it in the computer, it read you and logged you into the system. Do not worry, it is harmless. It is so you can be found if you get lost or if you were hurt, the computer would know by your biological levels. We are all logged in such a way."

"All right, then." She nodded slowly. Pursing her lips in a way that drove him mad with lust, she asked, "What is taming the dragon? Are you the dragon? Is it a sexual thing? Do I actually have to fight some beast? You said dragons are pets, so I have to tame a pet for you? What's the deal?"

"It is a pet of sorts, yes," he answered, trying not to laugh. Vladei could tell she was curious beyond measure. "It is up to you to tame it after we bond completely. It is a test of strength and endurance and greatly reflects the honor of our marriage."

"So if I don't then . . . ?"

"We are still married, just cursed with bad luck and hard years."

"Ah." Maggie nodded. Every depiction of a dragon Maggie had ever seen came to mind—fierce talons, sharp teeth, reptilian skin. No, thank you. Somehow she doubted the moves she learned in self-defense class would work against a beast. The thing would probably eat her before she could even get close enough to see if it had balls to kick. If she were to marry Vladei, she'd have to take the bad years. That was something else to consider, wasn't it?

"Tell me, temptress, if you are not going to release me from my ties, what are you going to do with me?" he asked with a twinkle in his eyes.

Temptress? That one word gave her such pleasure. Without thinking, she said, "I'm going to torture you until you explain this dragon thing to me. And then I'm going to demand you take me home to Earth—the Blue Planet."

He grinned. "Demand?"

The word was a challenge, just like everything else about him. What was she doing? Maggie couldn't believe herself, even as she walked up to him. Somehow, having the big, strong man tied up made her feel brave. She could touch him and if she wanted to stop, he couldn't do a thing about it. Wondering if touching him would bring the same sensations she'd felt from his hand, she reached for his chest. He stiffened as she ran her hands over his muscles.

"Tell me more about this marriage thing."

His held tilted back and his breathing deepened. "What do you want to know?"

"What will be expected of me?"

Vladei frowned. "Expected? I will not force you into my bed if that is what you ask. Though I do hope you will not wish to wait months and years. My body needs to be released often."

Maggie laughed. "I meant marriage-wise, everyday life. What will be expected of me then? Would I have a job? Would I be a housewife? Do I have to pick up after you and cook for you? Do we have servants? Where will we live? Now that you mention it, do I have a say when we have sex or just whenever you feel like it? What—"

"Oh." He interrupted, grinning. Tilting his head to the side, he shrugged. "You can do whatever you wish. Sex will be of mutual consent, though I may try to seduce you often. Actually, I know I will." He gave her a wickedly delicious look, as he meaningfully looked her over. "Oh, and the crew will gladly serve you as they do me."

Sex will be mutually consented to, though I may try to seduce you often. Actually, I know I will. It took all her willpower not to moan at that one.

"When you say serve, do you mean . . ." Maggie couldn't say the words. She was just asking hypothetical questions, wasn't she? And he was talking in absolutes.

I may try to seduce you often.

"What do you ask?" His eyes narrowed, but there was a sparkling to their liquid silver depths. He was a clever one. That much was clear.

Maggie swallowed nervously. "You . . . ah . . . sleep with the other members of your crew when there are no women around?"

Okay, it had to be wrong that the idea of him being touched by other men was very alluring. What was wrong with her? It wasn't like she wanted to share what was hers. Wait. Was he hers? Maggie was so confused.

"No," he stated. The word brought her back to reality.

"Oh," Maggie blushed, a little disappointed that she wouldn't get her male-male-Maggie fantasy after all.

"What? Did I say something?"

"No, no, I was just thinking." Without knowing why, she admitted, "It's just that you said 'serve' and I thought that maybe you meant, you know, *serve*."

"We do not touch each other without a woman present, but the men do like to watch the claiming between husband and wife. If you choose to reward them, you may invite some of the others into our room and allow them to find pleasure in watching. And, should you wish it, you may allow them to touch us—but it will always be as you wish, despite what I want. That is the law."

"You'd want . . ." Maggie couldn't finish the question, so instead asked, "The single men don't mind? No one gets jealous over such an arrangement? Not even the husband?"

On Earth there was no way a relationship like that would work—at least not that she'd ever heard of. Sure, in erotic novels it was great, but in "real life" it seemed egos would get in the way. Someone would always get jealous and insecure.

"I do not see why it would be a problem," Vladei said. "Bonded women release pheromones that are quite enjoyable to the single Dragoona male. And the pheromones from them can often enhance the married couple's sexual pleasure. Why would it be a problem if everyone is enjoying themselves? The men would consider it an honor to help you find release."

Maggie's mouth was dry, as she continued to just stand near him without touching. So the watchers in her dream were real. Vladei said it so casually, as if it was no big deal. In fact, by the look on his face, she got the impression he wanted her to "reward" some of the crew in such a way. It was clear these were very sexual creatures. But, could she be like that? Could she release her inhibitions and just go for what she wanted? "You would let another man touch me?"

"Touch? Yes. Put his cock in your pussy? No. Should we decide to bring another man or men into our marriage bed, their cocks will never enter your cunt. That is mine and mine alone. I will honor all other wishes you ask of me, but not that. There are some things that even I will not share. Your pussy is one of them." His hot gaze moved down to stare at her thighs. Cream already gathered there. His nostrils flared slightly, and she knew he smelled her desire for him. A slight grin curled the side of his mouth. "And, truthfully, I would enjoy watching other men touch you. If you are my wife and belong to me, there is no reason for me to be jealous."

"What of other women?" Maggie asked, her throat dry. Knowing it might be somewhat a double standard, a ménage à trois with another female didn't interest her. The idea of Vladei touching another woman made a wave of jealous anger rise in her chest.

"No," Vladei shook his head, not even stopping to consider the idea. "Another woman to pleasure would take away the focus of the first woman. We have found these relationships don't work as well for the women, as it puts the focus on the man. Only rarely do such things occur, but it is not normal for us. I myself do not wish it."

"Doesn't all this make it awkward among the crew?"

"My crew knows their place. They would never dare to make you feel uncomfortable, or else they'd be stripped of their position."

"Your crew?" she asked in surprise.

"Yes." He nodded. "You did not know this? I am . . . you would call it Captain? Admiral? President? Leader? I am not sure which one. This is my ship to command."

"You're the what?" she asked, her eyes wide.

He smiled. "It pleases me to know that you did not know. It removes any concerns I might have had that you would accept me only because of my position of power. I would like greatly to allow the others to gain pleasure as they watch us."

"And you're sure you wouldn't be jealous?" Maggie asked.

"Why would I be? If you are my wife, you would belong to me. They would only be here to add to our pleasure. Besides, I feel bad for the others. Until the gods are ready to give them women of their own, they will not have a steady presence in their bed."

Maggie nodded. Crazy as it sounded, she was drawn to the world he painted for her. She wanted it. And she especially wanted him.

Watching his eyes, she touched his nipples. They were hard, slightly bumpy to the touch. Curious, she ran her hands up to his shoulders, wrapping her fingers around to the back of his neck. Pulling his hair free, she felt the silky texture of it. His body jerked violently and he actually growled when she touched the ridge she found there. When he again looked down, his eyes swirled with glints of purple and blue. His chest heaved with ragged breaths.

"Like that, do you?" she asked, smirking. He didn't answer with words, but the intense look on his face was response enough. She felt her blood stir, pumping fiercely through her veins. Her hands seemed to have minds of their own as they continued to touch him. Walking around him, she explored his naked back and chest. Unable to help herself, she touched the neck ridge again. He jerked so hard his stomach contracted and his feet came off the floor.

She walked back around to his front, shivering when she saw the wild, untamed look on his face. She pushed his dark hair back, rubbing the ridge on his forehead. He moaned, softly.

Maggie glanced down. Seeing the blue tips on his hips, she bit her lip. Her voice husky, she said, "Tell me about consummation. Anything special or we just . . . consummate? I mean, if we do other things, does that count as consummation?"

"You must drink from me," he groaned, his eye closed tight, "and me from you. Once we share essences, it will be done."

Finding hooks along his hip, she slowly parted them, loosening his pants. She touched a blue point. "Is this a tattoo?"

He cleared his throat. "Yes. A marking of my . . . ah . . . rank. It's a tradition of sorts."

Was he blushing? She couldn't resist. Pulling his pants down over his hips, she freed his cock. It bobbed obscenely before her, tempting her, leaving her fighting the urge to demand he take her. He wore no underwear so it was easy to slip his pants down. Grunting slightly as she passed over a thin scar on his upper thigh, his body tensed. Before she knew it, her tongue had darted out and over the scar. His skin tasted divine.

He jerked, almost pulling free of her grasp. Maggie held tight to him, licking him once more. She wanted this too much.

Maggie pulled back and gasped. He was shaved clean, or maybe had no hair to begin with as his chest was also smooth. She was too stunned to see the place where he'd cut himself as a punishment. It didn't look too bad anyway.

Just like she suspected from her dreams, he was largely endowed. But that wasn't what startled her. It was the flesh of his cock. It was completely tattooed like a winged dragon. The blue tips on his hips were the wings and the mushroomed cock head was the dragon's head. It poked out at her like a serpent. Blues and reds created intricate scales from the tip of his shaft down over the balls. A tail wrapped around his upper thigh. The detail involved was amazing.

"It's a dragon," she said for lack of better words. Then it hit her. Wryly, she asked, "Taming the dragon?"

"It likes you," he smirked, grinning widely. "And it really is a man's favorite pet."

Men, she thought, resisting the urge to roll her eyes. Though to be fair, his was a dragon. Her dragon.

"Are you telling me you don't have real dragons?"

"No, we have those as well, but this is the dragon that must be tamed. Believe me, its appetite for you is fierce."

"Hmm." Maggie ignored his joke, reaching forward to touch his cock. It was the strangest thing she'd ever seen and yet it was highly erotic. She petted the dragon's head as if it were real. Running her fingers down the base of his shaft, she smiled. Being an alien's wife really might not be so bad after all.

Vladei groaned, giving a pained chuckle. "That feels nice. Hurry and ask your questions while I can still use my head. If you keep that up, I'll be in no condition to answer you."

Chapter Five

Maggie stared at Vladei's body as he jerked. He used his strong muscles to pull off his shoes before kicking off the pants she'd left around his ankles. When he was done, he was naked before her. It was time to make a decision. She knew what her body wanted, but did she follow instinct and take a leap of faith, or did she play it safe and use logic. She knew the answer, even as logic fought it.

"Did it hurt to get done?" she asked, eyeing the tattoo. It was so detailed, so perfect, so a part of him, just like she wanted to be.

"Not as much as it hurts right now," he grunted, giving her another adorably pained smile. "I've gone many days without release and you are testing my control."

His cock was in her hand, so hard and ready for her, and her body was wet and ready for him. Vladei made small sounds of pleasure as she stroked him. Maggie became mindless in the euphoria of his nearness. His body called to hers and her hands willingly answered that call. Soon her lips followed and she was kissing and licking at his chest.

He tasted good, salty, sweet. Oh, and his smell—potent,

raw, male. There was something primal to the way his body moved and tensed against her fingers and mouth. Before she realized it, she was biting at his flesh. He groaned, speaking to her in his rough language. The more she bit, the louder he cried out. She kissed a hard nipple, soon discovering that his darker flesh was the most sensitive. Sucking at his chest, she felt his muscles contract beneath her lips.

Then to her amazement, she felt his body shift as he lifted up. She pulled back, watching his arms come down from above. The chains moved, his wrists pulling at the shackles as he lifted himself up off the floor. The muscles of his arms bulged all the way up his neck and chest.

He glanced down his suspended body and grinned. Maggie panted in amazement. Seeing such a feat of strength was a definite turn-on. Slowly, she came to him, kissing at his stomach, running her hands over his chest. Vladei held the position and she knew that he wanted her to take his cock into her mouth. She kissed the tip, rolling her tongue over the dragon's head. He jerked. His legs wrapped around her, and she gasped in surprise as he thrust himself deep into her mouth.

She pulled back. He let her go. Maggie stumbled away from him. Panting, she said, "That position can't be comfortable. Maybe we should let you down."

Vladei slowly lowered his body in another great show of strength. Then, hopping lightly, he pulled his body into a flip, kicked at the sensor panel on his way around. The shackles were released, and he landed neatly on his feet. Rising up, he said, "I don't mind a little pain, but it will be as you wish. I want nothing more than to have you pleased with me."

She realized he could've done that at any time. Now that he was free, his head lowered, his eyes stalking. Maggie trembled before his predatory grace. His large body loomed closer.

"How do you want me?" Vladei came closer, breathing hard. He looked like a reined beast, fighting for control. When she didn't answer, he backed her up against the bed and urged, "Kneel before me so that you may drink my essence and we may finish the bond."

Drink his essence? Maggie trembled. If his cum tasted anything like his addictive flesh, she would gladly do so. She began to go toward the bed.

"Ah, but first . . ." He glanced at her and, with a mighty rip, tore her shirt apart. She gasped as he freed her breasts. Rubbing them in his euphoria-inducing hands, he sent hot waves through her body. His very touch left her bending to his will, not that she wouldn't have anyway. "Ah, beautiful. Later you will press them around my cock and let me enjoy their softness. I will take pleasure in fucking them."

No man had ever said such bold things to her. It wasn't a request. Vladei just assumed she'd be willing, as if such a thing were an everyday occurrence. These men were defiantly not like human males when it came to lovemaking. Just as they didn't understand sarcasm, they obviously didn't get embarrassed by sexual acts. His bold confidence excited her.

Suddenly, she understood the life he was offering her. She'd be pleasured and waited on by handsome men, without the jealousy of an insecure husband. In fact, her husband would enjoy watching her get pleasure from others, so long as she saved her heart and pussy for him.

Vladei proceeded to strip her of her pants. When she was naked, he urged her down on the bed. She kneeled before him, kissing a trail down his magnificent body. This was what she wanted. He was what she wanted. She felt it in her soul. He encouraged her mouth down so she could suck him. Maggie tried to tease him by lightly licking at the shaft. He groaned, obviously past the point of being teased as he maneuvered his cock into her mouth. She kept her eyes open, watching the erotic tattoo jutting out from his lean hips, as she worked her mouth over him, taking this thick length to the back of her throat only to pull away and do it again. Reaching down, she grabbed his balls, rolling them in her palm.

Maggie didn't mind oral sex but this time was slightly different. His scent, his salty sweet taste, it all took over, causing her to moan and suck wildly. She couldn't get enough. It's like when his hands touched her. His cock, his whole body, seemed to emit pheromones that just drove her body mad with lust. Her breasts tingled. Her pussy ached. She squeezed his balls tight, willing him to come.

Vladei tensed. The sweet essence of him flooded her mouth and she drank eagerly. His primal, warrior growl filled the room. Maggie pulled back, licking her lips, feeling as if she'd just conquered a wild beast. To her surprise, she found his cock was just as hard as before and looked just as eager.

Vladei lowered his chin. His silver eyes swirled with blue and purple streaks. He tossed her back on the bed, instantly crawling over her. "My turn."

His mouth moved over her breasts, sucking and biting her nipples until she was writhing beneath him. Maggie spread her legs, her pussy wet and needy, so ready to be dominated by the fierce dragon he wielded between his thighs. His essence did something to her, taking away any inhibitions. His large size didn't frighten her. She wanted it, wanted him to fuck her good and long.

His cock brushed her thigh and she was so sure he was going to give her body what it wanted. Instead, he moved down her stomach, rimming her navel before dipping between her legs. Vladei bit the flesh of her inner thigh, nibbling his way to the small thatch of curls guarding her pussy. She looked down and he flicked his tongue toward her. She hadn't realized just how long it was.

Gasping, she tensed as he delved down. His long tongue stroked her, working up inside her body only to pull out and twirl around her clit. She leaned up, watching his head between her legs. Damn, the man was gorgeous. He forced her legs further apart. Maggie thrust wildly against him, feeling as if he were her only anchor in the whole universe. Mindless with passion, she heard her own voice pleading with him for more, to never stop. It was too much, felt too good. She squirmed, clamping her legs down tight against his head. He growled, vibrating her with the husky tone of his voice. The tension built, and she came with a jolt. He groaned, noisily lapping up her cream.

Vladei arched back when the tremors subsided, throwing his head back in ecstasy. His voice hoarse, he said, "I feel you in me. We are joined. You are my wife."

She watched him stroke the dragon between his thighs, understanding what he meant. They were joined. Somehow, their bodies had become one. She felt his desire, his every motion—in the way his eyes took her in, the way his mouth curled at the side in contentment. The look on his face was more intimate than sex could ever be. Watching his large fist swallowing the tip of his thick cock, she grinned. Sex definitely had some advantages though.

"Now you must tame the dragon," he said.

Maggie pushed up, not the least embarrassed by her nakedness because she could tell by the heated look in his eyes how it made him feel to look at her. She pushed him on his back, slinking her body along his, caressing him with her whole body as he kissed her mouth. His long tongue teased her lips until she sucked it deep within her mouth.

Pulling back, she asked, "How does the dragon want to be tamed?"

Vladei sat up, pulling her onto his lap so she straddled his thighs. His large cock brushed her slit and she cried out. She'd just come, but her need was more urgent than before.

"This is crazy," she cried, moaning as she lifted up.

Vladei grabbed her hips, keeping her from thrusting down on him. He teased her with his cock, driving her mad with lust. "No, this is fate."

Maggie couldn't take it. Why was he hesitating? Why was he teasing her? She needed him in her. Why wasn't he fucking her?

Vladei growled as if hearing her frantic thoughts. He pulled her down on him. He filled her up, stretching her body wide. She gasped, the sensation more vivid than anything she'd ever experienced.

Is that why he'd hesitated? Is that why he'd been teasing her to the point cream was running down her thighs? Were all these nights of dreaming just to prepare her to fit him, really fit him? Had he been slowly stretching her pussy for him?

Maggie pressed her hands into his chest, working in shallow thrusts as she adjusted to his size. When her body began to loosen, she leaned back. Seeing them join was erotic enough, but the peeks she got of the tattoo only enhanced her visual pleasure. His cock was so deep, sliding in her cream. His hands touched everywhere he could reach, gripping her hips to thrust harder as the tension began to build. Soon he was tense, releasing himself inside her as she hit her zenith. Her whole body strained, until she felt as if her soul was merging to Vladei's. In that perfect moment, they became as one.

Breathing hard, she fell back. Vladei pulled out. She gasped as he again stroked himself. He was still hard.

"How . . . ?" she asked, swallowing nervously. That was twice now that he'd come, and he was still ready for more.

"The dragon wants more," he told her. Maggie shivered. "Turn over."

Maggie bit her lip. Vladei got up from the bed. Going to the wall, he ran his finger over the corner. A secret panel flipped out. She gasped. Bondage toys, masks, feathers, silks, liquids, whips—every sex toy she'd ever imagined and some she hadn't was in the secret cabinet. He grabbed one of the bottles of liquid, slathering it over his cock.

"Hands and knees," he ordered. The commanding, confident tone excited her. "I will try your lush ass now."

Maggie obeyed, tensing as he came behind her. She flipped her hair over her shoulder, leaning back to caress him. He forced her back down with a hand to her back. There was no hesitance in him as he slathered a generous amount of the cool liquid between her cheeks. It tingled and she jerked as he slipped a finger into her.

"Tight," he groaned, approval thick in his voice.

Urgently, he removed his hand. She felt his cock slip back and forth over her rosette before pushing forward. He was gentle with her, taking it slowly. She'd never felt as cherished as she did with Vladei. His emotion poured over her, his pleasure and desire for her. He hadn't stretched her here, but the euphoria she felt took her discomfort away.

Soon, she was bucking against him. The vision of his dragon cock being swallowed by her ass was in her head. Another orgasm tore through her, her muscles contracting and urging him to release his seed. As she fell forward, spent, she was sure he would be done. One glance over her shoulder told her otherwise. He was still hard.

Maggie moaned. Vladei gave her a sheepish grin. His body moved with more energy than should've been possible. It was like he was feeding off the sexual energy in the room.

"Come, we shower," he said, lifting her up. Maggie moaned again as he carried her to the laser shower. The green lights turned on, cleaning the sheen of sweat from their skin. Vladei kissed her, taking it slower as he built her passions to boiling once more.

By the time he lifted her up against the stall wall, she was as eager as he, though her limbs were numb from the previous pleasure. This time, he made love to her slow, taking it easy. His silver eyes stared into hers and Maggie knew she would never be more complete than she was at this moment. It defied all logic, made no earthly sense, but this wasn't Earth and her heart wanted what her heart wanted.

Tremors hit her, racking her to the core with pleasure. His release joined hers. She knew for sure that she wouldn't be able to take any more. Her body was drained.

Chapter Six

I wish for you to let me call witnesses so others may partake of our pleasure."

Maggie froze on her way to the bed. He'd just come four times and he wasn't finished with her. She glanced down at his still erect cock, having hoped he'd give her a small break.

Then his words hit her. He wanted to call in some of the men. She shivered. A very wicked part of her wanted him to do just that.

"Their energy will replenish you," he assured her, his tone low, his eyes glittering. "You will then be able to keep going. And, when the time comes, that energy will help us to conceive a child."

Maggie felt herself nodding at him, despite her sudden wave of insecurity at the idea of being watched. Vladei grinned and instantly crossed over to the door sensor. He talked into it, using his gruff voice. He pushed the button several times, pushing in codes before giving the same foreign order over and over again.

Glancing at her, he asked, "Is three enough or will you require more?"

Maggie opened her mouth. No sound came out. She merely shrugged. Vladei called two more.

Maggie hid under the covers, much to her new husband's amusement. He stood naked and proud, waiting for their guests. Seeing how he was excited took away part of her apprehension.

"Did you just call anyone?" she asked.

"No, they are men you know. They have been serving you these last days, and it is right that you should choose to reward them with this honor."

Maggie trembled. The same handsome men that had been walking around her room bowing to her for the last several days? Her body heated to think of them.

Vladei instantly sniffed the air. He grinned. "Ah, I see this pleases you. I am glad you approve of my choices. They are my most trusted crew members, and I have known them a long time. When you were receiving the dreams, each of them came to me hoping to be chosen to please you."

Maggie was stunned. What other species of man would hand-choose other men to please their wives? And hunky, Greek-god-type men at that? If such a thing were ever to happen on Earth, the husband would undoubtedly pick those whose attractiveness wouldn't compete with their own. Though, looking at Vladei, she had to say he was the most attractive Dragoona she'd seen so far.

"These men will pleasure us, but they will not come inside you. For that, it is custom for married couples to take what is called a "third." The third is granted freer privileges of our bed until the time when he finds a wife. Often the third will live with us, helping out around the home when needed, protecting you. You will never sleep with him without me, but we could all find pleasure together when it is so desired."

"And when he finds a wife?"

"We find a new third when we are ready," Vladei answered.

The door lifted and five men walked in. Maggie recognized them immediately. Vladei pointed to them in turn, as he introduced them. Obrin and Hasek had brown hair. Fal was blond. The three of them had brought her trays and taken them away. Kadian, another blond, was the man who'd picked up her hair tie. And Saban was the man who'd touched her foot. She stared at him the longest. He had a wickedly delicious look on his face. He nodded once to acknowledge her attention.

Maggie looked at Vladei. He barked an order, and the men instantly started to strip. Vladei came beside her on the bed and began to kiss her neck, drawing her body's attention back to him. The men stopped moving, their eyes swirling with passion as they watched.

A strange vibration worked over her flesh. Maggie could feel the sexual energy in the room, heating her to the point of near explosion. She closed her eyes. Vladei's hands worked beneath the covers onto her flesh, rubbing her body. The men groaned.

Maggie's eyes flew open in surprise at the sound. They all had dragon tattoos covering their erect cocks, though they were different colors. Vladei chuckled and tore the blankets off her. Gasping, she watched the men looking at her. Their breath deepened in approval and their cocks lurched, becoming fuller.

"They're staring," Maggie whispered to Vladei, torn between watching the men and the very arousing feel of her husband kissing her body.

"Would you like them to do more?" he asked, the subtle sound of hope in his voice.

Maggie nodded. Vladei barked an order. She'd meant that maybe one should dim the lights a little more and perhaps they could move or pleasure themselves or something. But, as they eagerly went down on all fours and crawled toward the bed in submission, she realized her husband had something else in mind.

Vladei stretched his body on top of hers, caressing her. He said something in his gruff tongue and Saban instantly went to the cabinet and pulled out ropes and lubricant. Fal went to the door sensors and dimmed the lights to a seductive level. Suddenly, the bed moved, detaching from the wall and rolling to the center of the room before lowering to the floor.

Maggie watched, her body automatically rubbing along Vladei's as they made love on the bed. He kept kissing her, ignoring the men as he sucked her nipples.

Saban bound the other four men's hands behind their backs. Their stiff cocks thrust out, denied. Two kneeled on each side of her. Then, Saban positioned himself above her head. His hands were left unbound. Maggie looked up. His large cock was over her head, the dragon-covered cock nearly as big as her husband's. She wanted to touch it, but held back.

Maggie shivered, surrounded by six very naked, extremely well-built men. All of them had rock-hard bodies and gave off a confidence that was arousing all on its own. She was amazed at how sex was so natural to the Dragoonas that this situation didn't seem odd in the least to them.

The men were all staring at her, wanting her, their cocks hard for her. But her heart belonged to only one of them. It was strange, but she felt it as sure as she felt anything. She loved Vladei.

"I love you," she said, reaching to lift his face to hers. She melted, as she looked into his eyes. For a moment, the others weren't even there. "Is that crazy?"

"Mm, no," he growled, kissing her deeply, so deeply that she had to squirm for breath to get him to stop. He pulled back, grinning. He adjusted his hips and his cock brushed her thighs. She was so wet. The smell of sex and desire was thick around them. The vibrations of arousal surrounded her until the air practically snapped with a life of its own. Unashamed that the others could hear them, he said, "I love you as well. I've loved you since that first vision I had of you."

Leaning up, Maggie kissed him. When she pulled back, her husband's euphoria was swimming in her blood, rushing to every limb, every section of her lust-filled body.

"They await to pleasure us," Vladei said. "It would please me for you to give them permission."

Maggie glanced around and nodded, eager to have them do so.

Saban's hands slid down over her shoulders to her

breasts. His callused palms were warm as he squeezed the globes. The man groaned. Maggie studied Vladei, watching for any hint of jealousy. There was no need. Her husband was too busy watching Saban's hands on her breasts. She felt Vladei's hips move against her.

The four bound men leaned forward, straining against their ties as they began kissing her shoulders and thighs. Maggie tensed. All six of them were breathing hard, moaning as they made love to her. There was something naughty and wicked and so very right about the way the tops of their heads brushed Vladei's tight body as they moved their mouths against her.

Vladei groaned. Saban kissed her neck. Maggie enjoyed the feel of the men's mouths, but she wanted more. Needed more. She wanted their hands on her body, on her husband's body.

"Can we untie them?" she asked, moving to bite Vladei's earlobe.

Her husband groaned. "I wasn't sure if you'd like that, but yes. You can do whatever you wish."

Maggie looked up at Saban, seeing first his large cock hovering as he stood. "Untie them."

The four men grinned as Saban left her to do as she ordered. He freed their hands and instantly they reached forward to touch her. Soon the bed was a frenzy of hands and mouths. Fingers glided over her body, squeezing and touching and stroking. Strong hands glided down Vladei's arms and chest. Maggie tried to touch the full length of her husband at once, reserving her hands for him.

Vladei must have sensed her hesitance and took her hand in his, moving it above her head to Saban's thigh. Running her hand up the man's leg, Vladei wrapped her fingers around the man's thick cock. Maggie moaned, as her husband worked her hand over Saban's arousal. She rubbed her hips up, taking her husband's shaft inside her with the same rhythm.

"I should like him to be our third if you so desire it," Vladei said into her ear. Saban groaned, staring down at her with desire.

"Third?" she whispered, glancing up to where her hand cupped Saban's dragon. Remembering what he'd told her, she shivered. Saban's eyes appeared to darken. Maggie found herself nodding. Both Saban and Vladei grinned, sharing a quick look. Saban groaned.

Vladei pulled her hips, jerking her down further on the bed. Saban kneeled, joining them on the mattress. He placed a knee by either side of her head so his cock and balls were directly above her face. The others looked at him with jealousy, but didn't stop their movements as they continued to caress her and Vladei, moving to touch Saban now as well.

Maggie lifted up and licked the root of his shaft from underneath. The clean, intimate smell of Saban assaulted her. He was muskier than her husband, but not bad. Saban jerked, moaning.

He pulled back, looking down at her. "How does my mistress want me?"

Vladei was busy kissing her stomach. He glanced up, his eyes hot as he smiled. "He wishes to know how you'd like him to come in you so we all may join together."

Maggie was still a little lost in how to answer. It was hard to concentrate with all the mouths and hands moving over her flesh. Her pussy was so wet, aching to be filled again and again. The four men beside her kept going around her wet slit when she would have them thrusting their fingers into her ass while Vladei took her pussy. The men only touched her, and knowing they wanted her was almost too much.

Maggie pushed up, needing to be fucked and soon. Since she'd just come several times with her husband, the need caught her by surprise. She ached and her pussy wept with cream.

"Should I take Saban in my mouth?" she asked Vladei.

"Ah, yes." Her husband nodded, eager for her to do so.

Maggie turned around. Before she could lean over, Saban kissed her, grabbing the sides of her face. His mouth moved differently and he tasted sweeter than Vladei. There was no love in the kiss, just pure sexual enjoyment, a friendship at best. She groaned, taking the pleasure for what it was.

"I am honored to be your third, mistress. I will make you and your husband proud," Saban swore when he pulled back. "My honor will enhance yours."

Then, gently, he urged her mouth down to his dragon. Maggie glanced around to the four men on the sides. Seeing that they still neglected their own cocks, she said, "Find pleasure."

They readily obeyed, taking themselves with one hand, while still kissing and touching her. Maggie expected Vladei's cock to thrust into her, but instead his mouth was on her ass, kissing and biting her cheeks. Then, spreading her thighs, he maneuvered himself so he was lying beneath her pussy. He pulled her down on his mouth, sucking her clit and fucking her with his fingers and tongue.

Saban maneuvered himself on the bed, working his body until his cock was just the right height for her mouth to take him in. Maggie gasped as Saban thrust forward, rimming her lips with his thick cock head. Her mind reeled, unable to concentrate as it was torn between feeling the all the wonderful sensations of the flesh. Her husband's mouth brought her such pleasure that she didn't stop to think as she instantly sucked Saban between her lips. The man groaned, wiggling back and forth. He tasted as different as he smelled.

Maggie smothered Vladei in her drenched pussy as she rode his face. She watched the erotic thrust of Saban's dragon coming in and out of her mouth. Hands were on everyone—touching Saban, moving along the cleft of her ass, and pinching her nipples, undoubtedly stroking over Vladei if the slight bumps along the backs of her thighs were any indication.

It was all too much. She was close. Her body tensed. Maggie groaned, sucking Saban harder, wanting him to come with her. She touched his hip. As she came, he jerked back, denying her his release. She gasped, jerking against Vladei's face. The four men groaned, jerking with her, coming heavily.

Vladei said something as he pushed her off his face. For a moment, Maggie was worried that she'd been too wanton. One look at his passionate face soothed the fear. The men bowed to her, smiling and sated as they quickly pulled on their clothes, leaving her alone with Vladei and Saban.

Maggie was still aroused. She no longer questioned her amazing sex drive. It was as Vladei said, the men had replenished her energies. She turned on the bed and Vladei kissed her, moaning into her mouth. Her taste was on his lips, mingling with Saban's. It was all too much. Saban came behind her and the two men instantly stood, drawing her up between them.

"This is better," Vladei said. He glanced at his friend then back at her. "It is good that we spend time alone."

A little worried, she glanced over her shoulder. "You're all right with this?"

Saban frowned, confused.

"I can't explain it, but I love him. You, I . . ." What could she say? She barely knew the man. Vladei was in her body, her blood. He was part of her soul.

Saban laughed. "You have a kind heart, mistress. I know well the place of the third and will enjoy fulfilling that place and serving you both."

Saban grabbed her ass before sinking his cock between her cheeks. Vladei did the same from the front, rubbing against her slit. Both men groaned in pleasure.

"You have sucked me well, mistress," Saban said. "If it pleases you, I wish to find release now."

"My cock is ready for you as well, wife," Vladei said, lifting her up off the bed so she was forced to straddle his waist. When he had her supported, she felt Saban move. She kissed Vladei passionately. When Saban came back he lubed her ass with the tingling liquid. Maggie tensed, realizing they both meant to take her like this.

Vladei thrust into her first. She cried out in pleasure. He was so big that she stretched around him. Before he was completely accommodated, Saban spread her ass cheeks and ran his cock along the moistened cleft. She felt him probe her tight hole as Vladei still filled her.

Strong muscles surrounded her as the men crushed her body between them. She felt their hands hesitate as they both kissed a side of her neck. Pulling Saban's hand from her hip, she drew it to Vladei. Both men groaned in approval. Soon they were thrusting against her, filling her completely.

Maggie whimpered. It felt so good. Then, groaning as she peaked, she felt both of the men jerk simultaneously, filling her up. Maggie dropped against Vladei. Saban was the first to pull out. Vladei grunted, weakened and trembling as he let her slide back down. The men lowered her down to the bed, lying on each side of her.

Saban was the first to move. "I have to report for duty. This time is for you two anyway. I'm just for pleasure, not this aftermath."

Maggie smiled at him before snuggling into Vladei's chest. When she heard the door open and close, she finally looked up at him. A moment's shyness overcame her, but he kissed it away. Then, pulling his head back, he said, "You please me greatly, wife."

"You please me as well." Almost scared, Maggie glanced down the length of his body. Finally Vladei's erection had gone down. She sighed with relief. After that last bout, she'd say she was definitely, completely, totally spent.

"I'd say it's tamed," she said, chuckling softly.

"Yes, unless you would like me to try and revive it?" Vladei offered, grinning tiredly.

"Mm," she moaned. Maggie couldn't open her eyes again. "Later. Sleep first."

He pulled her into his arms and held her tight to his chest. She kissed above his heart before pulling back.

"I love you," she whispered, before she could stop the words. Maggie refused to take them back, as she felt his response before he even said anything.

"And I you," he responded, unashamed. "The gods would not have brought us together if it wasn't to be a match of the hearts. Everything else we will need to know about each other will come with time."

Maggie smiled. He was right. Vladei was her fate.